RUTHLESS LEGACY

A Dark High School Romance

HAWK BAY DUET
BOOK I

CARA E. HOLT

CW01498350

reading ~ ~ness legacy! -Jay

Thanks.

Cara E. Holt
x

NOTE TO THE READER

This book is meant for those age seventeen and over. It contains swearing, sex, and scenes that some may find triggering including, kidnap, imprisonment, threats, use of knives, violence, intimidation, some dubious consent, and discussions about suicide.

If you are sensitive to the above triggers, please think twice before continuing.

CHAPTER ONE

ELIZA

As the police car pulls up outside my foster family's home, I groan internally at the welcome party awaiting me. My foster mum, Jackie, and my social worker, Hayley, are standing on the steps in front of their extended semi-detached house. Fuck my life. Hayley looks pissed off; no doubt annoyed that she has had to drive out here to deal with my sorry arse. Hayley is okay as far as social workers go. I do genuinely think she gives a shit about the kids on her caseload. And let me tell you, I've had my fair share of social workers. In the last five years there's been eight, to be exact. Kit and I take bets on how long the latest ones will last. Hayley has been our longest — she has stuck around for eleven months now. The rest of them all burnt out because of heavy caseloads. We are used to people not sticking around, though. No one wants two kids aged seventeen and fourteen, especially one like me. Let's just say I'm no angel. I like living life on the edge. Nearly dying can do that to you — make you re-evaluate your life. You can be here one day and gone the next, just like that. One selfish drunk driver and your life can be over, wiped out, and that is left are the photographs.

A slither of guilt runs through me as I take in Jackie's tired expression. To be fair, Jackie and Steve are okay. My problem isn't with them. I'm just angry. I'm angry at the world for the cards my brother and I have been dealt. There was a time when life was good. When we had two loving parents and a stable home. Before my selfishness robbed us of our home and family.

We came to live with Jackie and Steve six months ago, Hayley had pleaded with me to behave myself. She said that if I could just rein it in a bit, then this might be my last move. I've heard that shit before, though. Our last home was supposed to be our forever foster home and then they got divorced, and we were surplus to requirements. And the wonder why kids in care are screwed up? You try moving time and time again, only to be let down one more.

I no longer believe a word anyone tells me. I trust no one, apart from my brother. Kit is my world. He's all I have in this life, and I love him with every bone in my body. We have a real close bond. When you only have each other, and you're in the system, you stick together and have each other's backs. Kit is better behaved than I am though. He's a deep soul, and he channels his anger and resentment into his football and art. My brother is super talented, and yes, I'm biased, but he is a gifted footballer and artist and with his dedication, I think he'll go far. Me, ha, where do I start? Deep down, I'm quite smart, but I'm too busy having fun to knuckle down at school. I'm tough. Nothing and no one gets to me. I'm a wall of steel. I think the last time I cried was the day of my parents' funeral. After that day, I pulled up my big girl pants and told myself I had to ready myself for what was to come; that I had to be the strong one for my brother. It was my duty as his big sister.

Officer Higson parks at the bottom of the drive and turns around to address me from the front of the car, "Ready to face the firing squad, Eliza?"

I sigh. "Let's get this shit over with." I know what comes next, anyway. The lecture about disappointment and throwing my life away. I've heard it all before.

He pauses before getting out of the car. "Eliza, don't waste your life being angry at the world. Make a life for yourself that your parents would be proud of."

I frown. "You have no idea what it's like being in care. I bet you grew up with two loving parents and had everything you ever wanted. You have no clue."

He's silent for a beat. "Actually, my dad was a cop, and he died in a car chase when I was eight years old. So, I know exactly what you've been through, Eliza. We all have our crosses to bear. Jackie and Steve are good people. The genuinely care, but you may have pushed them too far this time. You're so lucky that Jackie doesn't want to press charges and add to your rap sheet."

I avert my eyes from his piercing gaze. "I know."

Higson climbs out of the car and comes round to open my door. I reluctantly follow him up the drive to face my fate.

"Hi Hayley and Jackie. I was hoping it would be a while before I was back here again," he says in a resigned tone. Jackie offers him a tight smile, her eyes quickly glancing my way before she looks away.

"Eliza," Hayley says, her face defeated, "I thought we made some headway last week. I thought I was finally getting through to you."

"Shall we take this inside?" Steve asks as he comes through the front door. He squeezes his wife's shoulders with a look of resigned disappointment on his face. My stomach knots with anxiety at the realisation that my desire to self-destruct could cause us to move again. I'm too good at acting without first thinking about the consequences.

Everyone piles inside and as we cross the hallway to the lounge; I glance up and see my brother peering around the top of the stairs. I offer him a confident smile and a wink, appearing far more assured than I feel.

We all take a seat. I notice that Jackie and Steve sit themselves at the opposite side of the room. Okay then. This is how it's going to be. Jackie takes genuine pride in her home. She loves watching home renovation shows, and she loves nothing better than dragging me around our local home décor store to buy new pieces for her house. I remember the first day we arrived here, and I walked in the lounge, painted all white but with shabby chic pieces of furniture that give it a modern farmhouse feel. I remember thinking that it felt like a real home.

"The car's at the station. There are a few scrapes, and you'll need a new bumper but it's not too bad," Officer Higson informs them.

Steve nods his head. "I'll come by later today and pick it up. I'm just glad no one is hurt." Steve shakes his head and looks at me. "I just don't get it, Eliza. A reckless driver killed your parents and yet here you are stealing cars and racing. Do you have a death wish?"

I snigger, earning me a sharp look from Hayley. "Well, I should have died five years ago, so I guess I'm lucky I've lasted this long."

Steve leans forward, his arms resting on his solid legs. "But you didn't die. You were given a second chance. The odds were against you, but you survived. You have a brother upstairs who worships the ground you walk on. Do you want him to down this path? Because you're not being a great role model for him."

I ignore his question and do what I do best — I go into defence mode. "So, I guess I should go and pack?"

Hayley clears her throat. "That's actually why I'm here."

I ready myself for this. Will it mean another school move? We are already at school number four. How long will it be before Kit resents my actions — actions that are having a direct impact on him.

"Jackie and Steve are surprisingly happy to have you stay, because they believe that with love and stability, the loving girl you are under all that armour could thrive. However, circumstance have changed."

Kit bursts into the room. "I'm not fucking moving again!" he tells them angrily. "I've actually got friends here."

My heart drops at the shattered look on his face. I've done this to him. This is all my fault. Everything about this situation and how we ended up in care is my fault.

Jackie stands and walks over to my brother, placing an arm

around his shoulder. "Kit, I know you're angry and upset, but just hear Hayley out. This is actually good news for the both of you."

I frown, how can she possibly think moving again is a good thing?

Kit leaves Jackie's side and comes to sit beside me. He reaches over and grips my hand in his, "Well, go on then."

"A family member has come forward to claim you both," Hayley announces. I blink. Sorry, did she just say a family member? I think my ears must be playing tricks on me. Maybe I've imagined it and heard what I wanted to hear.

Kit scoffs. "We don't have any family. Why do you think we've been in care for the last five years?"

Hayley shrugs. "Well, we were wrong. Your Grandfather is now your legal guardian and you'll be going to live with him."

I hold my hand out to stop her talking any further. "Rewind a bit. We have a grandfather?"

Hayley smiles. "Yes, and he's a good man. I've met him via video call."

"What side of the family?" Kit asks her, his voice hesitant. I know why. He doesn't want to get his hopes up that this could be real. Like we could finally belong to someone.

"Your fathers."

I nod, still processing this shocking news. "He said his parents were dead."

Hayley shrugs her shoulders again. "I can't explain that to you. But this man is definitely your grandfather."

I chew on my lip. "Where does he live?"

"He lives of the south coast, in a beautiful seaside resort. He's also very successful. His home is quite beautiful."

"How do you know?" Kit asks, his voice still hostile,

"He's shown me photos, and I've had a video tour of his house. He's already had bedrooms decorated for you both."

"I'm not fucking going," Kit protests, leaning back into the sofa and crossing his arms over himself defensively, then blows his dark hair out of his eyes.

Hayley offers him an understanding smile. "I know this is a lot to process, but he's your legal guardian, Kit. You will be going to live with him."

"Why now?" I ask her. Why has this mysterious grandfather come forward now, after all this time?

Hayley shakes her head. "I can't speak for your grandfather. That is a conversation you will need to have with him."

I look over at my brother. He's pissed off. I know he's been happy here. Probably the happiest he's been since we've been in care. He's made a good group of friends and he loves playing for the local team. I place my hand on his leg. "This is good, Kit. He's family. No more moving, no more feeling like we can't make roots in case we have to move."

"I'm just so tired of moving and staring again," he admits.

Hearing my brother say how much the system has broken him breaks my heart. And people wonder why I'm angry?

"I know, but this is different."

"Is it?" he asks me, sitting up straight, looking from me to Hayley. "What if he gets fed up with us and decides he doesn't want us anymore? What then? Another foster home? Another school?"

I can see Hayley struggling not to betray her emotions. "He won't get fed up with you, Kit. He's really looking forward to getting to know you and the school you are going to has the best sports facilities. There's even a pool."

I can see him waiver slightly. "Do they have a football team?"

She nods. "They do, the school is top-notch. The range of sports it offers is amazing."

Kit looks over at me and I smile in encouragement. "It sounds good, Kit."

Inside, I'm not really that convinced, but I put on my game face for my brother. I want him to feel good about this. He can leave the worrying to me. Am I cynical about this news? You bet.

For a start, my dad must have had a reason to say his parents were dead. If this grandfather is so great, then why did our dad have no contact with him? And why did we never meet him? I mean, if he gave a shit about us, then surely he would have been a part of our lives when we were younger? Something didn't add up here.

Hayley looks at her watch and gets to her feet. "I'll be back on Saturday to collect you; I'm driving you down there myself."

"You are?" I say in surprise. I presumed we'd be put on a train or something.

Hayley grins. "Yes, I am. I want to take you." She turns her attention to our foster carers. "Jackie, Steve, thank you for being so understanding with Eliza. She is very lucky you are so forgiving." She gives me a pointed look before she picks up her bag and car keys and heads towards the door. Steve and Jackie see her out.

"I smell bullshit," Kit states, his dark brown eyes filled with apprehension and fear.

"Well, it's happening, kid, so we're going to have to roll with it. We'll be okay. It's you and me against the world, yeah?" I hold out my fist.

He can't help it, he breaks out into a grin and taps my fist with his. "You know it."

I smile back at him. I'm pretty good at pulling him from his moods.

He chuckles. "I can't believe you stole Jackie's car." He shakes his head. "I mean, really bad-ass stealing a Ford Focus, sis."

"Hardy, har, har." I grin, relieved he's smiling again. Nothing is more important than my brother's happiness, and I'll move heaven and earth to ensure he gets it.

FIVE DAYS LATER, WE HAVE PACKED OUR BAGS, AND HAYLEY has arrived to take us to our new home. I'm still not entirely convinced that everything is, and will be, as wonderful as Hayley is leading us to believe. There are so many questions in my head.

"Have you double checked you have your lifeline charger." Steve teases me, as we all stand in the hallway, surrounded by our cases, filled with our belongings and our memory books from each foster home.

I roll my eyes, but I can't resist a smile. "Yes, I have my phone charger."

"Ready to go then?" Hayley asks us both. I nod my head.

Steve ruffles Kit's hair. "You keep your head down and keep training hard. One day I'll be watching you on the tv playing for Stoke City."

Kit laughs. "I think you mean United."

Steve smiles. "Just take care, okay?"

Kit nods and smiles at Steve. He's bonded with Steve over the last six months thanks to their shared love of football. "I will."

Jackie wipes a tear away. "Okay, let's get this over with before I start blubbering all over you both." She pulls Kit in fort a hug. "We're always a phone call away, okay?"

Steve gently nudges my shoulder. "You take care as well young lady. Use that fire in you to create a good life. You have so much potential."

I nod. "I will and thank you for putting up with all my shit. I know I haven't been easy." I almost choke on my words. I'm not good at apologising or admitting when I'm wrong.

Steve nods his head. I think he knows how hard it was for me to say those words to him. I pull the handle up on my wheeled suitcase and follow Hayley to her car. Kit has his chinchilla, Winston, in his carrier, and he places him between us on the back seats.

CHAPTER TWO ·

ELIZA

The car drives past the blue and yellow sign saying welcome to Hawk Bay. I already hate this place. I hate that I have been dragged from my semi-okay okay life in Heathley to this godforsaken place by the coast. I bet it is full of posh dickheads who play polo and chess for fun. How fucking dull. This place looks as far removed from where I grew up as you could ever imagine. Kit snores peacefully beside me, looking like he hasn't got a care in the world. I wish I could be as laid back as he is, just rolling with the punches.

As the car journeys further into that will be our new home, unease runs down my spine. Why did my dad run from this life of privilege? What made him so determined to leave it behind? Why did he lie to us about his past and where he grew up? Is this place really so terrible that he felt the need to keep it a secret?

As we wind through the main streets of the town, I notice a champagne bar and some cute expensive looking fashion boutiques. Jesus, this place reeks of affluence and wealth. The car eventually turns up a steep hill and the houses become grander and more opulent. They all have electric gates and long sloping driveways. It's clear that this part of town is where the money is.

Almost at the top of the hill sits four grand looking mansions, sectioned off from the rest. Hayley stops in front of the gates that lead up to them. I jab my brother in the arm until he looks up, bewildered and confused.

"We're here," Hayley announces with a cheery smile before she leans out and presses the intercom for the gates.

I nudge my brother again. "We've arrived," I hiss, and he immediately sits up in his seat and looks ahead as the car sweeps down the drive to where the large, imposing house sits. It has a large grand entranceway; huge stone pillars sit on either side of the doors. It reminds me of the mansion the Bingley's lived in from the movie version of Pride and Prejudice. It looks like it has stood here for centuries, with its sturdy structure.

"Wow, it's huge!" my brother says, his mouth wide open as he takes in the intimidating mansion style house.

"It's a beast of a house, that's for sure," I reply with a frown. Why would anyone need a house this big?

Hayley's smile widens. "See, I told you both. Your grandfather is a very wealthy man."

As Hayley pulls up in front of two large doors, they open to reveal a petite, round woman who looks to be in her early sixties. She smiles warmly and looks excited at our arrival. She has ginger curly hair and rosy cheeks covered in freckles.

Hayley kills the engine then opens my brother's door for him. I climb out last, and look up at the large mansion house, while Kit busies himself helping Hayley get our bags out of the boot.

"Welcome children." The lady beams, beckoning us forward with her hand. I shove Kit gently in the back to get him to stop gawping and start moving his feet. Taking the hint, he climbs the stone stairs to where she waits for us. "Welcome to Hawk Manor House."

She looks over at my brother first. "Well, aren't you a handsome young man. You are the image of your father when he was your age."

"You knew him?" I ask, my eyes darting up to hers at the mention of our father.

"I did. I was his nanny. No one knew that boy like I did." She smiles and shakes her head like she is pulling herself from a long-forgotten memory. "Well, let's get you inside and settled."

We hurry after her, inside the house, and Hayley follows behind us.

"Woah!" Kit exclaims, his head moving in all directions as he takes in the grand foyer. "This is epic!"

Epic is not how I would describe it. Opulent and indulgent would be more appropriate word choices. The floor looks like marble, and a black ornate staircase over to the left curves up to the next floor. Shiny chandeliers hang from the ceiling creating prisms of light across the walls and floors. I feel tiny standing in this vast space with its high ceiling and grand staircase.

"I'll show you both to your bedrooms first and then I'll give you a tour of the house. Miss Parker, will you be staying for some refreshments?"

Hayley smiles but shakes her head. "Thank you, that is a lovely offer, but I have to get back on the road shortly. I have a long journey home."

The housekeeper, whose name I don't yet know, guides us up the remaining stairs and down a corridor that runs along the east side of the house. As we follow her, I pause halfway up the curved staircase when I notice a large painting hanging from the wall. A painting of a woman who looks just like me. Her eyes are the same deep chocolate brown as mine, our chins have the same small dimple, and her skin is as pale as mine. I guess I now know which side of the family I get my looks from. She's sitting under a pink blossom tree reading a book, her attention lost in the words on the pages of the story in her hands.

"You're both in the east wing of the house. The west wing is your grandfathers."

"The east wing." My brother chuckles, putting on a posh accent, and I can't help but smile.

"This is your room, young man." She pushes open two large doors and I'm surprised when I see it's decorated in modern décor. Gone is the Georgian style and antique furniture. The walls are painted in navy blue and white, and the bed is a modern double with a black metal frame. Over to the right of the room there's a large television on the wall and beneath it sits an X-box and a PlayStation. It's the type of bedroom most teenage boys could only dream of.

"Hell yes!" Kit says with a long, low whistle. "Do you see this shit, sis?" he asks me with a huge grin on his face.

"I see it," I reply with a soft smile. My brother is my world and seeing him so happy makes me feel happy.

"Follow me, young lady."

With a wink and a grin to my brother, I leave him with Hayley to soak in his epic new bedroom and I follow the housekeeper further down the corridor. She pushes open two doors and I stop still in my steps.

It's pale pink. I mean really pink.

"Holy hell, did Barbie throw up in here?" The words are out of my mouth before I can stop them.

"You don't like it." Her face drops. "Oh dear, I did wonder when that interior designer suggested pink. My granddaughter is a couple of years younger than you, but her colour palette comprises of black and black." I wince at how upset she is that I don't like it.

I sigh and plaster on a reassuring smile. "I guess I can live with pink, it's just not very me, if you know what I mean?"

Her eyes sweep over me, no doubt taking in my ripped black jeans, biker boots and ripped leather jacket. "No, I can see that." She clears her throat. "Breakfast is at seven. Your grandfather will expect you to be punctual. He's a stickler for things running like clockwork."

"Oh," I nod, "we're not meeting him tonight?"

She shakes her head. "Ah, no, I'm sorry, pet. He is a very busy man. He wanted to be here, but business will keep him away until the weekend. I'll leave you to unpack. Your bathroom is through the door on the left. If you need anything, just dial down to the kitchen." She points at a phone over by the bed. I am kind of surprised it's not a bell and that a butler won't appear and say, 'you rang.' I chuckle to myself, earning an inquisitive look from her.

"I forgot to ask your name."

"Oh, silly me. Did I not introduce myself properly? I'm Edith. I'm the housekeeper," she says it with such pride, and I can't help but like this woman. "My husband, Rory, is the groundskeeper, and our son, Calvin, is one of your grandfather's drivers. He'll likely be taking you to and from school." She points to the corridor. "I'll go and check on your brother."

I walk further into the room. The walls are painted in a soft pink with a luxurious cream carpet that makes me stop and take my shoes and socks off. I sigh in delight when my feet sink into the softness. The bed is a white wooden four-poster with voiles closed around it and the bedding is pink with frilled lace edges. It is vomit worthy. I'm seventeen not seven! But I can't help being touched that they went to this effort to decorate it for me. There's a beautiful fireplace over by the right side of the room and above it is a flat screen television and a rather comfortable looking pale cream three-seater sofa. Over by the window there's a desk, and holy crap, there's an Apple Mac laptop and what looks to be a brand-new iPad. The biggest surprise comes when I open the door over by the far side of the bed. Jesus wept! It's a walk-in wardrobe and it's bigger than Jackie and Steve's living room. What draws me in further is the school uniform hanging up on the rail. The blazer is navy blue edged in yellow; the shirt is pale blue; and the skirt is tartan in, you guessed it, blue and yellow. Even the uniform screams money. The sound of a knock on my bedroom door pulls me from the room and a man who looks to be in his thirties, with curly brown hair, walks into my room and places two suitcases down on the floor by the end of my bed.

"Here you go, miss," he says with a warm smile. "I'm Calvin, your driver and I'll be taking you both to school tomorrow."

"We have our own driver," I say with a shake of my head. "Crazy!"

He grins. "I'll be out the front to take you to school at eight-fifteen tomorrow." He looks round my room. "Wow, this is pink. Well, I'll leave you to it," he says, pointing towards the door.

"Calvin, what's he like?" I ask.

Calvin's eyes soften. "He comes across as formidable, but he has good intentions."

I nod my head. "Thank you." What an odd way to describe someone.

"Anytime miss."

"It's Eliza," I shout after him, but he's already gone. With a tired sigh, I sit myself on the end of the bed and glance around the room. It is a far cry from our last home.

Hayley pops her head in five minutes later and gushes over the four-poster bed and walk-in wardrobe space.

We all headed downstairs for our tour of the house. Edith is clearly very proud of the house. The kitchen is enormous and surprisingly modern. There is a vast library that I cannot help but drool over, four reception rooms, and indoor pool, and a gym that is kitted out with all the latest fitness equipment. Kit practically drools when he sees it. Hayley announces it is time for her to go. It's weird to think we'll no longer have a social worker. That we are no longer in care. I feel like I need to pinch myself and check that this is all real.

"You two have a great future ahead of you both. I'm so pleased that you finally have a family again. Take care, both of you. I'll check in on both of you in a couple of weeks' time." She looks at us both like she wants to hug us, and I take a slight step back. I'm not a hugger. I don't do hugs and kisses. We watch her climb into her car, and she beeps her horn and waves at us as she heads back down the long winding driveway. I bet there is a small part of her that is relieved that she doesn't have to deal with my shenanigans anymore.

CHAPTER THREE

ELIZA

I spend the next couple of hours unpacking my belongings. I place the family photos up above the fire on the fireplace and place the small brown teddy my parents bought me when I was born on my pillows. Edith calls us down for tea and we drool over her homemade chicken and mushroom pie. Kit devours it and asks for seconds. He eats like it's an Olympic sport, not that you can tell. There's not a slither of fat on him. He's at the age where he's shooting up in height. It's late by the time we finish eating, so we head off to bed as we both have a big day tomorrow, starting our new school.

I'm not ready to sleep yet. Feeling bored, I walk over to the drawn, floor length curtains in my room and pull them open. To my surprise, there is a small balcony, with floor to ceiling double glass doors. The doors are unlocked, and I open them and step out into the cool evening air. It's dark now, being just before ten at night. I look up at the stars and soak in the quiet. The sound of someone whistling pulls my attention towards the rear right side of the property. As I listen more carefully, I can hear music. Restless and not ready for bed, I put my boots back on and decide to go for a little exploration of my new home. I sit my bum on the metal banister and reach out and grasp the down-pipe with my hands. Shimmying my way down until I am near enough to the ground to be able to drop down on to my feet. I pull the hood of my black jumper over my head and with a quick glance behind me, I run across the lawn towards the music. I push through the trees and over uneven earth until I come out on the grounds of what I presume is the neighbouring mansion.

"You never learn, do you Robinson?" a deep voice says, and I duck back, remaining hidden behind the trees. I follow the sound of the voice and see a group of big hulking boys surrounding another boy.

"Look, guys, it wasn't me. I swear," the boy named Robinson protests. He's on his knees in front of them, his palms pressed together as he begs them to believe him. He doesn't strike me as the kind of guy that would hang around with these meat heads.

One of the guys surrounding him laughs. "Don't try to deny it. Just be the sly little shit you are and take your punishment."

Another guy pulls his phone out and holds it out in front of him. "Let's make sure the entire school gets to see what happens when you don't follow the Ace's orders, shall we?"

One member of the group steps forward. The moonlight allows me to see his face. His hair looks to be a dirty blond colour, and he has a five o'clock shadow over his jawline. His eyes are pale, but I can't tell in this light if they're green or blue. Another one comes up behind Robinson and tips his head back, prising his mouth open with his fingers.

The guy in front of him picks up dirt from the ground and shoves it into Robinson's mouth. He splutters and tries to spit it out, but the guy behind him grips his jaw tightly. "Be a good boy and open wide."

The guy in front shoves more dirt into his mouth and Robinson chokes on it as more and more is forced inside.

My phone pings in my pocket and I stop dead still! Fuck!

"What was that?" the one holding Robinson's jaw in his grip asks, his eyes skirting into the darkness right where I am hiding. "Someone's there."

I take a slow step back and inwardly curse when my foot snaps a twig. Two seconds later, two hands reach out and grab me, dragging me forward.

"Get your fucking hands off me!" I hiss as my feet leave the ground and I'm dumped into the centre of their circle next to poor Robinson, who is still trying to spit all the dirt out of his mouth.

"Well, well, what do we have here?" One of the guy's steps forward and walks around me. His blond hair flops into his face. "What are you doing spying in the dark, huh?" He pulls my hood from my head and my long, wavy, scarlet coloured hair falls out and down my back.

"It's a girl," Blondie states as he continues to circle me.

"No shit, Sherlock," another guy states dryly as he steps forward to get a closer look at me. But it's the guy who's front and centre that has my attention. His dark eyes study me, like a lion watching its prey. I lift my chin in the air and meet his eyes, glaring back at him. He aims the torchlight from his phone at my face, making me squint. There's no denying it, he is beautiful. Like a sculpted god, with a chiselled jaw. His dark hair flops over his forehead and he fills out those jeans perfectly. There's an aura of menace and danger surrounding him.

"Do you mind?" I hiss, giving him evils; covering my eyes from the glare of the light.

"What are you doing out here in the dark, spying on matters that don't concern you, little girl?" He steps forward and as he reaches out, I flinch. He takes a piece of my hair and winds it around his finger. "I'm waiting for an answer."

I smirk at him. He thinks he's intimidating me. He's wrong. "Who I am is none of your fucking business. Is this what you do for fun around here, bully those weaker than you?"

He smirks back, his eyes never leaving mine. "What we're doing is not your concern. This is Ace's business."

I laugh. "What is that, the name of your little gentleman's club? Let me guess, do you have a secret clubhouse and get people to do hazing shit to join? God, you rich people are so cliché."

He steps closer to me, forcing me to raise my chin to look up at him, which just serves to piss me off even more. "Ah, I see. You're from the fair. A little gypsy girl. Were you hoping to crash the party and steal some cash, sweetheart? If you want to earn some pennies, you can always get on your knees and use that pretty mouth God gave you."

The other guys all laugh at his words. Someone kicks the back of my knees, forcing me into a kneeling position in the dirt. The ringleader steps closer and gripping my hair at the back of the neck, he tilts my head up. "Ah look, how pretty do you look on your knees? You want to suck my cock and earn yourself a fiver, Scarlet?"

I snigger and glare up at him. "I wouldn't suck your rich dick for a grand."

He grips my hair tighter and stares me dead in the eyes. "Ah, Scarlet, you'd have to pay me to let you suck my cock. Now, what do we do with you?" He tilts his head and continues to watch me. "Let her watch and see what happens when folk around here don't do as they're told." He forces me to my feet and spins me, so that my back is snug against his chest. His arm holds me around the middle whilst his other hand continues to fist my hair.

"Watch and learn, Scarlet. Rafe, carry on," he orders. His rich scent, surround me and despite the cold, I can feel the heat from his chest burning into my back.

The dark-haired guy's face breaks into an excited grin and he steps up, picking up a handful of dirt off the floor. "One handful for every one of your crimes."

Robinson's mouth is held open again, as he shoves more dirt down his throat. Another guy steps up and forces more down, then another guy. Robinson is coughing on the dirt and heaving, but they don't stop.

"Are you watching, Scarlet?" my captor asks me, his breath tickling my ear. "Now you'll run home tonight and tell that gypsy family of yours that if they send anyone up here again looking to steal from us, they'll end up in a far worse state than little Robinson here."

"You're a dick," I hiss, earning me a menacing chuckle. His stubble brushes against my cheek, sending a shiver down my spine.

"Throw him in," he orders, and two guys step forward and take Robinson by his arms and legs. He writhes and struggles in their hold, but they don't let go and I gasp when they place him a box that I hadn't seen there until this moment. A box that resembles a coffin. Two of the guys place him in and place the lid on the make-shift coffin and clasp it closed. Inside, Robinson is frantically banging on the lid, begging to be let out. Everyone steps back apart from the two that placed him in there, and they throw dirt on top of the coffin. Robinson pounds harder on the lid, begging and screaming to be let out.

"Cruel," I state, "making him think he's being buried alive."

"No more than what he deserves," the dark stranger replies as he continues to hold me against him. "You see, we're in charge around here. What we say goes. We make the rules, and we serve the punishment for those who don't follow them."

I laugh. "Have you heard yourself? Your what, like nineteen, maybe twenty. No one of that age has that much power. Let's call it what it is. You're bullies. You prey on the weak and vulnerable."

He laughs a deep, dry laugh. "I think that's more you and your gypsy family."

He starts slowly walking us backward.

"What are you doing? You need to let me go," I hiss, as I struggle in his iron grasp. I watch as a few more of the guys throw soil on top of the box they trapped Robinson in before they follow us and head off in front. Although two of the guys hold back, walking behind me.

"Have to say, she's quite pretty for a gypsy," blond guy says, winking at me and grinning.

"Yeah, well, you can look but you can't touch," I warn him, flashing my teeth.

"Ooh, feisty too. I like a girl with a bit of fight in her. Makes it more interesting in bed."

The other guy, Rafe, throws his arm over Blond's shoulder and looks at me then behind me at my captor who continues walking us backward towards the mansion house. "What are we going to do with her?"

My captor is quiet for a moment. "Scarlet is going to join us tonight," he announces.

Rafe cocks his head to the side, looking surprised. "Really?"

My captor doesn't answer him, instead he turns us so that we're both facing forward, and I can actually see where we're heading. The way becomes easier to see as the lights from the mansion provide some relief from the darkness of the night.

"Which one of you uppity bastards lives here then?" I ask gesturing my head towards the house before us.

"That would be me," my captor replies. Typical. He's my fucking neighbour. "The houses up on Hawk Hill are owned by the four founding families of this town. The Alderman's, the Colling's, the Ellsworth's, and the Savage's."

The blond guy holds his hands out wide to his side and twirls around in front of us as we walk. "AKA, the Aces."

I perk up when I hear my grandfather's surname. It feels strange knowing it's the family name, but at some point, my dad must have changed it. Hence why my birth certificate says Holton instead of Alderman.

"Let me guess, you're the Savage," I ask my sexy as sin captor. The name suits him perfectly.

"You ask a lot of questions, Scarlet, but you don't just get answers, you earn them," Blond explains to me with a wide grin.

I roll my eyes dramatically. "Forget it. I can figure it out for myself. And you three are the ringmasters of this little Aces club."

"The four founding families were once all very close. Now it's just the three families," my captor tells me, and I don't miss the hostility in his voice.

"But that is all set to change soon," Rafe says, chuckling, earning him a punch in the arm from Blond. "Just keeping it real for Arch."

So, his name is Arch. I wonder if that's short for Archie or Archibald. Nah, he doesn't strike me as either.

I'm surprised when we don't head towards the house, but instead continue round the side of the house towards a car that's parked on the drive. "Where the hell are we going?" I ask, but in answer all I receive is a throaty chuckle from Rafe and Blond. "This is kidnap, you know?"

"Is it though? I mean, you were trespassing on private property, so the way I see it, we have a right to apprehend you," Blond says with a wink.

My captor unlocks the car and opens the back passenger door and pushes me inside. He leans in and glares in warning. "Behave Scarlet." He moves aside and his two sidekicks enter the back and sit on either side of me, squeezing me in like a piece of meat in a sandwich.

My captor climbs into the front of his fancy Audi and starts the engine, and we head off into the night to God knows where. Blond takes out his phone and whistles and I peer at his screen. Gross, it's a titty photo. "Typical," I say dryly.

He smirks. "I don't even ask for them either."

Sighing, I turn my attention to where we are driving to. I notice we're heading out of town. We carry on driving for another ten minutes until he parks up beside a dirt track leading to some woods. Is this the part where they dump me in the middle of nowhere and leave me to find my own way home? My captor climbs out of the car and the other two follow. Blond reaches in and pulls me out by my arms, holding them behind my back. His other hand fists my hair at the nape of my neck, and we head into the forest. I try to control my racing heart. Why are they dragging me into the woods in the dead of night? What if they leave me here? I have no fucking clue where I am. Christ, I don't even know the address of my new home.

I stumble over a tree branch and Blond pulls on my hair to keep me upright. "What colour hair do you think she has under this dye job?" he asks the other two.

Rafe looks at me and smirks. "She's probably a ginger."

Blond chuckles. "I'm not impartial to a ginger chick. Summer Charlton is ginger, and she can give head like a pro."

"I'm sure you know all about the pros," I snigger.

"Quiet," Savage orders, and we continue on in silence, further into the confines of the woods. I can barely see a foot in front of me. It's so dark out here. In the distance I can hear voices and my eyes widen in surprise when the trees' part and I realise we have come out on top of a cliff. There's a group of roughly twelve other teenagers up here. Most of them boys, but three girls stand together over by one side. One of them grins like a cunning cat when her eyes set on Savage. She walks towards him, swinging her hips exaggeratedly. I wasn't sure why she was bothering. She has the body of a ten-year-old girl. The words eating disorder spring to mind.

"Baby, where have you been." She places her hands on Savage's chest and looks up at him, her lips puckered and her fake eyelashes fluttering up at him. I snigger and suddenly her gaze lands on me. "Who the hell is this?"

"None of your business," Savage tells her, firmly removing her hands from his chest and signalling to the blond guy who pushes me forward into the hands of my captor again. Savage wraps an arm tightly around my waist and with the other, he holds my hands behind my back between our bodies. "See this, Scarlet. This is Hawk Cliff Point. Down there is a thirty-five-foot drop into the cold sea. Tell me, can gypsies swim?"

"I can swim, arsehole," I hiss back at him. I hate being in situations that are out of my control. It doesn't sit well with me. "Why are we here?" I ask, feigning boredom to hide my increasing anxiety. I can swim, but I hate the water. I have feared it ever since my parents' car plummeted over that ravine into the icy river.

The blond one claps his hands together and makes the sound of a wolf howling. "It's initiation night, Little Red."

I shake my head. "So, I wasn't wrong about the hazing and stupid boy club."

"Listen up, Scarlet," Savage says directly into my ear, his breath tickling me, "everyone wants to be a part of this. The Aces have existed for generations. It's a tradition in this town. It's a privilege to be a part of our little society."

I shake my head, and even though he can't see my face properly; I roll my eyes and fake a yawn. "Wake me up when this is over."

"Okay, gather round my Clubs," Blond commands. "Tonight is the night you have been waiting for. We deem only a select few worthy. Worthy to take the chance to become a Club and be a part of the Aces. This is the ultimate challenge. Do the jump and you are in."

The group of boys all whoop and start patting each other on the back and bumping fists. Jesus, this is ridiculous!

One boy, who looks to be about fourteen, takes off his shoes and rubs his hands together focusing on the cliff edge. He walks towards the edge and takes up his position. Blowing out a nervous breath, he then makes a run for it, and jumps off the edge of the cliff, disappearing into the darkness of the night.

"Fuck," I hiss. Savage pushes us closer to the edge, so much so that the edge of my boots hang over the steep cliff face. There is a sound of something hitting water and suddenly a torchlight used by one of the others up here on the cliff shines on the boy in the water, who bobs up and down in the waves, fist bumping the air and whistling.

One by one, the other boys all take the challenge and jump off the clifftop into the cold water below. As I watch the last one jump, I can't help but wonder what the purpose is in bringing me along tonight. Rafe turns and shines the torchlight from his phone into my eyes.

"Now, it's Scarlet's turn."

I scoff, "I don't fucking think so. Besides, I don't even want to be a part of your shitty little club."

Savage's grip on my hands tighten and he pulls me back. "You think we'd let you be a Club, little gypsy. Only those deemed worthy get to join. You have to be from an influential family and loyal to this town and its traditions."

"You get to jump as punishment, Little Red," the blond one tells me, his eyes widening with excitement and adrenaline. "You interfered in business that has nothing to do with you and you were trespassing on private property."

Savage walks us to the edge of the cliff again, and my heart hammers in my chest. Anything but water. I fear nothing in life, nothing that is, but water. "You ready to take a little dip?"

"You can't make me do this," I protest angrily. When I get scared, I get defensive. Like a cat backed into a corner, my claws come out.

"Oh, you will jump, Scarlet. You'll jump or be pushed." He suddenly let's go of me and I jump back from the edge and turn my back on the deep drop to face the three boys and three girls who are still up here with me. "I'm leaving. You can't make me do this."

Rafe blocks my move to pass them. "Ah, ah, Little Red. There's no escape."

The nameless girl, who draped herself all over Savage before, taps her foot and looks bored. "Can you just fucking jump, tramp, and then we can all go. It's freezing up here."

I send a withering gaze her way. "Perhaps you should try wearing some clothes then," I suggest in a bored tone, my frosty eyes sweeping her body from head to toe. Who wears arse-hugging shorts and a cropped t-shirt on a bloody clifftop in the middle of the night?

"Come on, Little Red, I thought you gypsies were tough,"

Blond says to me, smiling, and it's while my attention on him that the little hellcat strikes. Out of the corner of my eye I see movement and suddenly I'm falling backwards over the edge of the cliff, down into the darkness and down towards the vast, cold ocean. I release a scream of fear as I plummet down and hit the water with a cold hard splash that takes my breath away.

CHAPTER FOUR

ELIZA

A ll at once, I'm back there again, seeing the car plummet down the hill and into the water. Watching helplessly as it sinks down into the murky water, taking my parents with it. I sit there struggling for breath and bleeding out, helpless to do anything. The sound of the water roars in my ears and the coldness bites at my skin as it makes contact. I'm frozen in panic, and then suddenly two arms reach for me, grabbing around my waist and pulling me upwards. I reach my hand out towards the car as it sinks into the river. I scream to my parents. I scream for someone to help them. I gasp as I come up above the surface of the water. "Go back, go back, they're dying, my parents, please go back," I scream, pounding on the chest of my saviour.

"Go back for who, Scarlet? What the fuck are you on about?"

Realisation hits me like a cold slap in the face. I'm not in the car with my mum and dad. I'm in the sea at Hawk Bay. I pound on his chest as I fight the angry tears threatening to fall down my face. "You fucking bastard."

"I though you said you could swim," he says angrily as he holds me against him, the force of the waves trying to take us further into the sea.

"I can," I hiss. "I just haven't been in the water for five years, not that it's any of your business, arsehole."

He looks down at me puzzled. His dark hair is slicked back

aways from his face and it places his chiselled cheek bones on display. Even soaking wet he is a beautiful monster.

"Lean on my back and put your arms around my neck, I'll get us out of here," he orders me, and wanting to get the fuck out of the water as quick as I can, I do as he asks without any argument. "I'll fucking kill Georgie for this," he promises, and he says it with such conviction that I don't doubt he will.

We reach the beach, and he drags my heavy and soaking wet arse down on to the sand. I suck in heavy breaths as I try to calm my racing heart. From where he sits beside me, he looks down at me and brushes my wet hair from my face, and just for a second or two, there's nothing but the two of us on the dark beach with the sound of waves crashing against the rocks. I am cold, wet, and extremely pissed off.

He grips my chin with his fingers. "Why didn't you just admit you have a fear of water?"

I scoff, "Why should I share anything about myself with you fucking vultures? You judge me, make presumptions, but you know nothing about who I am." I shiver. I'm fucking freezing.

"Holy fuck. Is Little Red alive?" Blond comes running towards us, the torchlight shining in my eyes, making me cover them with my arm.

"Stop shining that fucking light in my eyes, Seb," Savage orders him.

Seb, as I now know him to be, crouches down on his claves before me and looks me over. "Holy shit, girl. You sunk like a rock. I thought you were a goner for sure."

I shiver and wrap my arms around myself for some warmth. "Believe me, I've survived worse."

"See, I told you the little tramp would be fine," a whiny voice says, and I turn my attention to the little bitch as she comes into sight with her two friends and the third member of the Aces. I see red. This is all her fault; I storm her way and pull my fist back, then I smack her clean in the face. She squeals and covers her face with her hands. I'm furious and I pull my fist back again to give her another one, when two arms wrap around my waist and lift me off the ground.

"Put me down and let me fucking kill her," I demand, worming around, trying to get out of his grip.

"Just calm down, Scarlet, we need to try and get dry before we get hypothermia. I'll deal with Georgie tomorrow."

Georgie gulps at his words, as Seb checks her face. "Stop moaning. You'll likely have a shiner, nothing more. Besides, you fully deserved that. Now go home and keep your fucking mouth shut, Georgie, you hear me?"

She glares at Seb, but nods he head and backs off towards her friend who both swarm her, making a fuss over her, as they walk off into the night.

I yelp when I'm lifted off my feet. "Wrap your legs around me, Scarlet,' Savage orders.

I want to protest and tell him I can walk, but my legs feel like jelly and I'm shaking like a leaf. I can't feel my legs, or my arms, and my teeth are chattering. Winding my legs around his middle, he strides up the beach.

We walk for what feels like an age before the black car comes into view. Seb and Rafe climb in the front and Savage places me on the back seat, buckling me in, before he walks around the back of the car to climb in beside me.

"Crank that heat up man, as high as it will go,' he orders as he pulls his soaking wet hoodie over his head and then his t-shirt follows. He looks over at me and swears when he sees me shivering. "Fuck, Rafe, grab a blanket out of the boot, she's a mess." He reaches over to me and grabs the bottom of my hoodie.

"Get off," I say weakly in protest, smacking his hand away.

"You need these wet clothes off, Scarlet. We need to get warm and dry as quick as we can."

I'm too weak to fight him as he lifts my hoodie over my head, throwing it beside us. He reaches for my foot and pulls off one soaked boot and then the other, and then he undoes my flies and tugs my wet jeans down my legs. He pauses when he sees the four-inch scar on my right fly, and I glare at him daring him to even think about commenting. Then I'm in my bra and knickers in a car with three strangers in the middle of the night. My eyes bug out of my head when he pulls his jeans off and passes them to Rafe who, with a brief concerning look at me, hands him a thick white blanket.

Savage whistles to get my attention and beckons me with his head. "Get over here, Scarlet."

I shake my head vehemently as I sit there in my underwear, shaking, my teeth chattering. Suddenly his hands are around my waist, and he lifts me and deposits me, facing him, onto his lap. He wraps the blanket around us and pulls me tight against his chest and rubs up and down my arms to generate some heat. I'm so cold and tired that I let my head fall onto his shoulder. "Okay, go, get us to my place," he orders, and the car moves off, away from the line of the forest.

I close my eyes, feeling exhausted, and groan when he lifts my head. "Open your eyes, Scarlet. You need to stay awake. You hear me?"

I groan and shake my head. Why couldn't he just let me sleep?

"Open your eyes, Little Red."

I moan. Why wouldn't the handsome fucker just shut up and let me go to sleep?

"This handsome fucker needs you to open your eyes, Scarlet. Open them and look at me," he orders, gripping my chin tight between his fingers.

"Don't let her go to sleep, Arch. You need to keep her awake," I hear one of them say. Their voices sound far away, like they're at the other end of a tunnel.

"She's not listening to me. Fuck it," I hear Savage say before I feel his lips press against mine. His warm mouth moves against mine and my lips take on a life of their own and move against his. I moan when his tongue enters my mouth.

"Well, that's one way to keep her awake."

"Shut the fuck up, Seb," he replies against my lips before he continues to kiss me. I grasp onto his shoulders and shift in his lap, needing to be closer to him. His hands are in my hair as he kisses me. When he pulls away, I whimper. "Open your eyes for me," he coaxes.

My eyes flutter open, and I look into two chestnut-coloured eyes. The eyes of my captor. "There she is. Now stay awake for me, okay?" I nod and rest my head on his shoulder. I'm still shivering but a little less now than I was before. It's like his kiss breathed warmth into my body.

"Technically Little Red is a Club," I hear Seb say from the front of the car.

"She's not a Club," Rafe answers, cold and firm. "She doesn't belong in our world."

"Mores the pity. Little Red has fire in her soul," Seb comments. "I think Arch would agree with me too, huh?"

"Rafe is right, she's not one of us," he tells them both, his breath warm against my hair.

"So, have you heard when the Alderman princess arrives?" Seb asks from the front, as he drives us down the dark and winding road.

I feel Savage tense beneath me, and I snuggle into him, seeking his heat. I'm suddenly alert, keen to hear what they know about me.

"My dad seems to think she will arrive at Easter break." I don't miss the bitter tone in his voice when he replies. Is there bad blood between his family and mine?

"Well, you can always play with Little Red until the princess arrives," one of them suggests.

"Maybe I will," he says as his hands run up my back, and this time I shiver for a different reason.

The car comes to a stop. "Make sure you park her in the garage. I'll take it from here. I'll see you fuckers tomorrow." He opens the car door and stands with ease, even though I'm wrapped around him. He pulls the blanket tight around me and closing the door, he walks away from the car towards his house. I look over his shoulder at Seb who leans out of the driver's window and winks at me.

"I'll no doubt be seeing you again, Little Red," he says, and then he's driving off down the side of the house.

I hear Savage turn a key in the lock and he carries me inside. He climbs the stairs and I look over his shoulder at the opulent hallway. There are sleek marble floors, and a large, beautiful chandelier hangs down from the ceiling. We enter a large bedroom, decorated with black walls. He sits me down and I whimper as his body heat leaves me.

"You need to take off that wet underwear, Scarlet. I'll get you something dry to wear," he tells me, before he pads away from me in nothing but a pair of tight black boxers. His toned thighs flex as he walks. I blow out a breath as I admire his pert behind. My fingers are like jelly, but I manage to unclasp my bra and drop it to the floor. My knickers follow them, and I pull the now damp blanket back around my shoulders, covering my body.

He comes back into the room, now wearing low-hanging jersey bottoms, and I notice the tattoo on his chest. It's a fan of four ace cards for each suit of a card deck. "Arms up," he orders me.

If I wasn't desperate to be warm, I'd tell him there's no way he's seeing me topless, but I'm freezing and I need warmth, so I drop the blanket and lift my arms up for him. He pulls the top over my head, and I put my arms into the long sleeves, grateful to feel something warm and dry against my skin. He leans over by the side of me, and I startle at the close proximity, before I realise he's pulling back the covers on the bed. "Get in, Scarlet. We need to keep warm."

I drop into the warm and inviting bed and sigh as he pulls the covers over me and I feel the bed dip as he gets in behind me. I'm definitely warmer, but I still can't stop shivering.

"Come here, Scarlet." He pulls me against his chest and spoons me, and I'm enveloped against his warm body. One arm slings itself across my body. "What were you doing on my property tonight?"

Something stops me from telling him the truth. "Wouldn't you like to know?" I reply, my teeth chattering loudly.

"How long is your family in Hawk Bay for?"

I shrug my shoulders and this time my answer isn't a lie. "I honestly don't know." I really don't. I mean, I want to believe this is it. That this is our last move, but even though we have been claimed by family, I still can't let my guard down and let myself believe we're going to stay.

"Do you ever wish you could press pause, Scarlet? Ever feel like fate is creeping up on you and all you want to do is run in the opposite direction and not do what they expect of you?"

I chuckle weakly. "I never do what people expect me to."

"You like to live life on the edge, huh?"

"Yeah, but not the edge of a cliff."

This earns me a deep laugh from him, "Yes Scarlet, I figured that one out when I had to dive into that fucking water after you."

I yawn. The events of today have left me exhausted and I have no clue what time it is.

"Go to sleep Scarlet, I'll keep you warm."

I WAKE UP IN THE MORNING AND STRETCH. I SLEPT LIKE A log, which is unusual for me. Nightmares plague my sleep most nights. Wow, this mattress is so soft, it's like lying on air. I open my eyes and for a minute I'm disorientated. Then I remember. I remember the stranger who made me watch him and his friends shove a boy's mouth full of soil and pretend to bury him alive. Sadistic fucker. I roll over hesitantly and breathe out a sigh of relief at finding I'm alone. Thank Christ for that small mercy. The Savage boy is nowhere to be seen. I climb out of the warmth and comfort of his bed and search for my clothes. Shit!

I left my clothes in the car last night. I look down at the large male t-shirt that's skimming my thighs. This will have to do. Luckily, I don't have far to go. I look at the clock on the bedside table. It's only six-thirty in the morning, so I should be able to make it home before anyone realises I have been gone all night.

Opening the bedroom door ever so carefully and quietly, I jog to the stairs. I peep down to see if I can see or hear any movement, and when I don't, I dart for the stairs. At the bottom, I have a quick look around then head to the front door. I say a silent prayer as I carefully turn the door handle and send a quick thanks to my guardian angel when it opens. With one last quick look over my shoulder, I'm out of there like a whippet. I head round to the back of property, to where I know there is a gap in-between the fencing that separates the two properties and climb through. That's the first hurdle done. Now to get back into my grandfather's house unnoticed. As I make my way towards the house, I hide in the treeline listening for any signs of life. I make a run for it and when I hit the back wall of the house, I have to quickly duck down when I see Edith in the kitchen window. She sings as she goes about her chores. I crouch down and crawl along until I get to the back door, opening it ever so slightly to slide inside.

When I make it to my bedroom, I am gasping for breath. At least no one saw me. It would have been all kinds of awkward having to explain to my new guardian why I am sneaking back into the house at the crack of dawn in nothing but a boy's t-shirt. I climb into bed and snuggle under my covers. I should be able to get a half hour nap in before I have to get up.

It feels like my eyes haven't been shut for more than fifteen minutes, when Edith knocks at the door and bustles into the room, all sunshine and light.

"Good morning, Eliza. Time to get up and ready for your first day." She comes over to my bedside and places a glass of orange juice down on the side.

"It's too early," I groan, pushing my face into the pillow, hoping she'll go away.

"Nonsense. You start school at half-past eight. You need time to shower and change and eat a nutritious breakfast."

I lift my head of the pillow and stare at her. "Did you say school starts at eight-thirty? What kind of school makes kids starts so early?"

She chuckles at me and shakes her head. "The type that offers the best education money can buy. Come on now, up you get," she insists. "I'll see you in the kitchen for breakfast."

Groaning, I sit up and yawn. Today is going to be a long day thanks to those dickhead Aces and their stupid games. I smile mischievously to myself. They are going to get a shock today when I rock up to their posh private school and they realise they got their assumptions about me all wrong. Gypsy girl, ha! Wait until they find out who my grandfather is and that I live next door to Savage, in a house just as big and grand as his own.

The shower is amazing, I could stay in it all day, but breakfast calls. I frown as I stare in the mirror at my reflection. The navy and yellow uniform is not my style, and the yellow doesn't go with my burgundy-coloured hair. I have dried my hair and styled it in loose beachy waves, leaving it flowing down my back. I hate tying my hair up, because it exposes the large scar on my neck, and that leads to questions I do not want to answer. Don't get me wrong, I'm not ashamed of my scars. They are my reminder that I survived death. They are a reminder of what I have come through and of my inner strength.

CHAPTER FIVE

ELIZA

When I reach the kitchen, my brother is already tucking into a full English breakfast. He looks so grown-up and handsome in his new school uniform.

"Look at you," I tease as I take a seat beside him at the giant kitchen island. I run my hands along the white marble work top. "All smart and handsome."

Kit rolls his eyes at me. "Shut up." He looks over at me and grins. "Look at you, all cute and girly."

I sweep a quick glance over to make sure Edith isn't looking and then I give him the finger.

"Here you go, Eliza." She comes bustling over with a plate loaded with sausages, bacon, eggs, beans and even hash browns.

"Woah, Edith, this is way too much food for me." I stare at the full plate before me. "In future, poached eggs on toast will do me just fine, please."

Edith shakes her head at me. "Young girls today, so obsessed with their figures."

I go to protest that I'm not obsessed with my figure, I just like to lead a healthy lifestyle and feed my body with good food, but I decide not to bother. It would seem Edith likes to mother us, so I'm best leaving her to it.

I eat around half of what she's given me and grab a second cup of coffee. I can't function in the morning without coffee.

Calvin arrives to take us to school and Edith sees us off at the door, telling us to have a great day and to make sure we eat a good lunch. The woman is clearly a feeder.

We set off down the long driveway and I look over to Kit. "You ready for this?'

He nods his head. "Yeah, I can't wait to see the sports facilities."

I nod my head and smile enthusiastically, but secretly I'm pessimistic about how this will go. Not only are we new, but we haven't grown up with money. We come from a working-class are and our accents give that away. I'm not convinced that there will red carpet roll out for us, or a warm welcome.

I look to the front of our car, to our driver, Calvin. Time to pick his brains about this place.

"Hey, Calvin, what do you know about the Aces?"

Calvin looks at me in surprise through his front mirror. "How have you heard about them already?"

Ah shit. "Social media," I reply, thinking on the hoof. "I've been doing some snooping and saw some kid mentioned the Aces like it's some sort of elusive boys' club."

Calvin chuckles. "Yes, the Aces is a bit of an age-old tradition round here. It's the four founding families of the Bay. The Alderman's, the Colling's, the Ellsworth's, and the Savage's. The four families are the powerhouse of this bay. One of the four families has built or owns everything you see."

Kit chuckles. "The Savage's; they don't sound friendly."

Calvin shrugs his shoulders. "The Savage's are a very wealthy family. They own a large chain of well-known restaurants and clubs, and some health spa resorts. For as long as I can remember, everyone has held the Aces in revere, all wanting to be a part of their group."

"Did you know our dad?" Kit asks him, and I see Calvin visibly stiffen.

"Yes, I knew your dad. We grew up together. He was a good few years older than me, though."

I lean forward in my seat, eager to ask more questions about our father, but Calvin turns on the radio and turns his attention back to the road.

"Why does it feel like this place is full of secrets?" Kit whispers to me, a frown etched on his face.

"Probably because it is," I reply. Why does everyone shut down when we ask about our dad? At least at school, I may be able to do some snooping and find out more about why our dad ran away from this place and never looked back.

We pass through a grand entrance of two large gate pillars that have twin huge stone hawks standing on stone spheres, their wings spread like they are ready to take flight. The long driveway gradually reveals and very gothic, old looking building, complete with stone gargoyles and turrets. I feel like I'm stepping into a scene from HP. I mean who goes to school in a place like this?

Calvin waits behind other cars that pull up in front of the school, dropping off children at the front. It's a far cry from what we're used to. At some of our foster homes the local authorities paid a taxi firm to take us to school; nothing shouts 'children in care' louder than going to school in a taxi every day. Here, however, all the kids are being dropped off in a Mercedes or Range Rover. There are definitely no taxis here.

Calvin pulls up outside the grand school entrance, then opens my brother's door for him to climb out. I open my door before he can get round to my side, and step out. I look up at the large, imposing building — this place is enormous. I hope the map is easy to follow because finding our way around this vast place will not be easy. Calvin hands me my bag.

"Have a good day, both of you. I'll be here at the end of the day to pick you up." We both nod our heads and turn our attention to the school. People are already noticing us. I imagine around here, new people stick out like a sore thumb, especially new, poor people.

Laughter pulls my attention up the stone steps to a group of boys and girls who are hanging around the entrance. I freeze in place as I recognise them. The Aces. Archer, Rafe and Seb all hold centre court with their minions around them. I notice the bitch, Georgie, who pushed me off the cliff is there, too. I push my shoulders back and hold my head up high. Start as you meant to go on, Eliza, I tell myself. I climb the steps and as we near them; I feel three sets of eyes on us. Our path is blocked, and my gaze travels up the navy blazer to a set of cold, dark eyes.

"I think you're a little lost, Scarlet. The state school is over in the next village."

I raise my head and meet the eyes of Archer Savage, and then cock a brow. "Thank you, but I am exactly where I'm supposed to be. Now, if you'll excuse me, my brother and I need to enrol."

He doesn't budge and just glares coldly down at me.

"Ah, you must be the Alderman's." I pull my attention from Savage's frosty glare and up to the man who has appeared in the entranceway, who I presume is the headmaster.

"Come on up. Welcome to Hawk Bay."

Savage's nostrils flare and, honestly, I'm surprised steam doesn't come out of his ears. I hear gasps and whispers from behind me where his friends are all gathered.

"Excuse me," I say in a falsely positive voice. Out of the corner of my eye I can see his fists clench at his side. His glare has gone from frosty to downright hostile. He takes a step back and I shoulder check him on my way past. Arsehole. Last night I was good enough to drag along on their escapades, but today, because I have turned up on their territory, he is pissed off. Maybe he shouldn't have judged me and made assumptions about who I am.

As we pass his friends, I cast a sideways glance their way; Seb and Rafe are glaring at me with looks that could cut glass. I shrug my shoulders and keep my head high. They can kiss my poor arse because I'm here to stay.

"Welcome," the headteacher says in greeting as we reach him. "Please join me in my office and we'll get you set up for your first day."

I can't help but glance over my shoulder, and when I do, I see the three Aces with their heads together, talking and looking at me like I am a complete shock and surprise to them. Turning my back on them, I follow behind my brother. I'm not going to lie; it feels good throwing a curveball their way.

Half hour later we have our timetables and our iPads — yes, that's right, an iPad. The headteacher also gives us that talk that the school is a very elite school and that comes with expectations in regard to behaviour. His eyes focused on me when he talked about behaviours. I guess my school record doesn't read so well. I have been excluded a few times.

There's a knock on his office door and a girl pops her head inside. She's tall, about five-foot-seven, and she has a blonde, wavy, sharp bob that stops an inch below her chin. She also has pale blue eyes and a full, wide mouth; I notice my brother's attention shift upon her arrival.

"Ah, Verity. Just in time" The headteacher beckons her in and she smiles warmly at my brother and me. "Verity will be your guide for the day, Eliza. Maxon should be here any minute to take you, Kit."

Verity offers her hand out to me. "Hi."

I get to my feet and place my hand in hers, and she gives it a firm shake. "Welcome to Hawk Bay Private School. We're in English Literature together this morning and then we have Business Studies afterwards. Come on, let's get you to class."

Grabbing my bag off the floor, I glance at my brother. I smother my brother; I can't help it. "Will you be okay?"

He eyeballs me in embarrassment before glancing over to Verity and blushing. "Sure."

I nod my head and squeeze his shoulders as I pass him. I really want him to be happy here. I know he desperately wants to belong somewhere and finally settle.

"Okay," Verity says as we step outside, "first, welcome to HBA. In case you didn't know, the school building is over three hundred years old. It was once the home of Lord and Lady

Carrington. The school is big, but you will get used to it, eventually. Some pupils do dorm here, there are rooms up in the east and west towers."

I bob my head in surprise. I am amazed to hear it is also a boarding school. "Really?"

Verity nods her head, her blonde waves bouncing as she does. "Oh, yes, we have students from all across Europe. There are even a couple of students from America studying here. Our English teacher, Miss Hammond, is really great. She's so passionate about books." Verity beams when she talks about our teacher. "Our Business Studies teacher, Mr Harlow, not so much."

We walk for another ten minutes, and what seems like miles, until we come to a large mahogany door. "Lesson has already started, so we'll have to slip in quietly." She puts her finger to her lips to signal me to be quiet.

When we enter the room, everyone's eyes lift to us. The teacher stops mid-sentence, and smiling at both of us, gestures with her hand to the only two empty desks in the room. Verity heads to the one towards the back, and I take a seat in one in the second row from the front.

"Welcome, Eliza, I'm Miss Hammond. If you could open your book on your tablet to page one-hundred-and-fifty, we are currently analysing chapter four."

Letting my hair fall like a curtain, I pull out my iPad and open the book at the correct chapter. I can feel the stares of the rest of my classmates from behind me. I settle into the class, and Verity is right. You can't help but enjoy the class — Miss Hammond has a passion for the subject she teaches and it's somewhat infectious. Before I know it, the bell for the next class is ringing, and everyone jumps up, grabs their bags, and heads to their next class.

Verity appears at my desk, clutching the straps of her bag. "Ready for Harlow?" She casts a sideways glance at Miss Hammond. "Great class, Miss Hammond."

The teacher looks up from her notes and smiles warmly. "I'm glad you enjoyed it, Verity. How have you got with that book I lent you?"

Verity lights up before my eyes. "Oh, I'm already on chapter twenty. I could not put it down."

Miss Hammond nods her head in agreement. "I knew you would like it and you haven't even got to the best parts of it yet."

Verity blushes when she catches me watching her. "Well, we should get going. See you tomorrow, Miss Hammond."

Miss Hammond waves at us without looking up from her notes. As we walk to our next class, I study my guide. "So, Miss Hammond's, a favourite of yours, huh?"

Verity looks up and blushes. "Is it that obvious? She is just so beautiful. Have you seen the way her blue eyes turn a shade deeper when she's talking about books?"

I chuckle and shake my head. "No, I can't say I did."

Verity sighs, her mind somewhere else. "What I wouldn't do to be locked in a library alone with that woman for a night."

I almost choke on my tongue. "Oh, I see. I thought you were just girl-crushing over her."

Verity laughs and winks at me. "I like boys and girls. Why choose one when you can have both?"

"Whatever floats your boat," I reply with an arch of my brow and a smile. As we walk to our next class, I decide to try to do a little digging. "So, what can you tell me about the Aces?"

Verity stiffens at the mention of them. "What do you know about the Aces?"

I shrug and try to look nonchalant. "Not much, just that they run the school and have some stupid club that everyone clambers to become a part of."

Verity looks straight ahead and nods her head. "The Aces are the four founding families of the bay." She stops in her steps and places her arm on mine. "What you heard is correct, Eliza. They rule this place. Don't mock what you don't understand. This bay is old and steeped in tradition."

I'm somewhat taken aback by the change in her demeanour. Is she a part of the elusive Aces club? Maybe she's a Club, and she hangs off every word of the three Aces.

My steps falter when we walk into our next class, and I catch sight of the three boys who have been playing on my mind, sat right there at the back of the class. Verity leaves me at the door, and takes the last spot at the back, sitting down next to Rafe. He grins at her as he pulls his things out of his bag.

Okay, so now I understand loud and clear. Don't bad mouth the Aces around Verity. I take a seat three rows down from the front and pull out my things. A piece of paper hits me on the back of my head and I whizz around to look at the three prime suspects. Savage sits there with his arms folded, leaning back in his seat, looking like the king, lording over his domain. I meet his icy glare with one of my own before I turn back around to face the front. I lean down and pick up the crumpled piece of paper that has landed by my feet.

You're in trouble, Scarlet.

I scoff and shake my head; I lift my hand over my shoulder and give him the finger. He can kiss my arse if he thinks threatening notes will have any effect on me. You don't move from foster home to foster home, and new schools, without dealing with bullies. Bring it on Savage. Do your worst.

When I head out into the hallway at lunchtime, I'm met with sneers and snide comments. One girl calls me a tramp, and it takes all my strength not to charge her to the floor and pummel my fists into her face. When I reach my locker I sigh, it has a string of bin bags hanging of it and the words *dirty* written in red across the front. I pull the bin bags off my locker and open it to put my things inside. I can tell they're all waiting for some reaction, but they're going to be disappointed if they think a few bin bags and derogatory words are going to break me.

"Hey."

I look to my side to find Verity hovering.

"What do you want, Verity?" I ask her sharply. I will not waste my time on people who pretend to befriend me. Besides, she's one of their little Clubs.

"Seb's my brother," she blurts out. "I'm a Collings. I'm sorry I snapped before, but I'm an Ace and well, you may find our traditions a joke, but here it means something." She looks over my shoulder and stiffens. "I've grown up with the others. They always have my back, because it's Aces before everything else."

I dare a look over my shoulder and I see Archer, Rafe, and Seb, standing by their lockers, glaring down the corridor at me. "So, why am I being treated like a leper? I mean, technically I'm an Ace, too. By blood I'm an Alderman."

Verity looks at me, conflicted. "Look, it's way more complicated than it seems, Eliza. I wish I could say more, but it isn't my story to tell, but heed my warning. Don't go up against Archer. He hates you."

"Why?" I ask, throwing my hands up in the air. "Because I'm breathing his air? What have I ever done to him to deserve this hatred?"

Verity chews on her bottom lip. "It isn't anything you did. It's more what your family did." She holds her hand up to stop me before I speak. "Like I said, it isn't my story to tell, so please don't ask me. I love Archer like another brother, but he can be a mean bastard when he sets his mind to it. Just keep your head down and don't rise to it."

I snigger. Verity clearly does not know me well enough yet. "You think I'm scared of him?" I glare back over my shoulder at the person in question.

I pull my shoulders back and turn and walk down the hallway to where he stands.

"Oh, fuckity," I hear Verity curse as she rushes to catch up with me.

By the time I reach them, they are all standing shoulder to shoulder glaring at me. "Oh, look it's the Aces." I tap my chin.

"Let me just remind you what the first letter in your little acronym stands for. Alderman. You may not like that I am here boys," I say as I reach up and flick Archer's tie, and his jaw tightens, "but let me assure you, I am here to stay." I swivel on my feet and head off in the other direction. I don't have a clue where I am going, but so long as it is away from those arseholes, I don't really care. The sound of someone clapping stops me in my stride, and I find a guy leaning against the wall next to the exit.

"Got to say, you like playing with fire princess." He's tall about six-one and he's wearing his school shirt sleeves rolled up to reveal tattoo sleeves up both his arms. His dirty blonde hair flops into his eyes. The tatts and the feeling that he's not like the rest of these rich pricks has my attention.

"And you are?"

He chuckles. "Me? Oh, I'm trouble, sweetheart." He turns and heads out the side door, but before it closes, he looks over his shoulder at me. "Well, you coming?"

Curiosity has me following him outside. I catch up to him as he strides across the school grounds. "You're not a fan of the Aces then?"

He grins as he lights up a cigarette. "Something like that. Let's just say my family was a new addition to the area, a few years ago, and it hasn't gone down well with your elite princes."

"They're not my elite princes," I scoff.

He laughs at my answer, like he is part of some secret joke. "You're an Alderman, whether you or they like it. You are a part of their world."

I snort, and he leans against a tree and offers me the cigarette. I shake my head. If it had been a joint, then I might have been tempted. I lean against a tree opposite him and just observe him. "You don't belong in this world any more than I do."

He smiles a cunning and devilish smile. "That I don't,

princess. I come from new money, and they don't want the likes of us in their town."

"What kind of new money?" I ask him. Narrowing my gaze.

He walks towards me and stops before me, putting his hand on the trunk of the tree to the side of my head. He blows his smoke in my face and I cough. "The questionable kind, princess, but something tells me you've had brushes with the law before yourself." One of his fingers climbs up my leg until it reaches the edge of my skirt and I grip his wrist firmly to stop his progress.

"Careful. Don't touch what isn't yours."

"You heard her, Silver. Take your fucking hands off her," growls a deep voice from behind me.

I startle when I look over his shoulder to see the three Aces and Verity hovering behind him. Savage grinds his fist into his other hand, fixing a menacing look on the guy that I now know to be Silver.

Silver laughs, not turning to face them. "Oh, I see. This one is yours, is she Savage?" He laughs. "I have to say, I think you're going to have your hand full here. Must cut deep knowing she's been brought up poor."

Archer takes a step forward and his voice somehow becomes more threatening. "I said remove yourself from what doesn't belong to you."

Silver winks at me and drops a quick kiss on my cheek before he turns and shoulders his way past the three boys. Savage turns and looks like he's about to go after him, but Seb and Rafe hold him back. "Don't," Seb hisses in his ear.

My laughter has them all turning back to face me. "Well, this is hilarious. I really can't keep up here. Firstly, you feed me to the wolves and then you come to my rescue!" The fucking audacity of these three.

Savage stalks towards me, then leans both his hands on either side of the trunk beside my face. "Stay away from Silver."

I sigh, watching Silver's retreating figure with more interest

CARA E. HOLT

than I really feel. "I don't know. I kind of like Silver. I think he and I could have a whole lot of fun."

His jaw grinds in anger and I love that I am getting under his skin.

"You think he's genuinely interested in you, Scarlet? He's not, he's just testing to see who you belong to."

I place my hands on my hips, stepping forward so we are right in each other's space. "Oh, and who is it you seem to think I belong to?"

Savage glares down at me and softly brushes a hand over my cheek. A caress that does not match his icy eyes. "Haven't you figured that one out yet, Scarlet? You are mine."

"Yours to what?" I challenge. Who does this pretentious prick think he is? I don't belong to anyone.

He leans down so that I feel his breath across my face when he speaks. "You're mine to torment. Mine to play with. Mine to do with as I please."

"Wow, you really believe that, don't you Savage?" I chuckle. "Let's set the record straight here. I belong to no one. Not you. Not Silver. Not any prick in this little elitist bay or school. Now if you don't mind, I have lessons to get to." I duck under his arm, but he is quick and grabs me, pulling me flush to him.

"Stay away from Silver. Stay away or we won't be so nice to your little brother."

I eye him. "Leave my brother out of this," I snarl. Savage can threaten me, but no one threatens my brother.

Savage smiles, knowing he has me by the lady balls. "Then just be a good girl and do as you're told. You know our word is law around here. So far, we have given no orders for your brother to be ostracised, but I can change that in a heartbeat."

How is it he has worked out my weakness so quickly? Looks like I need to up my game if I want to be a step ahead of this guy.

"Fine," I snap. "I'll stay away from Silver, but not because you ordered me to; but because I don't like guys who get handsy without asking first." I look down at his firm grip on my arm and he releases me, causing me to stumble slightly on my feet. With one last glare his way, I storm past the others and back inside.

"Wait up," Verity shouts after me. "You don't know which way to go!"

CHAPTER SIX

ARCHER

W ell, that went well," Seb says, as we watch Scarlet make her way inside. "Man, if you want, I'll take her off your hands." He whistles. "Look at the way those curvy hips sway when she walks. Bet that girl can move."

I clip him over the head. "Quit it, fucker."

He chuckles as he lights up a joint. "Sorry, brother, but your future wife is hot as fuck. I mean, I really thought you'd end up with some fat spotty chick, but she," he whistles again, "she is fire and sin all wrapped together in a perfect parcel."

"And quit with the future wife shit," I growl, as I take the joint from him, inhaling deeply.

"Can I be a fly on the wall when she finds out what old Wilbur has really brought her back for?"

I ignore Seb. My gaze concentrated on the retreating figure of Scarlet. Who'd have thought the little firecracker I found spying on us last night was none other than Wilbur fucking Alderman's granddaughter. "What do we know so far?" I ask Rafe who has, as usual, remained quiet.

Rafe takes the joint from me. "They've been in foster care for the last five years and had six different foster carers. A drunk driver killed their parents. Little Red was in the car."

He pulls his tablet out of his bag and holds it out to me. The picture of her parent's car being pulled from the river is nothing but a crumpled wreck. "She was thrown from the car as it plummeted down the steep ravine. She was impaled on a branch. It went through her leg. Another branch entered her back. Little Red fractured four ribs and punctured a lung. Her right leg was broken in two places, a broken left wrist, a pelvic fracture, and concussion."

"No wonder she doesn't like water," I comment. "How did she get help?"

Rafe hands Seb the last of the joint. "Another driver saw the accident, found her and called for help. It was touch and go for a while, but our little Ace defied the odds and pulled through. She had months of rehabilitation therapy."

Seb whistles again. "Sounds like our queen is a little warrior."

"Our queen?" I echo, arching a brow in his direction.

"I thought you didn't want her?"

I clench my jaw. "What I want doesn't matter anymore. I'll do what I have to do to get my legacy." I hated her father and as he isn't around for me to exact revenge on, I'll focus all these years of hate on her. She will be mine to do with as I please, and I'm going to make sure she regrets ever setting foot in Hawk Bay.

CHAPTER
SEVEN

ELIZA

"Wow, your first day and you have them fighting over you." Verity sighs as she catches up with me. I'm livid, I'm hopping mad at the arrogant arsehole and his two cronies. First, he tells me I don't belong; then he tells me I'm his. Then he has the nerve to threaten my little brother. I hate him.

"Slow down, will you. By the way, your next class is that way." Verity points in the opposite direction to the one I'm walking in. She winces as I scowl at her, and feeling bad, I offer her an apologetic smile. It isn't her fault her brother is one of the three Aceholes.

I laugh out loud. Aceholes. I liked my new name for those three.

"What are you laughing so gleefully about?" Verity asks me, her blue eyes gleaming with curiosity.

"Nothing," I say grinning.

I'm that busy smiling at Verity, I walk smack into someone as we round a corner. "Shit, sorry."

"You should be," snipes a whiny voice that I sadly recognise.

"George," I greet with a sigh. Could this day get any worse? I can't fight the smile that comes to my face when I notice her right eye has some bruising from where I hit her last night.

She folds her arms across her chest. The first four buttons on her school shirt are open so that you get an eyeful of her breasts in her push-up bra.

"It's Georgie," she hisses. "I thought I told you to stay away from Archer."

I roll my eyes. The girl is obsessed. I wonder if her room is covered in photos of him. "Believe me, I'm trying, but the idiot seems to be stalking me."

Georgie steps into my personal space, and my hackles rise. "He's too good for the likes of you. You're the scum on our shoes. You can smell the poverty in the air." She sniffs my way as if to emphasise her point.

I clench my fists. Itching to smack her in her perfectly done-up face. But it's my first day at school and I don't want to piss off my new legal guardian by getting excluded.

"I'll give you one warning, George, and then I won't be responsible for my actions. You're right, I'm not like the rest of you. I grew up in a working-class town and I know how to fight. Now, if you don't want that little ski-slope nose of yours bent and broken, I suggest you keep out of my personal space."

Georgie bristles but holds my gaze. The girl has guts, I'll give her that much. "Just stay away from the Aces and we won't have a problem." She spins on her heels, her vanilla scented hair whipping me in the face as she glides down the corridor. "And my name is Georgie!"

Verity sighs. "Come on, we'll be late."

My next class is biology. I hate science subjects. They bore the pants off me. I have no plans to be a chemist or biologist, so why I have to take these boring classes is beyond me. Apparently, my grandfather has chosen my A-level classes. It looks like I get no say in the matter.

When I head to my next class, I'm shoulder checked, and droves of girls call me a slut under their breath. Water off a duck's back, ladies. It really is laughable that Savage thinks a few bitchy comments are going to have me running for the hills.

Verity finds me at my locker as I'm putting my things away. I can't wait to get home and just veg out and watch mindless television for a couple of hours. Today has been a drain.

"Well, you survived your first day," she says, smiling at me. "So, I was thinking, do you want to get burgers? There's a great little café a couple of minutes from here."

"Sure," I reply. I'm still confused why she wants to hang out with me. "Why are you being nice to me?"

She looks surprised by my question. "Because I like you, Eliza. You're a breath of fresh air in this place, and lord knows this Bay is so predictable."

"So, it's not because you fancy me?" I ask her, grinning, and she giggles at my question.

"See what I mean? No one would dare speak like that to me." She links her arm through mine. "You're beautiful, but not my type." She waggles her eyebrows and winks at me.

"Well, with the arseholes in this place on offer, I can see why you like girls."

Verity chuckles. "Ah, you're as straight as they come. I see the way you look at Archer. Like you don't know whether to climb him like a tree and strip him naked or wrap your hands around his neck and throttle him."

"Trust me," I snort, "I do not want Archer Savage."

I spot Calvin parked up, leaning against the Merc, and I head over to him. "Hey, Calvin. My friend," I gesture over my shoulder to where Verity hovers, "has invited me for burgers."

Calvin waves at Verity. "That's okay, Miss. I'll wait for Kit and tell my mum you're dining out. Do you want me to collect you after you've eaten?'

"I can drop her home," Verity announces, dangling her car keys from her finger.

When we arrive at the café, it's already busy with other kids from our school. As we enter, I spot a table over in the far corner and head that way, but Verity stops me in my tracks, tugging on my arm.

"You don't want to sit there," she tells me. She gestures with her head to another table near the door, but it's cold and there will be a draft every time someone enters.

"Sure, we can. The table is empty." I frown at her in confusion as I continue towards the empty booth.

"That's their table," she informs me.

I grin. "Perfect." I throw my bag down on the seat beside me and pick up the menu. A second later, Verity takes a seat opposite me.

"You really do have a death wish, don't you?"

I shrug my shoulders as I peruse the menu. "How much?" I say as I clock the prices. "Are their burgers covered in gold leaf?"

Verity looks at me like I've grown two heads. "What?"

"Nothing," I say with a shake of my head. Where I'm from a burger would cost a quarter of the price on this menu. Another reminder of the world I'm living in.

The waitress comes and takes our orders and returns a few minutes later with a Vanilla Frappe for me and a banana milkshake for Verity.

"Okay." I drum my hands on the table. "What is there to do for fun round here?"

"Oh, well there's usually a house party most weekends. Or there's the country club. When the weather's warm, we often all party on the beach."

I nod my head. "No nightclubs?"

Verity shakes her head. "Sorry, no. You'd have to travel two towns over to find a nightclub." She clocks my disappointment. "What kind of fun is it you're after?"

It's my turn to waggle my brows. "Where does the real fun happen? Any underground fighting rings or racing?"

Verity's eyes widen in surprise. "Oh, okay, I see." She looks around her and leans in closer. Her voice drops to a whisper, "I have heard of a place that the boys sometimes go to. I followed them there once. It's in Redwood, about a twenty-minute drive from here."

I rub my hands together. "Now we're talking. We'll go Friday night, yeah?"

Verity eyes me as she sips from her drink. "Why do I get the feeling life is suddenly going to get very colourful with you around?"

I grin at her. "Honey, my middle name is fun."

I look up when the door to the café opens, and the place suddenly falls silent. I frown when I see the three of them strolling in like they own the place. They head this way and I see Archer falter slightly when he spots me.

"This should be fun," Verity mumbles to herself as she puts her head down and concentrates sharply on her drink.

The three of them come to a stop at the end of our table and stare at me.

"Move. Now," Seb orders me coldly.

I sit back in my seat, placing my arm over the back of the one next to me and lazily observe them. "These seats are taken."

"Scarlet, pick up your drink and move off our table," Archer tells me with a bored expression. His eyes focus on the view outside the window, as if he can't even be bothered looking my way when he speaks to me.

I sigh, putting my hands on the table, making it look like I'm about to get up before I lean back in my seat with a smug smile. "Like I said, these seats are taken."

His jaw tics and before I can blink, I'm plucked from my seat and lifted in the air as he takes my place, and then places me down in his lap.

"What the fuck?" I attempt to remove myself from his knee, but he has a firm grip around my waist. "Get your hands off me, Savage."

He ignores me as Seb and Rafe take the two spare seats, either side of Verity.

"Verity,' says her brother, "you need to teach your new friend the rules around here."

Verity shrugs her shoulders. "I don't think Eliza likes rules."

I'm surrounded by Archer's woodsy scent. I can feel his warm breath on my face. "Let me up, now," I growl.

Archer keeps a firm grip on me. "You had your chance, Scarlet. Now you'll sit here like a good little girl and learn your place."

The waitress arrives with mine and Verity's order. "Hey boys," she says, smiling warmly at the three of them. She places my burger in front of me. "What will it be? The usual?"

I scoff at her flirtatious behaviour. Jesus, does everyone around here hang off their every word? I hate that I'm super aware of him. I can feel everywhere his body touches mine and I don't like the goosebumps it gives me. I do not want to be affected by his presence.

"So, what were you girls talking about?" Rafe asks as he reaches over and takes a bite of Verity's burger.

"Arsehole," she snipes, and he grins at her.

"What's yours is mine, sweetness."

Verity frowns but then releases the smile she's been fighting and pulls her tongue out at him.

I wrinkle my forehead, watching them. I can't help thinking there's a story there, between the two of them.

"Eliza was just asking what we all do for fun around here."

I snigger as I chew on my burger, and I feel four sets of eyes on me. "And I don't mean of the torture and bullying kind."

Verity looks at the three of them in question.

"Robinson," Seb states simply, and Verity hisses at the mention of his name.

"You look like you'd enjoy being tied up and tortured, Scarlet," Archer says in my ear. "You could do with a good whipping to bring you into line."

My wriggling to get free of him has caused my shirt to rise up from out of my skirt and my breath freezes in my throat when I feel his thumb rub across my skin.

"I'm sorry to disappoint you, Little Red, but there are no brothels taking on in Hawk Bay." Seb chuckles, and Rafe joins in laughing at his joke.

"Damn, guess I'll have to sell my wares on the street corner then," I reply dryly. The whore jokes are so predictable. I don't come from money, so I must be a slut who opens my legs at every opportunity. Rich people are so predictable.

"I might have a party at the weekend," Seb announces, looking directly at me. "But you're not invited."

Verity clears her throat and throws daggers at her brother. "It's also my house, Sebastian, and I can invite who I want. In fact, Eliza is sleeping over." She looks over at me and winks. I love that she is sticking up for me.

"I'm not sure your parties are my kind of thing, Seb. High tea and croquet aren't really my bag."

From behind me, I feel Archer's chest move as he laughs at my response. My, my, so he does actually know how to laugh. I thought his face was set in a permanent resting bastard look.

"The village is a buzz of gossip at the return of Wilbur Alderman," Rafe says as he leans back in his seat and plays with the lid on Verity's drink.

I look over at him. "What do you mean?"

I see Rafe look over my head at Archer and then at Seb in some silent conversation. "Dear Grandad hasn't lived here in the village for the last seven years. Last I heard, he was living in London."

Well, this was news to me. I want to ask more, but I don't want to admit to them that I know nothing about the man who is now my guardian. My phone rings in my bag at the side of me and before I can reach for it, Archer has it out of my bag and answers it.

"Hello." He frowns as he listens to the person on the other end. "Yeah, this is her number." He hands the phone to me. "Your social worker."

I flush red as I take the phone from him and hold it to my ear. "Hi, Hayley."

"Hi, Eliza. I just wanted to touch base and see how your first day has gone."

I'm conscious that everyone is listening in. "Yeah, all good. I'm out right now. Can I call you later or tomorrow?"

"Oh, sure. I just wanted to make sure you were okay. I'll call you tomorrow."

"Speak soon," I reply, ending the call and slipping it back into my bag.

I feel Verity's inquisitive gaze when I lift my head. "What?"

"You have a social worker?" I can see the sympathy in her eyes, and I hate it.

"Little Red here has been in foster care for the last five years. She's a poor little orphan," Seb happily shares, grinning coldly at me. Why do these three hate me so much?

I lift my chin high. I've nothing to be ashamed of. It wasn't like I was in care because I was neglected. "When my parents died, we didn't know of any living relatives, so we went into care."

"Oh wow," Verity says, her eyes are full of empathy. "That must have been awful."

I shrug my shoulders. "It was what it was." I bite into my burger, effectively ending that conversation. I glare at Seb. It looks like these fuckers have done their homework on me. I need to get the details on these three and fight fire with fire.

Archer's phone rings and as he lifts it to his ear, I snatch it from him and answer the call. Two can play this game.

"Hello, Archer Savage's phone," I say in my best cheery voice.

"Hello. Who is this?" The male voice on the end of the line asks me, the surprise in his voice clear.

Archer tries to grab the phone off me, but I lean out of his way.

"Oh, my name's Eliza."

"Wilbur's granddaughter," he states rather than asks. "Well, Welcome to Hawk Bay, Eliza, you're earlier than expected. I'm Edward, Archer's grandfather. I shall look forward to meeting you, Eliza. Now, would you mind putting my grandson on the phone?"

"Of course, and it's a pleasure to meet you, too." Grinning

widely at Archer, I hand him his phone and he snatches it from me.

"Yes." His jaw tics as he listens. "I know. I will. I'll call a meeting." He taps my waist and lifts me, getting to his feet and placing me back down.

"Aces business, sweetheart," Seb says with a grin as he gets to his feet and takes a large bite of his burger.

I rise out of my chair behind them. "Well, if it's Aces business, then Verity and I should be there as well."

This brings a chuckle from all three of them, clearly finding my suggestion laughable. Archer firmly, but gently, pushes me by the shoulders back down into my seat.

"First, you're not an Ace. Just because you have the surname doesn't automatically mean you're a part of us. You earn that right. Second, female Aces don't attend our meetings."

"We should follow them," I suggest to Verity, as I watch the three boys climb into Archer's black Audi.

Verity shakes her head. "Hell no. I am not getting caught out snooping on the boys. Besides, I trust them and if it is anything I need to know, they'll share it with me."

I sigh, resigned that she isn't going to change her mind. "So, what's with you and Rafe?"

Verity looks up from her phone at me with guarded eyes. "What do you mean?"

"I don't know," I reply with a shrug of my shoulders. "I just got vibes that there is history there."

"Oh that. Yeah, Rafe is unofficially my fiancé."

I choke on my drink and bang on my chest to get a breath. "Fiancé? So, he's your boyfriend?"

Verity shakes her head, putting her phone down and giving me her full attention. "No, we're not together. Although we hook up occasionally. It's an agreement between the two families. Once we're both eighteen, they will announce our engagement."

I stare at her, opened mouthed for a few seconds, processing this information. "But do you even have feelings for each other?"

Verity considers my question. "Yeah, we care about each other. I mean, I have known him all my life and we've known for a long time that it was our family's intention for us to marry. The sex is good between us when we hook up and we've both agreed that until we are officially engaged, we'll both play the field and enjoy life."

Wow, I have heard some fucked up things in my life, but this is a new one for me. Arranged marriage. What century are we living in?

"You're shocked speechless," she says with a nervous giggle. "Welcome to life in the elite. It happens all the time. Georgie has been hopeful for years that her family could broker a marriage deal for her and Archer. It's all about mergers and strengthening the power and status of the families."

I offer her a tight smile, as I don't want to make her feel uncomfortable. "Do you think it will happen? With Georgie and Archer?"

Verity laughs. "Hell no, Georgie's family doesn't have enough pulling power. Plus, Archer is already promised elsewhere."

A knot forms in my stomach and I'm confused why, as I honestly don't give a shit who Archer Savage is supposed to marry. "Oh, okay. Who is he promised to?"

Verity shakes her head, her eyes wide and expressive. "Ah, you'd have to ask him about that."

I nod my head and take a sip of my drink. "Does Rafe know you're bi-sexual?"

"Oh yeah," she replies laughing. "He knows." I get the feeling there's something she isn't saying but I leave it at that. She has really opened up to me today and I don't want to push her.

CHAPTER EIGHT

ELIZA

Verity drops me off at home and I head into the kitchen to tell Edith all about my first day before I head up to my room. As soon as I shut the door, I pull off the stifling uniform and head straight for the shower. As the water cascades over me, my thoughts drift to Archer and the fact that he already belongs to someone. My mind flicks through some of the girls at school and I wonder which one of them is his.

I change into sleep shorts and a vest top and settle down on my bed to get some homework done. Only my first day and I already have four pieces due in later this week. There's a knock on my bedroom door and Edith pops her head inside.

"Can I come in?"

"Of course," I reply, smiling and gesturing for her to enter.

She sits on the edge of my bed. "I just thought I'd let you know I've just heard from your grandfather, and he will be here on Friday. He's just wrapping up some business in London and then he and Lexi will return to Hawk Manor."

"Lexi?" I ask. I haven't heard her mentioned before.

Edith's mouth pinches. "Yes, your grandfather's partner. Her son, Chester, will also be with them. He'll be enrolling with you at the academy."

"Oh, okay. How old is he?"

"Seventeen. So, he'll be in your year."

I can tell from her tone of voice that she doesn't think much

of Lexi or her son Chester. I get the feeling that Lexi is probably young enough to be my grandfather's daughter.

Edith pats my leg. "Anyway, I'll leave you to it. I'm going to retire for the night, but just call me if you need anything."

"Edith," I shout as she heads to the door, "thank you for making us feel so welcome."

She beams at me. "Oh, honey. We're thrilled to have young ones in the house again and looking at your brother is like looking at your father when he was younger."

"Do you have photographs of him when he was a child? It's just I've never seen any. He never spoke about his childhood or his family."

A look of sadness crosses Edith's features. "Ah, yes, I'm sure I can dig out the albums for you. We can all have a look together."

"I'd like that," I tell her with a smile.

"Now, don't stay up too late," she tells me, giving my hand an affectionate squeeze. "If you want any supper, just call me."

"Edith, I can make my own supper. Seriously, go home and rest. By the way, do you live here or in the village?"

"We have a little cottage on the grounds, my dear. Your brother is in his room getting his homework done too."

"Thanks Edith. See you in the morning."

"Sweet dreams, my dear."

After she leaves, I feel an ache in my heart. I've forgotten what it feels like to have someone genuinely care about me, like Edith does. We will finally meet our grandfather this weekend. I'm not sure how I feel about his impending arrival. I'm naturally curious about him, but I can't help that feeling deep in the pit of my stomach that tells me there is a reason my dad left this place and never looked back.

I AWAKE BOLT UPRIGHT IN THE DARKNESS OF THE NIGHT AND rub my eyes. My vision adjusts to the dark and my breath stops in my chest when I see the silhouette of someone sitting in the armchair in the corner of the room. I'm dreaming, right? There isn't really someone here in my room with me. I rub my eyes and when I look again, there is a male figure looming at the end of my bed. I go to scream, but a hand clamps over my mouth and I'm pulled out of my bed and onto my feet. Fighting whoever is holding me prisoner, I'm pushed forward until I'm standing before the stranger. He's wearing a mask over his face. A white mask that looks sinister against the darkness.

"Time to see just how tough you really are," he tells me in a cold and calculating voice.

I'm hauled through the house and down the stairs. I fight them every step of the way, but it's no use. As much as I hate to admit it, they're stronger than me. I'm under no illusions about who the three guys are behind the masks. It's Savage and his aces.

"Let me go, you arseholes," I hiss as they bundle me into the boot of a car and close the door. The engine starts, and the car takes off. I try my best to untie the rope that holds my hands behind my back, but it's no good — its tied too tight. I'm fuming. How dare they steal me from my bed in the middle of the night like this.

The car comes to a stop after what I guess to be about ten minutes, and I hear the car doors opening and closing. I growl when the boot is opened, and I'm hauled to my feet by Seb. His mop of blonde hair, giving him away despite the mask.

"Now, now, little kitty. Play nice," he taunts me as he pulls my back flush to his chest. Archer comes in front of me, his body pressing flush to my front so that I'm sandwiched tight between the two of them. He runs a lazy, cold finger up my thigh, stopping at the hem of my shorts.

"Time to see if you have what it takes to be an Ace." His gaze skims down my body and pauses on my pebbled nipples. "Does this turn you on, princess?" he asks with an evil smile.

"It's cold, dickhead," I snipe in reply. "And just to be clear. I don't want in on your stupid juvenile club."

Archer's laugh is loud and cold. "Oh, Scarlet. You don't get a choice. The elders have spoken." He runs his hand over my cheek tenderly. "You're in our world now. There are no choices, only duty. We've been told to initiate you and that is what we're going to do." He cups my face in his hands, his sharp eyes holding mine prisoner. "You ready to play, Scarlet?"

"Fuck you," I growly. Two nights in a row these fuckers have disrupted my sleep and anyone that knows me knows I'm not a nice person to be around when I don't get my sleep.

"You've got a fifteen-minute head start and then we hunt you. If you can avoid capture for the first hour, then you pass, but if one of us finds you," he shakes his head and tuts, "that will be bad news for you, Scarlet."

Archer and Seb step back and I'm shoved forward and almost stumble to the floor.

"Tick tock, Little Red," Rafe says, looking at his watch and reminding me I'm on the clock. Part of me wants to tell them they can shove their elitist game up their arses and stay exactly where I am, but another part of me, the part that loves danger and excitement, is itching to run and play their little game.

With a chain of expletives, I run off into the dark of the night and don't look back. I'm in the middle of a thick forest. As I run, branches and nettles catch at my bare feet and legs, and I run into a twig that cuts across my cheek. I have no idea how long I've been running, but I snake off to my right and do a zig-zag pattern ensuring that I'm not running in one direction. One thing in my favour is that I am a fast runner. I've hightailed out of illegal factory parties and fight rings more times than I can count on my two hands.

I run for what feels like another five minutes until I find a rock crevice that I can hide under. I shove my body underneath the cold wet rock and tuck myself in, as tiny as I can, and then I sit and wait. I'm on high alert, listening for any slight noise or sound. An owl hoots in the night sky and I jump a mile. My heart is pounding in my chest and adrenaline courses through my body. I want to believe I can beat them, but they have an unfair advantage. They have grown up here and will know these woods like the back of their hands. I also get the feeling that they've done this before. I curse myself for wearing a white vest top and pale blue shorts, not exactly the best colours when you are trying to blend into the night.

What will they do to me if they capture me? I remember the wicked glint in Archer's eyes when he told me I'd regret it if they caught me. I can't believe I'm out here in the dead of night playing manhunt, a game for ten-year-old children, but here I am. For what feels like forever, I hide. I've no watch on so I can't tell the time.

I rest my head against the rock face and close my eyes. I'm exhausted. I hardly got any sleep last night thanks to the Aceholes, and now here I am again out playing their games when I should be fast asleep in bed. My eyes snap open when I hear a twig snap over to my left and I freeze, trying to breathe as quietly as possible. Fuck, I fell asleep!

"Come out, come out wherever you are," calls a menacing voice that I recognise as Archer's. I should have known he'd be the one to hunt me down. Out of the three of them, he's the darkest of them all. I should know, I can recognise a soul as dark and damaged as my own.

I stay still, praying that my breathing doesn't sound as heavy as it does in my mind. My heart beats ten to the dozen as I look into the blackness of the dense forest night. These stupid boys and their stupid club that I want no part of, and yet here I am playing their games in the dead of night. I also can't deny that being out here and knowing the three of them are hunting me and not knowing what they'll do when they catch me is kind of giving me a rush. The same rush that I get when I'm fighting in a ring or when I'm joyriding.

"I can sense you, Scarlet. I know you're here somewhere," he announces into the night, his voice confident and menacing. "I can smell your fear."

I scream as I'm yanked from my hiding spot and pulled tight against a body. I fight and hiss and kick and he just laughs coldly, like he's loving every minute.

"Well done, Scarlet. You lasted longer than most of the girls who have gone before you. Two hours is good going."

I shiver against him. My body seeking the warmth that he offers. "Why is it anything involving you normally ends with me cold and wet?"

He cocks a brow and smirks at me. "Are you admitting that you are always wet around me?"

I glower at him even though it's dark. "You know what I mean, and the day you make me wet in that way will be the day that hell freezes over, and the dinosaurs return from extinction."

He chuckles, still clutching my body close to his. "We both know that's a lie. I'm afraid you're not going to like the next part of this."

I don't have time to ask what he means before I feel a sharp prick in my arm, and I look down to see him withdrawing a needle.

"You drugged me, you bastard," I hiss. How dare he fucking drug me. "I'll kill you for this," I promise him, before my eyes roll back

"I'm sure one of us will kill the other before all this is over, Scarlet."

I jerk awake and, in a panic, look around me that the last thing that happened to me was Savage putting a needle in my arm. I'm trussed up like a pig in a slaughterhouse, my arms tied above me with chains as I dangle from a metal rod that runs the length of the room. The tips of my toes can't quite touch the cold, hard ground. It looks like they've brought me to a cellar somewhere. There are no windows, only some wooden stairs that lead to a door, where light shines through the bottom, letting me know I'm not alone. I'm also stripped down to just my panties. I wasn't wearing a bra when the fuckers kidnapped me from my nice, warm bed. In this position, my breasts are thrust out and the cold air has made my nipples stand to attention. There is no point in trying to get free. I'll just end up making myself tired and sore, so I'm better waiting for the three Aceholes to return and see what they intend to do with me. I listen intently for any noise, but I can't hear anything, no voices, no movement, just silence.

I have been in some situations because of my shenanigans over the past few years but never a situation quite like this. This is a new one for me. I've no idea what time it is, but I know they can't keep me here all night. At some point, they will have to return me to my home, otherwise Edith will know I'm missing and call the police. Will she think that I have run away? I hate the thought of worrying Edith unnecessarily.

I'm jerked from my thoughts when I hear the door being unlocked and light floods the dark space. The silhouette of three figures looms in the doorway, still and silent, until they slowly descend. Their heavy footsteps echoing in this large, empty space. The kings of this fucking stupid club. Well, fuck them and fuck their games.

Archer tilts his head and observes me as he comes to a stop a few feet in front of me. He's wearing black joggers and a black vest. There is nothing on his feet. He drinks me in, with a fire burning in his eyes that tells me he enjoys seeing me like this, strung up and helpless. And that's what I am — helpless.

They could do anything to me down here and I am powerless to stop them, and I hate it. I hate not being in control.

Seb and Rafe come up beside him, both staring at me. Seb groans and grabs his junk through his pants. "Man, how fucking good does she look strung up like this? God, what a turn on."

Archer doesn't answer, he just continues to watch me, like a predator eyeing its next hunt before going in for the kill.

"So, come on, don't keep me in suspense," I snap. "What is next in your little game?"

Archer steps forward, and I'd take a step back if I could, but I can't. He runs a single icy finger from the centre of my collarbone down between my breast coming to a stop just before my belly button; making me shiver. He watches my every reaction, studying me like I'm some kind of fascinating enigma.

"Normally we ask you if you're willing to commit to us as your Aces and we all have our turn with you," he tells me. His voice cold and firm.

I laugh. "There's one slight problem. I don't want in on your stupid juvenile club. So, no thank you."

He laughs, his finger continuing its slow move down my body until it comes to a stop at the lace of my knickers. "White. I'm disappointed. I'd imagined red."

I cock a brow at him, hoping that my body doesn't betray the effect he is having on me. "You fantasising about my underwear, Savage? Fantasise away, because you'll never have me."

He smirks at me as his fingers, dips slightly inside the top of my knickers and he runs his finger back and forth across the skin there. "I could have you right now if I wanted and there would be nothing you could do except take it." He leans in, so his mouth is at my ear. "And you know what I think? I think you'd love it. I think you'd scream and beg me for more, Scarlet."

"In your dreams," I reply with a snigger.

Savage steps back until he's standing beside his sidekicks who have remained silent throughout this entire conversation.

"Do it," he barks, and Seb steps forward with something in his hand. My eyes widen in fear as he stalks towards me. He grins at me. It's a sinister grin that causes a rush of cold to run up my back.

I'm powerless to move. All I can do is wait as he reaches me and he wraps my hair around his fist and tilts my head back, so I have no choice but to look at him. He drops a quick and chaste kiss on my lips, and I hear a growl from behind me. Seb smiles wider in response and chuckles.

CARA E. HOLT

"Sorry Little Red, but they have chosen you for initiation and now you must choose your final challenge."

I scream out in shock and pain as blistering heat burns my flesh. My eyes move to where I feel the pain and they widen when they find its source. A fucking branding iron? I kid you not! The fucker has branded my flesh. It hurts like a bitch too. As he pulls the object of my pain away from my chest, I get to see what the hell they have permanently marked me with. I'm uncertain, but it looks like an ace card.

"You marked my skin," I hiss, glaring at Seb and then in turn at Rafe, then Savage.

"Your initiation mark, Little Red. Let the games begin." He spins on his heel and as he passes Archer, he squeezes his shoulder. Rafe gives me one last frown before he also makes for the stairs, leaving me alone with my nemesis.

Archer walks over to a cabinet, taking a key from his pocket. He opens it and pulls out a bowl and pours a liquid into the bowl. He also grabs some gauze and then he's stalking towards me. He wets the gauze in the bowl and takes another step towards me and I jerk back. Pain races along my arms as I jerk against the chains holding me in place.

"Be still," he orders me as he reaches out and presses the gauze against my blistering skin.

"Holy fucking snake balls," I say with a sharp intake of breath. That hurt like a motherfucker!

"The scars on your back and thigh and neck. They're from the car accident?"

My angry eyes fly up to meet his. "None of your god-damn business."

"I like them," he tells me. "They make you look fierce. They show the world that you are a warrior and that you have survived and come back stronger." One minute he's so cold and hard, and then he says something that makes me feel like he knows who I am deep inside. Like he has peeled back my skin and taken a good look at the broken and haunted girl I am inside.

68

I snigger. "Like you'd have any idea what it takes to survive in the harsh world outside of your little elite Bay. You know nothing Archer Savage. You have everything you want there for the taking. you can just reach out and have whatever and whoever you want."

"Not everything I want," he says with a frown before he returns to the task of treating my burn. He gently applies some cream and I watch him in silence. His touch is gentle and careful. The exact opposite of his hard and unyielding armour. "There. That should do for now. Keep putting cream on at night and it should heal, okay?"

"Why, thank you," I reply, my tone dripping with sarcasm that brings a half-smile from him. He puts the bowl and gauze down and picks up a bottle and offers it to me, bringing it to my lips. I jerk back, concerned that he might be trying to drug me again.

"It's just alcohol. To help manage the pain."

Warily, I let him put the bottle to my lips and I drink. It spills down my chin and down my chest. He pulls the bottle away and, with the back of his thumb, he wipes it from my chin and catches the droplet between my breasts before he sucks his thumb into his mouth. I watch him, zoning in on his mouth and when I lift my eyes, his are on mine, burning into my soul. He releases his thumb with a pop and grasps my chin between his thumb and finger.

"You really are an anomaly, aren't you, Scarlet? Are you here to make me answer for my sins?"

I chuckle in response. "I'll leave that for the priest to do when you go to confession. I imagine you'd be there for some time, too."

He smiles in response, and moves to the wooden post, unhooking the chain that has been holding me suspended. As my feet touch the floor, I find they buckle underneath me. He reaches an arm around my waist and holds me against him. "I've got you." The same words he said to me that first night when I slept in his bed. Knowing my legs won't hold me, he lifts me, and I wrap my legs around his waist. A part of me wants to tell him to put me down, but I know I'll not be able to hold my own weight, so I park our next battle for now.

When we reach the top of the stairs and come out into the light, I glance around me and take in where I am. It looks like a high-end lodge. It's open plan. There's a large media wall with a large television and a long glass fire screen. It feels warm and inviting and that cream fur rug before the fire is begging me to curl up on it and just close my eyes.

"Is this yours?" I ask him as he stalks through the inviting room and up the stairs to the next level.

"It belongs to the three of us," he answers, carrying me into a room where there is a large black four poster bed. Looking around the room, I somehow know instantly that he sleeps in here when he comes here. He carries me straight through to a bathroom where there is a modern walk-in-shower, and he places me down on the sink unit before turning and switching the shower on.

"There are towels in there, I'll leave some clothes out for you to change into, I'll put them on the bed." He gestures through to his room.

"I'm not sleeping here. I need to go home," I tell him with a frosty glare.

He smirks. "You'll do whatever I decide, Scarlet. If I decide to keep you up here for the next two weeks, then that is what would happen."

I fold my arms and laugh. "Oh, really? I think my grandfather would have something to say about that."

He cocks a brow. "Oh, he wouldn't say anything. In fact, he'd probably encourage me."

I frown at him. I hate it when I feel like he is insinuating something that I don't understand or know. And honestly, I have no idea what kind of man my paternal grandfather is, so he could very well be right. He likely knows him far better than I do right now.

"I'll be downstairs," he tells me with a gruff bark before he stalks out of the room, leaving me alone.

I enter the shower and sigh as the warm water cascades down my body. Closing my eyes, I imagine two arms snaking round my naked waist. One heads south to my sex whilst the other cups one breast, making me shiver with pleasure. A cold sharp slap of reality hits me as I realise I am standing naked in Archer Savages shower and imagining him touching me. What the actual fuck? Have I lost my effing mind? I grab the shower gel and scrub my body vigorously, imagining I am erasing away any thoughts of Savage in any way other than him being my enemy.

I dry myself off and walk into his room to find a black designer label t-shirt laid out on the bed. Yet again I end up dressed in his clothes. Why does it feel like he is branding me in every which way possible? I use my fingers to brush through my tangled hair and then I head downstairs to seek out the devil in his lair.

I find him sitting in an armchair by the fire. He leans his arms on his thighs and he stares into the flames, looking like he is miles away from here. I clear my throat and his sharp, dark eyes snap to mine. I feel his gaze briefly drift down my body before he returns them to meet my eyes.

"I've made you a warm drink." He gestures to the table beside the sofa, where a cup sits. I could kill for a brew, so with a brief nod I enter the space and, taking the cup, I sit down on the sofa and curl my legs up beneath me. When I look up, it is to find him watching me.

"What?"

He shakes his head. "Nothing." He reaches to a notepad beside him and pulls out a folded piece of paper and holds it out to me. I cock a brow and wait. "Your options for your challenge."

I want to tell him to shove the paper where the sun doesn't shine, but curiosity gets the better of me and I snatch it out of his hand and sit back in my seat. I open the folded white paper and read:

Option 1: Sex with each of the Aces.
Option 2: Break into the Silver mansion and steal the silver horse on the mantle piece.
Option 3: Steal the headmaster's car and crash it into the school fountain.

I laugh. Well, option one is definitely a firm no! Now option two or three are both up my street. I am not a novice at breaking into houses. It was a little game I used to play with some guys I used to hang out with back during my stay at my third foster home. But option three calls to me like a beacon. Stealing a car is like child's play for me. I love the rush.

"What if I decide not to take on any of the challenges?"

He half-smirks as he lifts his cup to his mouth. "Then we'll bring the challenge to you, and you'll lose your option to choose, and trust me Scarlet, you won't like the challenge you'll have forced upon you. Besides, Wilbur has insisted you are initiated, and you wouldn't want to disappoint him, would you?"

I nod my head. Something tells me he is right about not liking the other option. I fold the paper back up and place it on the table beside me. "How do I prove if I have completed the challenge?"

"If you go for option two, you'll bring that statue to me. If you go for option three, well, we'll see the car at school. Option one, well, I'd be a participant, so I think I'd know when that one's done."

I laugh at his humour. "Yeah, don't hold your breath. I suggest if you have an itch, you get sweet George to scratch it for you."

He licks at his bottom lip as he watches me. His eyes burn with mischief. "If I have an itch, Scarlet, I have plenty of offers available to me. I don't need some orphan Annie to fulfil my needs."

And there you have it. The cold sharp slap of reality to remind me he is nothing but a cold, calculating arsehole. "I want to go home."

He arches a brow. "And where might that be? Do you even have anywhere to call home?"

I glower at him. I hate that he seems to know what buttons to press with me. We've barely met and yet it feels like he knows me and what makes me tick, whereas I know nothing about Archer Savage. I, however, plan to change that. I will learn what his weaknesses are, and when I need to, I'll use them against him.

As I fall into bed that night, one person plagues my thoughts, and that is Archer Savage with his icy demeanour and God-like complex. A part of me hates him, another part of me is all too interested in who he is and what makes him tick. Do I take their challenge? Do I want to be a part of their elite yuppy group? They have made it crystal clear from my first day that they don't want me here. What is their game? Is it sad that some part of me longs to belong, to feel a part of something, because I haven't had that in so long?

CHAPTER NINE

ELIZA

B y the time Calvin drops me at school the next day I'm still no nearer to deciding whether to ignore their challenge and to tell them to stick it where the sun doesn't shine or whether to prove to them I can complete any challenge they set me. I'm so deep in my head, placing some of my notebooks in my locker, that I don't notice Silver until he's leaning on the locker beside mine.

"I'm having a party at my place tonight. You should come."

I look up into Silver's pale green eyes; he has his school shirt rolled above his elbows, showing a large snake tattoo winding down his arm. There's a small cut under his eye that makes me suspect he's been brawling recently. I close my locker and lean sideways against it, so we are facing each other.

"And why would that be?" I ask him, looking disinterested.

"Because, princess, I know how to have fun and you'll feel at home in my world."

I chuckle, arching a brow. "And that world would be?"

I stiffen when he leans into my personal space and tucks a piece of my hair behind my ear. "The one that isn't ruled by rich, privileged pricks. You can bring Rafe's little Wifey if you like."

He knows about them?

My poker face mustn't be on form today because he leans into my ear and says, "There's a lot I know about your Aces, princess, and I'm willing to share if you are?"

I'm about to tell him no, when I remember the challenge and

the second option of stealing the silver horse statue from the Silver mansion. I still haven't decided to do their stupid challenge yet, but should I decide to, what better opportunity than a party at the Silver house with lots of people around?

"I'll think about it," I tell him with a non-committal shrug of my shoulders.

He grins at me, but his eyes shift attention behind me, over my head. "The kings are descending. I'll catch you tonight, princess." He presses a kiss on my head. "Oh, and wear something sexy."

I pick my bag up off the floor as I catch sight of the three Aces heading my way. Before I can turn on my heels and head off in the opposite direction, two hands push me against the wall of lockers.

"What did he want?" Archer demands, crowding into my space.

Playing it cool, I adjust his tie and smile dryly at him. "What have I told you about keeping out of my business, Savage?"

He grins coldly at me. "I told you to stay away from him, remember?" He grips my ponytail and tilts my head up to look at him.

"Aww, you jealous Savage?"

He smirks. "Jealous, of a lowlife like him. You think I'm interested in your dirt-poor pussy? Play by our rules, Scarlet, or pay the price."

I snigger. "You and your boys don't scare me, Savage. You can hunt me, tie me up, brand me, but you'll never own me. I play by my own rules, so do your worst to me. See if I care."

Archer shakes his head and tsks at me like I'm a disobedient child. "Don't say I didn't warn you." He releases my hair so swiftly, making me hit the back of my head on the lockers. Fucking arsehole.

IT'S AFTER MY FIRST CLASS THAT I NOTICE A CHANGE. AS I leave the classroom I'm spat at, called a whore, street rubbish. When I get to my locker and open it, rubbish tumbles out of it all over the floor, including stale food and used sanitary items. I hear droves of laughter behind me and know I'll turn around to find an army of phones recording my reaction. Clenching my fists tightly — I take a deep breath and turn to face the swarm of students. I spot Archer and his boys standing over by the water machine, watching and waiting for my reaction. Keeping my eyes trained on his, I slowly suck one finger into my mouth and then another and then hold them up to him in a big fuck you sign before picking up my bag and heading to my next class.

In my second class, I sit myself down and ignore the catcalls and whispered name calling and pull out my iPad. Fuck all of them. They think I can't survive this shit, well they're wrong. About ten minutes into the lesson, I feel damp on the back of my thighs; I lift a thigh off the seat, and I grimace. There is a slime like substance all over the seat and now all over my skirt and thighs. The boy sitting behind me laughs and I glare at him. Jumping up from my seat, I grab my bag and head for the door. I hear the teacher demanding that I return to my seat, amongst the mocking laughter of my classmates, as I exit the room.

I head to the nearest girl's bathroom and unzip my skirt and examine the mess. I wet some paper towels and then try to wipe off the gooey slime. It leaves a dark stain, but at least I get most of the sticky shit off. I hold it under the dryer and do my best to dry it out. It is still damp, but it will have to do for now as the bell for lunch has just gone and I don't want to be caught in the girls' bathroom in just my knickers.

With a scowl on my face, I leave the bathroom and head for the cafeteria. I grab a chicken salad and some French bread and storm over to an unoccupied table in the corner of the room.

"Hey, there you are," Verity says as she throws herself down opposite me. "Woah, who pissed you off?" she asks as she takes in my face.

"Arthur-fucking-Savage and his Aceholes," I hiss. "I swear one day I will fucking destroy Savage."

I scoff and blink. "What have I done? I stood up for myself. Fuck their club and their stupid rules. I'll talk to who I want to, when I want to. In fact, if I want to fuck Silver right here in this cafeteria in front of everyone, then I will, because no one controls me."

Verity sighs and reaches over and pats my hand. "Oh, honey, it's cute that you think that way, but if you don't play by their rules, they will release all kinds of hell on you and they will give the school free rein to destroy you."

"Let them fucking try. You don't spend five years in foster care without developing a thick skin. It will take more than rubbish in my locker and slime on my seat to tame me." I break off a piece of my bread with more aggression than is needed and shove it into my mouth. "Oh, and by the way, we are going to a party tonight at Silver's."

Verity chokes on her drink, her expressive eyes widening. "Oh no we're not. My brother and Rafe will skin me alive if I step foot on Silver territory.

I put out my bottom lip. "Oh, come on Verity, please. I need my wing woman."

"Do you have a thing for Silver? Because honestly, my money was on you and Archer hate fucking each other."

I snort in disgust. "Never will anything happen with Archer. As for Silver, maybe. He's more the kind of guy I go for and he is easy on the eye."

Verity sighs and looks at me in despair. "Eliza Alderman, you'll start a war if you go down that path. I'm telling you, it's not worth it."

I roll my shoulders. It's never a good idea to tell me not to do something because for me that is like a red flag for me to go and do it.

Later that evening, I'm putting the finishing touches to my make-up when Verity arrives. She waltzes in, her Chanel perfume leaving a trail as she sits herself at the end of my bed.

"I hope you know what an amazing friend I am being for you tonight. If Rafe or Seb find out where I am, I'll never hear the end of it."

I look at her through my mirror as I apply my mascara. "First, Rafe doesn't own you, you are not his little Wifey yet, and Seb is not your keeper either." I stand and hold my arms out. "Will I do?"

I'm wearing my signature ripped skinny jeans, heeled boots and a crop, ripped band t-shirt from a vintage t-shirt company I found online. I've finished my look off with thick winged eye liner and a deep red lip. My hair hangs in beachy waves down my back.

She whistles. "Girl, you look hot. Are you sure you don't want to try some girl on girl loving?" She winks at me playfully.

"I'll stick to boys, thank you, but you do you, honey. Okay," I say, grabbing my phone, "let's check these Silver's out."

The Silver Mansion is on the other side of the bay. It's set back off the lane with electric gates that have been left open for the partygoers. When we pull up, the place is already packed, and we have to park on the lane up to the house and walk on foot. It's a modern building but made to look like it's from the Georgian era, with large symmetrical windows. The music is loud and can be heard from back here on the lane. Inside though, it's super modern. White marble floor, black chandeliers and a wrought iron black stair rail that weaves around in a curve to the next floor. As soon as I step inside, despite the grandeur, I feel more at home here. The people at this party don't scream money and privilege, they scream public education. I take Verity's hand in mine, and we weave through the house until we come out into a large open-plan kitchen that has bi-fold doors that open the full length of the room. A kitchen island holds an array of alcoholic drinks. I grab a can of fruit cider and offer Verity a coke, because she is driving tonight.

"So, where are the Aceholes tonight? Planning world domination?"

Verity shakes her head. "No clue. They were all in the den at our house when I left."

"Ladies! You came," says a voice I recognise, and I turn to find Silver heading our way, with a drink in one hand and a spliff hanging out of his mouth. He's shirtless, showing off his muscular physique. He does a low whistle as he looks me over. "Princess, you look like my kind of trouble tonight."

I wink at him and grin. "Trouble's my middle name."

"Don't I know it," he agrees, placing an arm over my shoulder. "And you brought the other Ace Princess as well. Do your keepers know you are here tonight?"

I snigger. "I don't have a keeper."

He nods, giving me a knowing look. "You keep telling yourself that, beautiful. Come and meet some of my mates."

He leads us out into the back garden to where a large group sit in a sunken seating area with a fire pit in the middle.

"Braeden, move over," he orders, and the boy with a closely shaved head shuffles over to make room for us. The chatter dies instantly when we sit down, and everyone stares at us. I look around at the staring faces with wide eyes.

"Never seen two pretty girls before, people?" Silver asks the crowd.

One guy takes a drag on his spliff and leans back in his seat. He has a ring piercing through his lip and two in one eyebrow. "Elite girls, huh?"

"Not just any elite girls either," says the girl he has one arm around, her hair is platinum blonde and cut in a blunt bob. "She's an Ace."

Verity flushes and looks uncomfortable.

"You after starting trouble, brother?" says a guy sitting over to the left. I see the resemblance between him and Silver immediately. They have the same alluring pale green eyes, only his brother is stockier and has more tattoos.

"Just being friendly to the new girl in town," he replies, offering me the spliff.

"And who might you be, new girl?" His brother asks, his assessing eyes landing back on me.

"Eliza Holton."

"Eliza Alderman," Silver corrects, and his brother instantly sits up straighter in his seat.

"Going for the big prize, huh?"

I sigh. "When you two have finished talking in code. My friend and I might be from the other side of the Bay, but we're here to have a good time. So can you all quit with the staring and just let us be?"

"Now I see why you invited her," his brother says with a look on his face that makes me think he is plotting something. "You heard the girl," he says to the crowd of people, "stop staring."

At his command, everyone turns away and resumes conversation, like the awkward stares never happened.

I hand the spliff back to Silver. With some weed in me, I feel like I can finally relax. "So, Silver, do you have a name? It feels weird calling you Silver all the time."

He grins and leans back in his seat, his arm still draped casually over the back of my seat. "Damon. My names Damon." He eyes me for a few seconds. "Tell me, princess, what do you do for fun?"

"First, quit with the princess thing. I'm no princess, and it's really pissing me off. As for fun, I like to fight, fuck and, on occasions break the law."

Damon laughs, his eyes never leaving mine. "My kind of woman. You fight, huh?"

I nod. "I've fought in a few underground fighting rings. I love it."

"You any good?"

I cock a brow. "Is the Pope a Catholic?"

"Well, beautiful, you are in luck. There happens to be a ring a couple of towns from here. Fight nights are Fridays and Saturdays. My brother often fights there, but I should warn you, your ball and chain is also a regular in the ring."

"My ball and chain?" I ask, even though I have a fair idea who he is talking about.

"Savage."

I scoff and look over at Verity, who is deep in conversation with the pretty blonde girl next to her. "Let's get one thing clear here, Damon. I'm not Savage's. Never have been, never will be. I'm free and single and if I want to hook up with someone here tonight, I will, and if I want to fight, I will. I'm under no one's control."

Damon grins and leans in, taking a hold of my chin between his thumb and forefinger. "I hope I'm on the top of your list of potential hook-ups, beautiful?"

"Maybe, if you play your cards right," I tell him with a wink.

I pull Verity away from the girl she is hitting on and we head inside for a bathroom break and a refill. We hang out in the open-plan kitchen and people watch for a while.

"Please tell me you aren't going to hit it up with Silver, because honestly, that would be a terrible idea," Verity asks me, a deep frown marring her pretty face.

I shake my head and grin. "No, I'm not. Well, at least not today. Tonight, I'm just testing out the waters. Seeing which side of the Bay I like to be on."

"Silver has an agenda, just as much as you think Archer has," she sighs, "look I don't want to say he's only showing interest because of who you are."

"But," I prompt her.

"He knows you're an Alderman. He knows you are an Ace by birth right. Just ask yourself if he would show as much interest if you weren't."

I love Verity for caring, but I can look after myself. I'm not stupid. I know Damon's interest in me is partly because of who I am and because, for some reason, it seems to get a rise out of Archer. "You don't need to worry about me, Verity. I have always been able to look after myself and cover my own back." I look over Verity's shoulder and see the blonde she was talking to earlier walking our way. "I'm going to make myself scarce. You can thank me later." I gesture my head at the approaching girl before I pick up my drink and head through to the front of the house.

I find what I am looking for in the large living room at the front of the property. There, sitting on a marble fireplace, taking centre-stage is the silver horse statue. It looks heavy, and it's also a little big to sneak under my jacket, so I'm not sure, should I decide to steal it, how I'll get it out of here without being seen. I walk through the house until I come to a door which houses the home's security cameras. Checking there is no one behind me, I sneak inside and close the door behind me. I find the footage of me walking down the corridor into this room and erase it and then I locate and turn off the camera outside of this room and the one in the living room. I also turn off the one that covers the front door of the property. That will make going undetected a little easier. I pull out my phone and dial the number for the police.

"Hi, I'd like to make a complaint about a house party where drugs are being taken."

I pocket my phone and, smiling to myself, I stick my head out of the door and check the coast is clear before heading back through to the kitchen. I chuckle when I find my friend. She's standing between the legs of the blonde girl — who sits on the kitchen worktop — kissing.

"I need your car keys," I tell her and without pulling her lips away from the girl, she reaches in the pocket of her skirt and holds them out for me. I slip them into my jeans pocket and wait. About ten minutes later, I hear a guy holler across the room that the cops are outside, and everyone panics and breaks off; heading for the various exits. I check quickly that no one is in the lounge, and I reach up and grab the statue and pick up a random coat that someone has left behind and shrug it on and fold it closed over my chest to hide the large statue I'm holding there. With one quick glance around, I head out a side door and into the tree line and make my way through the darkness until I come out near Verity's car. I unlock the boot and I take off the borrowed jacket and wrap it around the horse before placing it in the boot and closing it. I snake back along the treeline and slip back into the house via the side door.

I peek around the hallway and see Silver's brother at the door, talking to the police. A hand grabs mine and I'm pulled back around the corner.

"Careful," says Silver, "don't want to be caught underage drinking at the house of the enemy." He has me caged in against the wall.

"Who said you're the enemy? Maybe the Aces are my enemy."

He smirks. "You might not have grown up here, beautiful. But you are an Ace by blood and therefore I am the enemy, but that doesn't mean that enemies can't fraternise." He leans in and places his lips against mine. He holds them there for a beat, as if waiting to see if I'll push him away, and when I don't, he takes a step closer and kisses me. I respond, kissing him back. I'm not going to lie, it's a good kiss and Silver is hot. I pull away and rest my hand on his chest, noticing the tattoo of a horse. "What's with the horse?"

He looks down at where my hand rests over his tattoo and he places his hand over mine. "It's where my family first made their money. Betting and horse racing. You could say it's in my blood. We have stables here."

I bob my head up and down as I take in this new information. "I used to ride. When my mum and dad were alive. It's been a long time since I rode."

"Well, princess, you're welcome down here anytime for a ride." He smirks at me, and I roll my eyes at his attempt at sexual innuendo. "Come on, I'll run you home."

"I'm good," I protest as we create some space between us. "I just need to find Verity."

"Then let's find your friend." He takes me by the hand and leads me out into the hallway, just as his brother is closing the door. He looks at his brother and then down at our joined hands and smirks before he disappears into a room over on the right. We find Verity in the third bedroom we try, her and the girls jump apart from where they were fooling around on the bed when Silver opens the door and turns the light on.

"Oh, hey," Verity says, running a hand through her unruly hair. "We were just passing some time until the police fucked off."

"You don't say," Damon says with a devilish grin. "Parties over and Cinderella here needs a ride home. Unless you're otherwise engaged?"

Verity rolls her eyes at him as she shuffles to the end of the bed and puts her shoes back on. "I'm good, thanks," she tells him. Kayla huffs, annoyed we have interrupted them, and she grabs her own shoes. She leans in and drops a kiss on Verity's lips. "Call me." As she passes Damon, she pulls her tongue out playfully at him and he chuckles.

We follow Damon to the front door, and he holds it open for us. Verity passes him with a wave.

"Thanks for the invite tonight," I tell him as I pause on the doorstep.

"Anytime, beautiful. Oh, and if you want to be on the fighting line-up for this Friday, I can set you up?"

"You could?" I ask, my eyes lighting up with excitement.

He nods. "Leave it with me." He leans in and places a kiss on my forehead. "Be good."

I take a step back and hesitate, and he cocks a brow in question. "By the way, that kiss, don't think it means anything."

His mouth lifts at the corner as he tilts his head and studies me. "Never crossed my mind that it did, princess. Good night."

Taking a step backwards out into the night, I shake my head, smiling, before turning and heading down the drive to Verity's car.

I climb inside and Verity waits silently while I put on my seatbelt. "Do you want to tell me what went down between you two?"

I laugh and shake my head. "Nothing for you to worry about, Verity. So, Kayla's cute?"

Verity bites her lip and nods her head. "Isn't she gorgeous? Those legs of hers go on forever." She starts the car, and we head for the other side of the bay. "Oh, and you can call me Vee. That's what those in my close circle call me."

I chuckle and nod my head, and I can't help the pleasure I feel in knowing that she now classes me as part of that inner circle. "Let's head home. Are you still staying at mine?"

"I sure am," Verity replies.

CHAPTER
TEN

ELIZA

We pull up at the Alderman mansion ten minutes later. I've barely unbuckled my belt when I'm yanked from the car and pushed up against the window of the rear seats.

"Where the fuck have you been, Scarlet?" I look up into the livid eyes of the number one thorn in my side.

"Nice to see you too, Savage."

"Don't roll those eyes at me, Eliza. I'll ask you again, where the fuck have you been tonight?" Steam is practically coming out of his nostrils, he's that fired up.

I sigh and place a hand on his chest. "Well, judging by your pissy attitude, I'm guessing you know where I've been. Let's just cut to the chase, shall we?"

He grips my chin and forces my head back as he leans closer into my space. I hear a yelp and look over my shoulder to see Rafe throwing Vee over his shoulder and walking towards his car, throwing her into the passenger seat. "Catch you later," he tells us before he screeches off down the drive. It looks like Vee is in for a telling off too.

Now I am alone with my nemesis, and when I look him in the eye, I swallow. What is it about him that has my blood rushing to my head every time he's near me?

"Did I or did I not tell you to stay away from Silver?" he demands, leaning into me so are bodies are touching in every place possible.

"Yes, you did, but you also challenged me to take something from his house. Not sure how you expect me to do that without actually going to his house."

He scoffs, "Don't play innocent with me." He pulls his phone from his pocket and places it in my face. "Want to explain this to me?"

I frown when I see the photo of Silver kissing me. Who the fuck took that? My frown deepens as I consider that maybe Damon sent it to him.

I sigh in exasperation, and I knock on his forehead with my fist. "Have you never seen a boy kiss a girl before, Savage?"

"You let him touch you," he seethes. Looks like I've really poked the bear tonight.

I meet his fierce gaze with my own. "I did, and I might let him do it again."

"Over my dead body," he growls at me. His dark eyes burning with rage.

I shake my head in exasperation. "What is it with you? You hate me. You've made that clear, so why does it matter who I lock lips with?"

He steps right up, so our bodies are flush with each other's. "I do hate you. I hate you with every breath in my body."

I hold my hands up in the air. "So, stay out of my way then and I'll stay out of yours."

"Did you like it?' he growls. "Him kissing you?"

I grin widely. "Oh, I liked it a lot." That isn't quite true. The kiss was pleasant, but it didn't light my spark. Damon Silver is firmly in the friend zone. The angry guy in front of me though, he is in another zone altogether.

CHAPTER ELEVEN

ARCHER

I'm burning with rage right now. I was having a game of poker with some of the lads when that photo came through on my phone. It shouldn't have bothered me, but it did. No matter how much I hate her, she's mine. She is my toy. She is mine to destroy. No one else gets to touch her.

I throw my cards down on the table and get to my feet. "We're out of here." Seb and Rafe don't question me. They just place their cards down and follow me out of the room.

"Everything okay?" Seb asks as we head outside to our cars.

I turn and show them my phone screen. Seb takes in the photo and whistles. "Silver sure is playing with fire. How do you want to handle this?"

"I'll deal with her first and then him," I bark as I stalk to my car. Seb jumps in with me, and Rafe follows us in his own car. We drive to the Alderman Mansion.

"You think he knows about the contract?" Seb asks me.

I grip the steering wheel tighter. "I know he's using her to get to me, so he must know something."

"How though?" Seb asks, looking bewildered.

"We must have a spy in our midst, and when I find out who, they'll wish they were never born."

"What about Little Red?" he asks, his eyes not leaving my face as we speed through the streets of the sleepy bay.

My fist clenches around the steering wheel again. "She needs to learn which side she is on."

Seb sighs. "She wasn't brought up here with us, man. Her loyalty is with her brother and no one else. You still sure about your plans for her?"

My head snap rounds to glare at him. "Why wouldn't I be?"

He shrugs. "I don't know, Arch. I kind of like the girl. She's the type of girl we need as our queen."

"Have you forgotten what her father did to my mother? Her family is the reason she is dead, and she'll pay the price for what they did to my family."

Seb nods. "I know man, I do, and we'll have you back no matter what, but..." he pauses, "but she's kind of perfect for you. Her fire and defiance. Not to mention she has a dark side that craves danger, just like you do."

"She is a means to an end, nothing more, and when I'm done breaking her, she'll be nothing but the shell of a woman her father turned my mother into." As soon as my grandfather had shared the news that they had tracked down the two Alderman heirs, I knew this was the perfect way to get revenge for my mum. He may well be dead, but his daughter is alive and kicking and so she'll be the one I destroy. She'll pay for the sins of her father.

We pull up in the driveway and I kill the engine and sit and wait for her to arrive home. Rafe pulls up a minute later and once he's parked up, he joins us in my car.

"Is Vee with her?" he asks me. I nod and he swears under his breath. "I'll deal with her," he announces firmly.

I hold my hands up. "Of course, she's your fiancé."

We wait and eventually they pull up in Vee's car. They are both grinning and laughing. I hope they enjoyed their fun, because they'll soon be punished for their actions.

"You liked it, huh?" I repeat. My blood boiling inside. I run my thumb over her bottom lip and then her top one, and the little vixen snaps at my finger with her teeth. I grip her chin firmly. "No one touches these lips"

She laughs, her eyes burning with hatred and anger, and it's making me hard. I love her defiance; it sings to my soul. She is beautiful, but when she's angry and fired up like this, she is breath-taking. Her chocolate brown eyes glare at me. "I'll kiss who the fuck I want, Archer. You don't own me."

Oh, Scarlet. But I do. And I can't wait to see her face the day she realises why her precious grandfather has really brought her to this town. I press my body into hers, pinning her against the car. I feel every curve of her body, her breasts pressed up against my chest, her stomach exposed in that sexy crop top she's wearing. Fuck, I hate her, but my body wants her. My dick strains against the confines of my jeans, begging me to sink myself balls-deep in her and fuck the disobedience out of her. I press my lips against hers and, at first, she squirms and tries to pull away, but then she stops fighting me. I should have known she'd feel too good. Her lips are soft and inviting, and I plunge my tongue inside her mouth, kissing the breath right out of her. When I pull away, we're both panting and shocked. Fuck, I shouldn't have kissed her.

Crack! She slaps me hard across the cheek, and it stings like a bitch. I blink in shock. A girl has never hit me before and certainly not after I've kissed her. "Hit me like that again, Scarlet, and I'll pull your jeans down and spank your arse so hard you'll not sit down for a week."

Crack! She hits me again; the sound echoes out into the silent night. I see red. I grab her by the waist and throw her over my shoulder. She punches and hits at my back, demanding I put her down, as I stride further into the grounds of her grandfather's property. The empty cottage door bangs open as I shove it aside with my foot. I throw her down on the dusty wooden kitchen table, face first, and press my body over hers.

"Time to learn your place, Little Red." I keep her arms pinned behind her back as I reach round and unzip her jeans. I grasp the back of her jeans and yank them down over her arse. Fuck me sideways. The sight of her bare arse bent over this table is a sight I'll be jerking off to for days. She's wriggling and calling me every name under the sun, but I'm oblivious to it. I rub my hand over her pert cheeks, and I lean my mouth against her skin and bite into her flesh. She yelps and I smile in delight when I see my teeth marks on her flesh. I want to mark every inch of her skin. I crowd over her.

"I wonder, are you wet for me, Scarlet? Shall we see?"

"Fuck you, Savage," she spits as I suck her earlobe into my mouth. I reach my hand around her front and smile to myself when I sink my fingers between her folds and find her dripping wet for me. Little red is as turned on by this as I am.

This wasn't my plan tonight. I insert a finger inside her, and she whimpers, and it isn't in protest.

"You like that, my little traitor, don't you?" She groans when I pull out then push back inside her. I pump my fingers in and out of her wet sex and she moans my name. I love hearing her say my name. There is something my sick, dark side gets off on having her here compliant and needy. I pull my fingers from her flesh and bring them to my nose and inhale her scent. Fucking perfect. I suck her juices into my mouth before I bring the palm of my hand down hard on her pert arse cheek, the sound resounding around the empty room. She yelps, but it ends in a moan, and she wriggles her hips. Bringing my hand down again, hard, it leaves a red hand mark on her arse cheek. I lean down and kiss it better. I don't think I've ever been this hard. I think I'm going to explode in my pants. The need to fuck her and own her roars through my veins. The need to fill her so deep with my cum is instinctual. I want to see her sore because she has had my dick pounding her sweet pussy for hours. I plunge my fingers back inside her, three this time and she takes it like a good girl. She moans my name, begging me for her release, and I love that I have the power to give it to her, or not.

I pull my fingers away and I grab her waist and spin her round. She raises a hand to slap me again, but I catch her wrist in my grip and press my body into hers, so she falls back into the table.

"Now are you going to do as you're told, or do I have to spank you some more?" I hiss.

She glares at me, her eyes mix of hate and lust. "I fucking hate you, Savage."

CHAPTER TWELVE

ELIZA

"Get dressed," he orders me coldly. I sit up and dress as he quietly stands there, glaring at me. His cold treatment should bother me, but it doesn't. It's better this way, and it's not like what just happened changes anything between us. I still hate him, he still hates me, and that's the way it will stay. I'm even more annoyed that he got me going and then didn't let me come.

We walk back to the front of the mansion in silence. As I walk behind him, I see him clench and unclench his fists as he walks like he's itching for a fight.

"Before you go, I have something for you," I tell him, heading towards Vee's car.

He arches a brow and glares at me coldly. "You have nothing I want."

I open the boot and with my hand on my hip, I gesture for him to take a look. With an irritated sigh, he stalks over and looks inside.

"I completed your stupid challenge. You have your fucking horse statue. Looks like I'm in your little club now. Goodnight, Savage. Sweet dreams." I blow him a kiss, keeping my bitch gaze fierce as I turn and walk towards the back of the house. It is late and I can't risk trying to go in by the front door.

My thoughts are all over the place as I climb into bed. Both Damon and Savage have kissed me tonight, but there's only one kiss that's now stuck in my brain on replay. There is only one kiss that has awoken something in me that I haven't felt in a long time. Tonight, I feel truly alive and when my eyes finally close, it's not the usual nightmare of the night I lost my parents. No, tonight its dreams plagued with his dark eyes and the feel of his hands on my body.

CHAPTER
THIRTEEN

ELIZA

I jump in fright when Vee dives on my back the next day at school. I was lost in my own mind, replaying last night's events. In the shower this morning, all I could think about was the feel of his fingers inside me. Last night was a stupid mistake, but damn if I didn't enjoy every second of it.

"Jeez, Vee. Don't sneak up on me like that," I chastise her as she wraps her arms around my neck from behind and kisses my cheek.

"Someone is jumpy this morning. Did Archer spend the rest of the night waterboarding you for being a bad girl?"

"Funny," I say sassily, pulling my tongue out at her.

"Ugh, Georgie just doesn't know when to quit," Vee groaned, and I follow her eyes to see Georgie pressing herself up against Archer and whispering in his ear. Archer's eyes briefly find mine and I quickly turn away and concentrate on my locker. I'm not bothered, not at all. I hate Archer Savage and last night was a big, stupid mistake.

"So how did Rafe deal with your disobedience?" I ask my new friend as I close my locker and we head down the hallway to class.

Verity grins. "He spanked me. Honestly, my arse cheeks are sore as shit," she says rubbing at her bottom. "But it was worth it for the angry sex we had afterwards."

I arch a brow. "What is it with those boys and spanking?"

Verity stops in her steps and grabs my arm. "Hold up, who has been spanking you?"

I'd walked into that one without thinking. "No one," I scoff. "As if I'd let that moody, arrogant bastard anywhere near my arse."

Verity gives me a look that tells me she doesn't believe me, and I roll my eyes and look away. I could talk to her about what happened last night, but then it meant nothing, so there is really nothing to talk about.

As we walk past the Aces, Georgie lets a peel of high-pitched laughter ring through the corridor. I don't look over. I won't give him the satisfaction.

I take my seat in class and stare out the window. My grandfather is coming home tonight. I'm a bundle of pent-up anxiety. What if he doesn't like us? What if he decides he's made a mistake and we have to go back into foster care again? What if his partner decides she doesn't want us here invading their perfect lives?

I feel him walk into the room before I see him. Instead of taking the seat behind me, he takes the seat to the side of me. I don't know which is worse, having him behind me all lesson or at the side of me where I can see him, and where I am aware of every time he shifts in his seat. We don't speak all lesson. He doesn't acknowledge me. Looking at us, no one would have a clue about what went down between us last night.

I grab some lunch in the cafeteria and throw myself down beside Vee with a deep sigh. I haven't even put my drink down on the table when two strong arms wrap around my chest and lift me from my seat. "We've let you flout the rules for long enough, but now you need to fall in line."

I glower up at Vee's brother. "Put me the fuck down, Seb."

He chuckles, walking, with me dangling in his arms. "No can do. You're an Ace now and us Ace's always sit at the top table."

I struggle even harder when I see where we are heading. Towards their table. The Gods' table. Archer sits leaning back in his seat, watching me with lazy disinterest whilst Georgie sits beside him yapping away about God knows what.

"Why is she here?" she demands of Archer in that whiny voice of hers.

Archer turns his attention on her, and he glowers at her coldly, making her flinch. "Move. Now."

Georgie's eye screw up as she scowls. "You're joking, right? She's nothing."

"Move," he orders firmly.

With a huff, Georgie picks up her plate and moves around the table to sit next to one of her girlfriends. Seb plonks me down beside Archer and takes the seat next to me, tucking straight back into his burger. Verity has followed behind us and gives me a quizzical look before she takes a seat opposite us.

"Why the fuck am I here?" I hiss at Archer, whilst I take in the open-mouthed stares of all my fellow pupils who have just watched me be man-handled over here. My eyes fall on my brother, sitting just a table over with some boys from the football team. He's frowning in concern, so I offer him a smile to reassure him that I am okay with what just happened. It seems to settle him as he offers me a quick smile back and then returns to talking to his friends.

"Will they expect him to join?" I ask, my voice barely a whisper.

"He's the blood of one of the four, of course he'll have to join," Archer replies in a bored tone.

I turn my face to look at him. "What if I don't want him to? What would I have to do to stop him from being a part of this?"

Archer is silent for a beat as his eyes burn into mine. "This is our legacy, Scarlet. This life is what we are born into. We don't get to say no. We bow to the traditions set by our forefathers, and we play our parts."

"And what is my part to play?" I ask him as a cold shiver runs down my spine.

"That is a question for grandaddy Wilbur." Archer places

something in my hand. "You're to come to the clubhouse tonight for your swearing in ceremony."

I look down at my palm and I find a small sized playing card in my hand. The ace of diamonds. "What if I don't want to?"

Archer smirks. "Like I said, you don't have a choice, Scarlet. The sooner you come to terms with that, the better." And with that he is done with me. He turns his attention to Rafe and they talk about an upcoming fight.

By the end of the day, I'm weary, and with a quick hello to Calvin, I fall into the backseat of the car and close my eyes.

"Hard day, Miss?" he asks me, his eyes meeting mine through the mirror.

"You've no idea," I reply with a weary smile, just as the car door opens and my brother climbs inside.

"Hey, Kidder." I ruffle his hair, and he groans trying to push me away. "I feel like we hardly see each other these days. How's it going?"

He grins. "I love it here. Have you been in the indoor pool yet?" I shake my head. "It's amazing," he tells me. "And the football coach is the best. Did you know he once played for England?"

"I didn't, but now I do. So, have you made the team?"

He sniggers in response. "Of course, I have. Stupid question."

I pull my tongue out at him and we both laugh.

"Hey, what's going on with you and Archer?" my brother asks me, his face turning serious.

I frown. "Nothing. Why?"

Kit looks to see if Calvin is listening before he carries on. "Are you one of them now? Because Jasper says only the Aces, or the Clubs, sit at their table. And Rory Johnson says that you're his."

I chuckle. "Don't believe all you hear about their silly little club, okay? I'm not in their club and I'm not Archer's or anyone else's at that school. You got it?"

He nods, still watching me. "Being a Club is kind of cool though, you know? Did you know our family was one of the family's that founded the Aces?"

I nod. "I did. Like I said, it's just a bunch of bored rich boys and a silly club. You just concentrate on your football."

⚜

WHEN WE PULL UP THE DRIVE, THERE IS AN UNFAMILIAR CAR parked up. A black Bugatti. Even I gawp when I see it.

"Woah! Who's is the Bugatti?" Kit asks, drooling as he stares out the window at the car.

Calvin laughs in response. "That is Wilbur's car. They arrived home about an hour ago."

I gulp. They are here. I am filled with anticipation and nerves at meeting the man who raised our father. The man my father left behind and never spoke a word about. The man that holds the chance of stability for my brother in the palms of his hands.

We head inside and I immediately look through the door of every room we pass to see if they are there. When we reach the kitchen, Edith is busy at the stove. She smiles warmly at us both.

"How was your day? Kit there's a strawberry protein shake waiting for you. I added the peanut butter, just as you like it."

I eye Kit as he passes me, and he just shrugs his shoulder and blushes. He already has Edith wrapped around his little finger.

"Don't let him run rings around you, Edith," I tell her, and she bats away my comment with her hand.

"Ah, it's my absolute pleasure to look after the both of you. Now go on up and get showered and changed. Dinner will be in the formal dining room tonight with your grandfather and Lexi. Make sure you put on something nice."

I nod my head as I grab an apple out of the fruit bowl and follow my brother up the stairs. It looks like we won't be meeting our new family members until it is time to eat.

I throw my school bag down and pull off my shoes, throwing them down next to my bag. I've no sooner lay back against my pillow when my phone rings. When I don't recognise the number, I frown.

"Hello."

"Hey there, princess. I got you a slot in the ring tonight. You better be as good as you say you are."

I grin. "Hey Silver, that's great, and I'm really that good." Years of boxing training with my dad had paid off and I was a machine in the ring. Plus, I loved the adrenaline rush of a fight. I also loved the pain. It soaked through the numbness and the guilt from the accident and made me feel something.

"I've texted you the address. You okay getting here?"

"Yep," I reply. Verity didn't know it yet, but she was my lift there. "I'll see you tonight."

I step into the shower and look down at the red puckered skin from where those fuckers branded me. It's still sore, but it's healing, slowly. I am expected at the secret clubhouse tonight, but that would mean I might miss my slot in the ring. Part of me wanted to attend this ceremony whilst another part of me wanted to give it the finger and not turn up. I grin to myself. I have never been very good at taking orders.

I um and ah for about forty minutes on what to wear and I eventually settle on a purple skater dress and black ballet style pumps. It's a bit girly for my taste, but I can't see ripped jeans and a t-shirt being suitable for a formal dinner. I leave my face void of makeup apart from my signature burgundy lip, then I head to Kit's room and knock on for him.

He opens his door wearing a pair of black trousers and a pale blue polo top. "Aww, look at you all smart and posh."

He shoves me playfully and pulls his tongue out at me. "Look at you trying to look all sweet and demure."

I arch a brow as we walk together down the stairs. "I am sweet and demure."

Kit laughs. "As sweet as a sour patch kid."

I grab his head in a headlock and ruffle up his hair. "I'll give you sweet, you little shit."

We're both laughing and play fighting when the sound of someone clearing their throat pulls us from our silliness. A tall man, about six-foot-two, wearing a white shirt and navy trousers, stands in the doorway watching us. His hair is silver grey, and he has pale blue eyes just like those of our fathers. When I turn my face fully to look at him, he does a sharp intake of breath. Like he has seen a ghost.

"My lord. You are the image of Catherine." He studies me intently with a wistful look on his face.

"Catherine?" I ask him curiously.

He nods his head and gestures to the painting on the wall above me on the staircase. "Your grandmother and my late wife. You are her double."

"I wondered who she was." I take a step towards him and offer out my hand. "Hi, I'm Eliza."

He smiles as he looks at my outstretched hand before he leans in and kisses me on my cheek. "Welcome home Eliza, and you must be Kit." He holds out his hand and Kit takes it and gives it a firm shake. "And you are the image of your father. Come on through and you can both tell me how you are settling in."

When we enter the formal dining room, a tall slim woman with long blonde hair sits to the left of the head of the table with a glass of red wine in her hand. As I suspected, she's at least twenty years younger than Wilbur. Opposite her sits a boy with dark hair and dark eyes, and a sun-kissed tan. He reminds me of the obnoxious guy from the original gossip girl. I have recently binge watched the whole series.

"Eliza, Kit, meet Alexis, my partner, and her son, Chester."

"Lexi," she corrects him with a tight smile. "Welcome to Hawk Bay. It's so lovely to have you here."

This brings a snigger from Chester. He rolls his eyes when she glowers across the table at him.

"Ignore Chester," my grandfather says with an amiable smile. "We usually do."

I chance a side glance at Kit; he is looking as weirded out as I am. Dysfunctional is a word that springs to mind.

I take a seat beside Chester, and Kit sits beside Alexis. "How do you like the house? I hope you both like your bedrooms, I had a hand in the design," Alexis tells us both proudly.

"The bedrooms are great, thank you," I reply, lying through my teeth.

"Yeah, I'm sure baby pink is really your colour." I look up into the mocking deep blue eyes of Chester. My grandfather clears his throat and gives Chester a warning glare.

"How are you finding your new school?" Wilbur asks Kit, and my little brother's face lights up in delight that he is showing an interest in him. He has missed having a real father figure in his life.

"It's the best," Kit replies. "The sports facilities are amazing."

My Grandfather smiles, looking pleased. "Nothing but the best for the Alderman's. And you Eliza?"

"Yeah, school is okay. I've made a friend, so she is helping me settle in."

"Who?" Chester asks me, leaning back in his seat and eyeballing me over the table.

"Verity Collings."

My grandfather is suddenly alert. "I'm pleased to hear you are making friends with the founding families. Have you met Verity's brother and the Savage and Ellsworth boys?"

"Oh, I've met them alright," I say coldly, realising too late I haven't hidden my animosity.

"It's important, Eliza, that the four families remain a united front," Wilbur tells me, his brows furrowed together at me.

"Oh, you don't need to worry. The boys have given me a great welcome to town." I smile. If only he knew what these boys have put me through. Though thinking about it, my grandfather is an

Ace, or he was, so he likely does know what the Aceholes have put me through.

Wilbur breathes a sigh of relief and leans back in his seat. I look up to find Chester watching me with avid interest. When our eyes meet, he smirks and winks at me. Yeah, there is no doubt this guy is one hundred percent another conceited arsehole. God, was this whole town full of guys with massive egos?

The meal goes surprisingly well. Wilbur listens avidly to Kit when he tells him all about his first football game next weekend and he looks thrilled when our grandfather tells him we'll all come and watch him. I mean, I always go to Kit's games. I am his number one cheerleader, but to have other family members coming to his games now would be strange.

"We have a charity dinner to attend in a few weeks. It will be a great opportunity to introduce you both to everyone. Alexis will help you find a dress, Eliza. You are an Alderman now and you need to look the part." He looks over at Alexis. "Book her in at the salon as well. We need to do something about the hair colour."

"No," I say firmly and everyone in the room turns their attention to me. "I mean. I like my hair this colour."

Wilbur clears his throat and is about to reply when Alexis places a hand on his arm. "Choose your battles. I'm thinking a burgundy-coloured dress will go perfectly with your hair, Eliza. What do you think?"

"I'd prefer black," I reply in honesty.

"Why doesn't that surprise me?" my grandfather comments, giving me an assessing look. "It's unbelievable how much you look like my late wife." For a brief moment, I see a flash of emotion cross his face before he reins it in. At the mention of his late wife, I side-eye Alexis who is rolling her eyes before she takes a large sip of her wine.

"I'd like to know more about why my dad always told us he had no family," I announce, and I feel the atmosphere in the room drop a few degrees.

We all startle when the doorbell chimes. Clearly no one at the table is expecting visitors. A few seconds later, Calvin appears at the dining-room door.

"Apologies for the interruption, but there is someone here for Eliza," Calvin informs Wilbur, his eyes briefly meeting mine.

"Who is it?" my grandfather barks, clearly annoyed at my mystery caller interrupting our meal.

"It's Mr Savage Junior."

My grandfather's expression quickly changes from one of anger to one of delight. "Oh, invite him in, Calvin." Wilbur beckons enthusiastically with his hand.

I am about to express that I have no desire to see Archer Savage when he appears in the doorway looking like sex on a stick. His dark hair is styled back off his face and he's wearing a black leather jacket and dark blue jeans.

"Archer, son, come on in." Wilbur beckons, getting to his feet and offering his hand out to Savage. Archer pulls his attention from me, and with a cool nod he places his hand in my grand-fathers.

"I'm sorry for the interruption, but Eliza has an appointment this evening."

I blink. He what? I open my mouth to protest, but my grand-father beats me to it.

"Well, of course, that is okay. We were more or less finished with dinner, anyway." He looks from Archer to me and smiles in satisfaction. "I must say, I am thrilled to hear the two of you are spending time together. Eliza was just telling me how welcoming you have been."

"Of course," Archer agrees. His eyes mine and though no words are spoken between us, I know inside he is smirking away. "Eliza is one of us. We look after our own."

"That we do," my grandfather agrees. "Well, don't just sit there Eliza, leaving this young gentleman waiting."

"What time do I need to have her home, Mr Alderman?"

"Oh, no curfew tonight. Tonight is an important night. You two just enjoy each other's company."

I gawp at him, in shock as I get to my feet. Kit looks over at me with a cocked brow and I shrug my shoulders. I make my way over to Archer and as soon as I am in touching distance; he reaches for me and kisses my cheek. "Eliza, you look lovely."

"Uh, thanks," I reply, looking up at him with a false smile. The fucker is forcing me into his plans, and he has my grandfather eating out of his hands.

"Enjoy your evening, Eliza. I'll see you both up there," Wilbur tells me with a cunning look in his eyes. He shares a brief look with Archer that has me tilting my head in observation, but before I can assess it any further. Archer places a hand on my lower back and guides me out of the room.

"What the fuck are you doing here?" I hiss at him as we make our way through the grand hallway to the door.

"I'm doing my duty," he replies dryly, walking towards his car and leaving me trailing after him.

"Well, newsflash buddy. I don't want to go to your clubhouse. I have my own plans."

He sighs as if bored and turns to face me. "Get in the car, Eliza."

I scoff and stand my ground, folding my arms and glaring at him in challenge.

"Your grandfather is watching," he tells me with cool disdain, and I turn to look back at the house to see Wilbur looking out from the dining-room window, a glass of wine in his hand, watching us closely.

I plaster a smile on my face and wave at him before I turn back and make my way to Archer's car. "Acehole," I spit as I open the passenger seat and take my seat.

Archer climbs in and starts the engine. "I like it when you're obedient and do as you're told."

"Kiss my arse," I reply, glaring across the car at him as we drive away from my new home.

"Are you sure you don't want me to spank it? You seem to like that," he replies with a smirk.

I give him the finger with a haughty glare and turn my attention to the scenery outside of my window. "I take it we're going to the mystery clubhouse?"

"Clever girl," he says mockingly. "When you are told to come to the clubhouse, you come, Eliza. Night or day."

Even though I won't admit it to him. I am curious about the clubhouse. The centre of this bullshit, stupid, elite club. He turns west towards the hills, and I perk up in interest. I haven't been to this side of the bay before. We follow a narrow winding road up into the hills and as we turn the corner, I sit up straighter seeing the outline of a building. The building looks old, I'm talking fifteenth century old. It looks like an old coaching house, stuck out here in the middle of nowhere.

He parks the car and climbs out and I realise I am still sitting here gawping at the place like an idiot. I climb out and jog to catch up to him.

He stops in his purposeful stride, and I almost walk straight into his back. He grips me by the arms and looks down at me and there is a look of hesitation in his eyes. "Look, just don't ask questions tonight, okay? It'll be better for you if you just go along with this."

"And if I don't?"

He frowns, tilting my chin up to look up at him. "If you don't, you won't like the consequences. Look, Eliza, this club that you think is a joke, well, to the people who are members, it's serious. It's an immense honour and very important to those who are a part of it. Once we go inside there, you don't mock or joke or you'll face the wrath of the elders."

I gulp as I look at his face and I realise he is seriously trying to warn me here. I nod. "Okay, I'll behave."

"Good girl." He takes my hand in his again and leads me towards the devil's lair.

Archer takes out an ancient looking key and places it in the lock of the black wooden door. We enter a large hallway that has wrought-iron chandeliers lighting up the room. Archer walks over to a sideboard, reaches into a basket and pulls out a face mask. The mask is black and along the top it's edged with the symbols from all four decks of cards. He puts it on, and it covers his eyes and nose, leaving his mouth clear, but giving him some sense of anonymity. The mask makes him look even more sinister and deadly, which I didn't think was possible. I roll my eyes when he holds out a white mask of a similar design for me.

"Seriously?" I ask, raising my eyes heavenward. "Are we sacrificing a goat tonight as well?"

His answer is to glare at me as he waits for me to take the mask.

With a weary sigh, I snatch it from his hand and put the mask on. What the actual fuck is going on here? I feel like I've stepped onto the set of some weird cult movie.

With his hand at the base of my back, Archer guides me towards a pair of doors. When we enter, the room holds a group of about fifteen men and women, all wearing masks, all milling around drinking champagne and making small talk. The room is circular, and the floor is covered in black and white floor tiles, like a chessboard. In the centre of the tiled floor is a mosaic of an ace card. Wow, I mean they really take this Aces thing seriously. Archer offers me a glass of champagne and I take it from him and neck it in two gulps. He cocks a brow and, taking the glass from me, grabs another from a passing waitress.

"So, what now? Do I have to drink blood or sign my soul away to the devil?"

Archer's lips quirk up at the corner as he leans to whisper into my ear, "Something like that."

"I hope this is you attempting to play a joke, Archer? I got you the statue. Was that not enough?"

Archer looks off into the distance as he replies, "Nothing is ever enough."

His words send a shiver down my spine, and I suddenly want to run from this place and never look back.

A masked male figure moves to stand in the centre of the circle and claps his hands together to draw everyone's attention. He looks at me and beckons me with his finger. I can't see his face properly because of the mask, but he has grey hair, and I would guess him to be in his seventies at least.

"Come forward," he orders, and Archer gives me a nudge in the back until I find myself slowly walking towards him until I reach the centre of the circle. "Tonight, we initiate a new Ace. Tonight, we welcome her into the fold, and as part of our family."

I take a step back when I see him reach behind him and pull out a knife. What the fuck!

"Eliza Alderman, do you accept your place in this society? Do you pledge your loyalty above all others to those who stand in this room with you?"

"Yes," I say hesitantly, looking around the room at the silent figures.

"Do you accept that the laws of the society are absolute and must be obeyed at all times? That any order given by an elder will be obeyed without question?"

"Err, I...yeah," I say, the hesitancy in my tone clear. I didn't know shit about their laws, so let's hope there was nothing in them I should be worried about. Should Archer have given me a club rule book to read before I signed up for this shit?

"Do you swear you will abide by the society's rules and traditions and that you are one with your brethren?"

"Yes," I say, my voice barely a whisper.

"Then step forward, child and take your oath in blood."

I hesitate, and I can feel the eyes of everyone in the room on me. I take an unsteady step forward and gulp when he steps closer to me with a knife in his hand.

"Eliza Alderman, you are now a member of this society." He moves towards me and the cold knife glints against the candlelight, making my heart stutter in my chest. I feel like time stands still as his arm nears my body.

"Blood of my blood. Kin of kin. For now, and always," the man chants and everyone in the room repeats it after him as he slices the knife across my thumb, causing me to hiss in pain. He then slices his thumb and wipes his lips with his bloodied finger. For a minute I stand there staring, before I realise he is waiting for me to do the same. With a shaky hand, I run my thumb along my bottom and top lip. I try to veer away from him when he takes me by my arms and leans down and presses his bloodied, stiff lips against mine. Then he hands the knife over to the next masked man, who cuts his thumb, and he leans down and kisses me. This continues until every member present in the room has drawn blood and put their lips to mine. I do a double take when Vee is before me, placing her lips to mine. She winks as she pulls away. I falter even more when I find my grandfather standing before me with the bloodied knife in his hand. He looks at me with such pride and satisfaction when he leans down and presses a quick, firm kiss to my lips. The last one to step up and take the knife is Archer. When he steps forward, the man who conducted the ceremony holds the knife out to him.

Archer slices it across his palm, but instead of reaching for my hand, he squeezes his fist over a silver goblet, and I watch with morbid fascination as his blood drips into the cup. When he does reach for my hand it's to slice across my palm and draw blood. He holds it over the cup and squeezes my fist until my blood pools and falls into the cup. He takes the cup and places it to his lips and takes a drink before offering it out to me. I hesitate. I mean, I'm not really down for drinking anyone's blood, not even my own. Archers' dark eyes burn into mine in warning, so with an internal eye roll I take the cup and drink. I didn't know there was also red wine in the cup, so I'm relieved that I can't actually taste or notice the blood.

"Mea per sanguinem," Archer says and everyone in the room repeats the words back to him.

The older man who resides over the whole thing holds the palm of his hand out to me and resting there is a key, much like the one Archer used to enter the building with. I reach out and tentatively take the key, closing my bloodied palm around it. "Welcome to the Aces, Eliza Alderman."

Everyone in the room breaks into applause and then the dimmed lights resume their brightness, and everyone breaks off and resumes socialising and drinking like the strange ceremony didn't just happen.

"Well, that was weird as fuck!" I exclaim, letting out a breath of relief that it is over. I really don't have a clue what I've signed up for here, but my grandfather is here, and he wouldn't let me be involved in anything dangerous or sinister, right?

Archer grasps my hand in his and gently tugs me from the room. As we pass another tray of champagne, I grab a glass, bringing it with me. I need the alcohol tonight to help me process things.

"Where are we going?" I ask him.

"Wait and see," he replies as we climb a staircase up to the higher floor. He guides me through various rooms until he reaches a door that he unlocks with a key. I'm surprised to find that it leads outside to a stone staircase that leads onto the roof of the old building.

I falter in my steps. There's a terrace up here. The night sky is so clear from here. The stars shine brightly, not a cloud in the sky. Fairy lights line the edge of the roof.

"It's beautiful up here," I say as I wander further on to the roof and gaze up at the stars. When I stop and look back, Archer is standing with his hands in his pockets, watching me.

"What?" I ask him with a tilt of my head. Why is he looking at me like that? He stalks towards me, and I'm frozen in place as he descends on me. When he reaches me, he cups the back of my neck and tips my head back until I meet his eyes.

"What is it about you?" he asks me as he searches my face for some kind of answer. Before I can ask him what the hell he is going on about, his lips crash down on mine, and I forget everything else but the feel of his mouth against mine. I whimper, leaning into him, and kiss him back with fervent need.

Archer walks us backwards until he stumbles back onto a stone bench. He lifts my legs so that I am on his lap, my thighs either side of him. He holds me tightly as he devours me, and I can't get enough. I want more. I want to be closer to him. He reaches behind me unzipping my dress. I should stop him. I should say no, but when he runs his hands up my thighs and bunches my dress up to my waist and then up and over my head, I make no protest. My bra quickly follows until I'm on his lap in nothing more than my black lace thong. When he pulls his mouth from mine, I whimper in protest, and he shushes me as he trails soft kisses down my neck, and he finds a pebbled nipple. I run my fingers through his hair as he licks and nips at my breast.

"Why didn't you kiss me like all the others?" I ask breathlessly, as he worships my skin.

"That was you swearing your allegiance to me. You're my initiate," he explains as his fingers trail between my legs.

"My allegiance to you? Are you kidding me?" I hiss as he sinks a finger inside of me.

"Oh, but I'm not Scarlet. In the eyes of this society, you are mine. That ceremony you just took part in where you drank our blood. That was you making yourself mine."

"I'll never be yours Savage," I hiss in protest as my hips ride his fingers.

He grabs my hair and pulls on it, making me lower my face to his. "You'll be mine in more ways than you could ever have imagined."

"What does that mean?" I ask, my question nothing more than a whispered moan as I chase my impending orgasm.

He swears and turns his gaze away from me for a second before facing back towards me. "Nothing, forget it."

"No," I tell him as I grab his chin and make him look at me. "What is it you're not telling me?"

"Fuck, guys,"

I jump when I look over Archer's shoulder to find Vee, Rafe and Seb have all just come up onto the roof.

"Oh shit," I hiss as I cower into Archer's body to shield the fact that I'm wearing nothing but a black lacey thong and I currently have Archer's fingers inside of me.

Seb chuckles. "Looks like Arch and Little Red started the celebrations without us. Welcome to the family," he says, grinning. "I say we go party and celebrate. What do you say?"

"Can you, like, all turn around, I'm kind of more or less naked here, Seb," I hiss, exasperated at him chatting away like walking in on us is a normal everyday occurrence.

Vee gives me an apologetic smile before she shoves at her brother and makes him turn away. I lift myself up off Archer and, keeping my eyes on Seb and Rafe to make sure they haven't turned back around, I dress at record speed.

"We're done," Archer announces, standing up and picking up his mask from the bench. He isn't at all bothered by what we were just caught doing.

Seb spins around and waggling his brows at me, he replies, "I don't think Little Red was done."

"Funny," I hiss, grabbing my mask and stomping past him. It's hard staying mad at Seb though, he's just so easy-going.

"You four can do what the hell you like. I have a fight to get to."

"A fight?" Rafe asks, looking from Archer to me.

"Yes, a fight. You know. Where two people get in a ring and hit each other until one of them wins," I reply sarcastically, tapping my foot in annoyance. I'm itching to get in that ring and welcome the pain.

"You're the new girl fighting tonight. The Red Raven?" Rafe asks, the surprise clear in his tone.

"That's me."

Rafe looks at Archer. "Did you know it was her when you placed your bet?"

Archer looks over at me, and he nods his head. His face is devoid of any emotion. "I had a hunch it was her."

"Well, you better be good, Little Red, because if you lose, Archer here can kiss goodbye to twenty grand."

My eyes bug out of my head, and I stop in my tracks. "Say it again? Did you just say twenty fucking grand?!"

"Seb," Archer says in a warning tone.

"Twenty, baby," Seb repeats, grinning at me while I stand there open-mouthed staring after Archer who is climbing into his car.

"You can't fight in that dress. Here," he throws a bag on my lap and when I look inside, there's a pair of my gym shorts and a sports bra, there are also my clothes from that first night I arrived in the bay when I took a plummet into the sea. I'd forgotten he had these. How on earth did he manage to get my shorts and sports bra?

"You're taking me to the fight?" I say in surprise, as I climb into the car and take the seat next to him.

"I put good money on you tonight and I intend to see you win." He starts the engine, just as Seb climbs in the back and closes the door.

"How do you know I'm any good?"

He shrugs his shoulder as he pulls away from the clubhouse. "Just a hunch. Besides, if you lose tonight, I'll spank you until your arse is red raw."

"Promises, promises," I say with a grin, and he actually smiles at me with a look that says, be careful what you wish for.

CHAPTER
FOURTEEN

ELIZA

The underground fighting ring is in a derelict old mill a few towns over in a quiet industrial park. I'm amazed at how busy this place is and surprised that no one knows it's here.

"Is it always this busy?" I ask as I climb out of Archer's car and the others pile out of the back.

"Yes. Fight night is popular. Besides, the main event is on tonight. Archer is fighting Luca Silver."

I look over the bonnet at Savage. "Why?"

He shrugs his shoulders. "Because fighting and fucking are my favourite past times, Scarlet," he says with a wicked grin. Seeing Archer smile is a rare thing, but I have to say I like it and I have seen it twice in one night, tonight. It's a little disarming for my poor heart.

"I didn't know you knew how to smile," I tell him as I meet him around the front of the car.

"There's a lot you don't know about me Scarlet, and trust me, you don't want to." He holds out his hand and I automatically slip mine into his. I do it without thinking and I have no idea why. The guy on the door clearly knows all the guys as he greets them all with a fist bump and Archer congratulates him on the birth of his new baby boy. Seeing Archer smiling at people and being sociable is an unfamiliar experience. Maybe tonight I will see a whole other side to him.

Inside, the place is heaving, but we don't have to push our

way through the crowds. They part for us instantly; everyone greets Archer and the boys with respect and makes room for them.

"Well, well, here he is our main event." A tall Indian guy jumps down from a podium and grinning grips Archer in a hug. "And you brought a girl," he says, eyeing me like I'm some kind of illusion. "Don't tell me you finally got trapped by some pussy, Archer."

I pull my hand from Archer's and cock a brow at the guy. "For the record, I'm not his and I'm here to fight."

"Are you now?" The guy says with a wide grin. "And who might you be?"

"She's the Red Raven." I look behind me to see Silver walking up to us.

"Eliza, meet Dev." He glares at Archer and then smiles warmly at me. "You ready for it?"

"I was born ready," I tell him with a playful wink as I feel two hands land on my hips from behind me and I don't need to turn to know who they belong to.

Silver's eyes rest on the hands. "So, you've claimed her, huh? Not trying to run her out of town anymore?"

"What I do is none of your concern, Silver. You stick to your side of the Bay, and we'll stick to ours."

Silver chuckles and nods his head. "Yeah, but which side of the bay does princess belong on, huh? Because I got to say, she looked much more comfortable and at home on my side."

I fake a yawn. "Okay, enough with the ego competition. Is there somewhere I can go get ready?"

Silver laughs and beckons me over to him. "Come on, I'll show you the way?"

Before I can take a step in his direction, I'm pulled back against Archer's chest. "Rafe will stay with you tonight. It's not safe for an Ace female to be on her own in here," he whispers into my ear.

"No one here will know who I am."

Archer chuckles in my ear, and it sends shivers down my spine. I like it when I make him laugh. "You really believe that. Look around you. Everyone knows about the new Alderman heir with the filthy lips and scarlet hair."

I do as he says and look around at the crowd and sure enough, people are looking over and whispering. "So much for a quiet life," I reply with a sigh as I step away from Archer and head over to Silver.

⚘

HALF HOUR LATER, I STEP INTO THE RING TO RAUCOUS CHEERS and excitement. The place is buzzing, and everyone seems to have gathered around to watch me fight, even though there are other fights going on.

"Ladies and gentlemen, I have a treat for you tonight!" Dev announces into the mic. "We have fresh blood in Westview. Tonight, a new fighter, the Red Raven, will face the formidable Hell Cat!"

The crowd cheers and starts chanting Hell Cats name as my opponent steps up into the ring.

"Well, look who we have here?" she says, grinning as she circles me. "It's the little rich girl. Are you lost, honey? Are you sure you want me to rearrange that pretty face of yours?"

I grin as I look into the eyes of the girl from Silver's party the other night who'd asked Silver's brother why we were there. She was as hostile then as she is now.

"What's up? Scared you're finally up against some real competition?" I ask her with a confident smirk.

She laughs as she bobs on her feet, eager to fight me. She holds out her glove and I tap mine against hers. It is all banter, but in the ring, you always have respect for your opponent. Dev rings the bell and we begin. Hell Cat bounces on her feet and attempts to throw the first punch, but I duck and get a jab in on her side. We're well matched in size, and she is nimble on her feet, but I'm faster and I'm quicker with my jabs. When the final bell rings, I know I've won.

"Your winner and one to watch good people: The Red Raven!" Dev raises my arm in the air and the crowd goes wild, chanting my name.

As I step out of the ring, Rafe hands me a towel. Seb and Verity are with him, but Archer isn't here, and I feel a twinge of disappointment.

"He's gone to get ready for his fight, but you should know he stayed and watched enraptured until the final bell," Vee tells me, giving me a knowing wink. "I have to say. You were on fire in that ring, girlfriend. Rafe, wasn't she hot as sin in there?"

Rafe shrugs as he drapes an arm over her shoulder, and he gestures for me to follow them. Seb passes me a bottle of water. I go to take my bag off his shoulder, and he shrugs me off. "I got it Little Red," he insists with a smile and a nudge to my shoulder.

"You were the one who stuck the tongue in, weren't you?" I ask him as we walk behind Rafe and Verity.

Seb's response is to laugh. "Busted. I had to take my one and only opportunity to go for it Little Red. Although Archer's likely to kick my arse for it later."

"Is he telling me the truth when he says everyone has to do what I did in there tonight?" I ask him quietly and he wraps an arm over my shoulder, pulling me into his side.

"He is Red. All of us have. So don't sweat it or worry about it. Besides, you're one of us now and we protect each other with our lives. I'll always have your back and so will Archer." I snigger in disbelief. "It's true Red. If there is one thing about my friend. He's loyal, and he'd do anything for another Ace."

"Even kill someone?" I ask, joking.

"Even that," Seb replies with a serious face, and I wonder for a moment if I want to know just how true that statement is. Nothing would surprise me in this fucked up bay.

Seb pushes through to the front of the ring, and we stand alongside Vee and Rafe, who are all touchy feely tonight. It's strange to watch as even though I know they're more or less engaged, I've never seen them be affectionate with each other like they are tonight.

Seb catches me watching them and he nods his head. "Struggling to get your head around them? Truth is, they're perfect for each other."

"It doesn't bother him that she sleeps with other people?"

Seb shakes his head. "They're both enjoying being young and free before the reality of our world traps them in its clutches."

I take a swig of my drink as I process his words. "Are you expected to marry someone your family chooses?"

He grins. "Maybe I am. Maybe it's you?"

Laughing in response, I jab him in the ribs. "You could do a lot worse."

Seb kisses my head affectionately with a chuckle. "I'd be more than happy to have you, Little Red."

"Would you though?" I ask him, my playful expression turning sober.

He sighs and takes a drink from his bottle of beer. "What do you think? They had already planned our lives out for us before we took our first steps. It's fucked up, but that's how it is."

"You could say no," I suggest casually.

"It's not that easy. Here he comes." He gestures with his head towards the ring, and I forget what we were talking about the minute I lay eyes on Archer. He steps into the ring in just his black shorts, his chest bare and his hand of aces tattoo there above his heart. His eyes briefly find mine before he turns his attention to his opponent. Holy smoke, he looks good up there. My ovaries swoon and beg me to make babies with him.

The bell rings and the match begins; I'm enraptured watching him fight. I'm with him every punch and jab and from the side-lines I push him on.

"Fuck him up Savage," I shout as he jabs the older Silver brother in the stomach and dodges a right hook from him.

When the bell rings and Dev announces Archer as the

winner, I cup my mouth with my hands and whoop and cheer. Seb offers me his fist and I bump mine with his. Archer was savage in the ring. Silver's brother gave a good fight, but Archer dominated him from the second the bell rang.

Archer shakes hands with Silver and he says something in his ear and Luca Silver laughs and nods. I gulp when Archer jumps down out of the ring right in front of me. Seb throws him a towel, and he wipes the sweat off his face. My tongue begs me to lick the bead of perspiration dripping down his chest and I have to give my head a shake.

"You fight good," I tell him, and I get a smirk in response. I don't get a chance to say anything further to him as a girl comes bounding over and pushes herself in front of Archer.

"Hey Arch." She places her hand on his chest. "I was wondering when you'd be back in the ring. Are you coming back to mine?"

I blink, staring at the back of her head. Who the fuck is this?

"Give him some space, Freya," Seb says as he swings an arm over her shoulder and manoeuvre's her away from Archer. "Come get a drink with me and let Archer cool down."

Freya looks like she wants to protest, but with a quick glance back at Archer, she lets Seb guide her away.

I'm dying to ask Archer who she is, but my pride won't let me. I mean, it's not like we're anything to each other.

"Looks like I earned you some good money tonight," I say with a cocky smile. My hands in the pockets of my jeans as I drink in how good he looks right now.

He laughs as he opens a bottle of water and quenches his thirst. "Come on, let's get out of here."

"What about her?" I gesture with my head behind me, and he looks over the top of my head.

"What about her?" Archer asks me, his face devoid of any emotion.

I shrug. "She seems to think you're going home with her. Like it's a regular thing."

He towels his hair and passes me his empty bottle. "I don't give a flying fuck what she thinks, besides who I fuck is none of your business, Scarlet."

His eyes burn into mine as I swallow. I hate that I want him. I hate that his presence makes me constantly aware of him and I hate that I'm burning with jealousy that he had a regular thing with her

"You're right, none of my business," I say with a flippant smile. Fuck Archer Savage and the sweaty boat of hotness he sailed in on. No matter how good he looks right now, he's still a complete arsehole, and I must never forget that or let my guard down.

"You're quiet. That's a first," he observes as he throws the towel around his neck. Dev whistles and beckons him over and Archer gestures for me to follow him.

Dev hands him an envelope full of cash. "Good fight tonight. Are you back next month?"

"I'll let you know."

Dev holds an envelope out to me. "Same for you, Red Raven. You're welcome back here anytime. You can fight, for a tiny thing."

"Thanks, I think. And yeah, I'll be back."

When we make our way back to the others, Seb has returned, and Freya is nowhere to be seen. "Lets' go." Archer throws his keys to Rafe. "You can drive."

Just as we reach the car, I hear someone shouting my name and turn to see Damon jogging over. Archer's jaw tightens as he leans against the car and glares at him.

"He's like a fucking puppy at your heels," he mutters under his breath, his brows furrowed.

"Hey," I say as Silver reaches me. I'm conscious of the tension between these two. I kind of like how furious Archer gets when Damon is around me.

"Can I have a word?" he asks me, not giving the others a second glance.

I nod my head and step to the side with him. "What is it Silver, I'm beat and need my bed."

"Your bed or his?" he asks with an arch of his brow.

I fold my arms over my chest and give him a pointed look. "Whose bed I sleep in is none of your business. What did you want?"

"I heard Chester has returned to Alderman Manor."

I nod my head with a frown. I didn't know he knew Chester. "What of it?"

He looks over at Archer from the corner of his eye. "Look, just be careful around Chester, okay? He's not a good person."

I nod my head. "I can do that, but can you tell me why you're giving me this warning?"

He sighs and takes a step backwards. "Just trust me on this one, okay?"

"Okay." I turn and head back towards the others.

Everyone else is in the car except Archer who is leaning against the bonnet, arms folded and a scowl burning into the back of Silver's retreating figure.

"You going to stand and glare at the back of his head all night, or are we going?" I ask him as I walk past him and climb into the back of the car and take a seat next to Seb.

A second later, Archer climbs in beside me. There isn't a lot of space with the two of them in the back here. Rafe starts the engine and turns up the music. Rita Ora sings about a boy being her poison and I can't help but chuckle to myself. Archer Savage is my poison. He's no good for me, but I still want him.

"What did he want then?" he asks me, and I can tell it's killing him that he doesn't know what Damon said to me. I could lie and say he asked to see me some time, but I don't want to put a target on Damon's head. I kind of like the guy, as a friend.

"He warned me to be careful of Chester, my grandfather's partner's son. Do you know him?"

Archers shakes his head. "He doesn't go to college around here. I've seen him a few times in the Country Club."

"Want me to get some intel on him?" Seb asks, and Archer nods his head and says, "Might be worth checking him out."

"You guys can do that?" I ask, looking from one to the other. They both grin at each other.

"Little Red, there's nothing we can't dig up on someone. Why, we knew all about you within twenty-four hours of you being here."

I shake my head. This is really a world away from the one I knew. Who knew a sleepy coastal town in the East of England had weird old societies and traditions with seventeen-year-old boys who held so much control just from their surnames and their birth right.

CHAPTER
FIFTEEN

ELIZA

By the time I'm dropped back home, it's gone midnight, and the house is in darkness. I unlock the front door and sneak in as quietly as I can and re-set the alarm. I pause in the hallway when I notice my bedroom door is ajar. When I came down for dinner earlier, I know I closed it. In fact, now that Chester is living here, I need to ask Calvin to put a lock on the inside of the door for me.

I cautiously open my bedroom door and peer inside. As my eyes readjust to the darkness, a cold shiver runs through me. That sense of foreboding, that something isn't right here. I switch on the light and my breath stops in my throat. My room has been completely trashed, and when I say trashed, I mean ruined, but it's what's written on the wall above my bed that pulls my full attention.

In big red capital letters, it says: 'Leave town or regret it.'

Shaking, I step further into the room, hugging my arms around myself as I take in the damage. My pillows are shredded, and my mattress looks like someone has hacked it to pieces with a knife. A sob rips from me when I see that the photograph of my family is ruined, someone has scraped out the faces of both my parents and my brother. Is this a threat against Kit? With shaking hands, I pull my phone from my coat pocket. I swear to myself when I realise my first thought is to call Archer. Could this be him? Could he be luring me in with a false sense of security? His words to me on my first day at school were that I didn't belong here and that I needed to leave. Is he playing psychological games with me?

I slip my phone back into my pocket and, hugging my coat around me, I leave the house and cross the grounds to Edith and Rory's Cottage. The house is in darkness, and I feel bad for waking them up. I knock firmly on the door, and the sound echoes through the silence of the night. I see a light come on in the hallway and I breathe a sigh of relief when the door opens, and Calvin greets me in nothing but his boxers.

"Eliza," he says, looking at me in confusion, rubbing his tired eyes.

I hug at my arms. I hate feeling this shaken and vulnerable. "I'm sorry to wake you, but I didn't know who else to come to." Behind him, Edith steps into the hallway, tying the belt of her dressing gown as she comes closer.

"Eliza, my dear, what's the matter?"

"Someone's been in my room whilst I was out. It's completely trashed. I'm sorry to wake you, but I didn't know what to do."

Edith moves past her son and ushers me inside. "Come in my dear." She drapes an arm around me when I enter and guides me into the house. "Calvin, get dressed and go and take a look. Call the police on your way over there."

Calvin nods and disappears out of the room. Edith guides me over to a comfy-looking sofa, and she sits herself down beside me. "Oh, you're shaking. Wait here while I wake Rory. Honestly, the man could sleep through a bomb explosion. Then I'll make you some tea. Tea makes everything seem better."

Edith comes back a couple of minutes later and hands me a warm cup of tea. "Thank you."

"Rory is going over to the house now. Did it look to be just your room that they've been in?"

"Shit!" I jump to my feet, almost spilling boiling hot tea all over myself. "Kit. I didn't check on him. What if they went into his room when he was in there? I have to go back over now."

Edith hushes me. "Hold your horses, young lady. You are not

going anywhere near that house until the police arrive." She pulls a mobile phone from her dressing gown pocket and holds it to her ear. "Calvin, can you check on Kit please for Eliza?" She pauses, listening. "Oh, thank goodness. Don't let him come over on his own, will you?" She nods and puts the phone down beside her. "Kit is fine. He was fast asleep in his bed," she pauses, a concerned look crossing her face, "it looks like it is just your room that was targeted."

I gulp, clutching at the cup of tea in my hands. "There was a message on the wall in red paint. It said leave town or regret it." I shudder as the image of those words flits through my mind.

She places an arm back around me and her sweet vanilla scent surrounds me. "Do you know of anyone who might have done this?"

Archer crosses my mind immediately, but he was with me all night. Could he have got someone else to do it for him, though? Maybe one of his clubs. "No. I barely know anyone here yet. Why would someone want me gone?"

Edith sighs. "You're an Alderman, Eliza. Your grandfather is a rich and powerful man. Someone may be trying to threaten you to get to him. Try not to worry, we'll sort this out."

Edith's mobile phone rings and I startle, splashing my boiling hot tea all over my hand, and I yelp in pain.

"Oh dear. Get some cold water on that hand," she instructs me as she answers her phone. "She's fine, Wilbur. Shaken up, but fine. We'll keep them both here until the police arrive."

I run the cold tap over my hand and wince. Why can't I just have an easy life? Just for once. I just wanted to come here, keep my head down and get to eighteen.

I hear Edith enter the kitchen and she comes up beside me and inspects my hand. "That's looking red. Come on, let's get some cream on it." She guides me over to a small circular dining table and I take a seat. I look around the room while she rummages in a cupboard and pulls out a first aid kit. The kitchen is warm and cosy, with cream shaker cabinets and pale blue tiles.

A shelf full of recipe books lines the wall between the cooker and the sink. She takes a seat beside me and carefully takes my hand and dabs it with a wet cloth.

"Rory is bringing Kit over now. Your Grandad wants you to stay here at the cottage for now."

I nod my head. I'm eager to see my brother and confirm to myself that he is okay "How did they get in? I mean, I thought this house had top-notch security?"

Edith shakes her head, frowning. Her red curls fall over face as she leans over my hand and applies the cool cream to my burned skin. "It does. Whoever did this somehow knew how to by-pass the security settings, which suggests that this is no amateur." She places some gauze over my hand. "There you go. That should do it for now."

The front door opens, and I jump to my feet and hurry into the hallway. When I see my brother, relief washes over me and I rush to him and fling my arms around him. "Are you okay?"

He scoffs, squeezing me tightly. "Am I okay? It's you who's had their room trashed. Are you okay, sis?"

I pull away from him and tenderly push his hair out of his eyes. "I'm fine," I say with a reassuring smile, attempting to ease the worry etched across his face. "It's just a room. Probably just someone from school playing a prank."

"Is it those Ace boys?"

I side glance at Edith, who has stopped what she is doing at the mention of the Aces. "No," I tell him with a firm shake of my head. "I was with them this evening. It couldn't have been them."

"Sis, they have kids at school that could have done this for them."

Edith comes up and hands Kit a cup of tea. "Let's leave the police to investigate who has done this. Now you two sit down in the living room and I'll make you both some toast."

"I don't think I could eat right now," I protest.

"You're in shock and something in your stomach will do you

good. Now go on and relax. Put whatever you like on the television."

Kit and I head into the lounge and stick-on Netflix. I try to concentrate on the tv show but I'm distracted. This had to have been the Aces, right? Who else in this town would benefit from me leaving?

Kit falls asleep, so I cover him with a blanket. He looks so peaceful and I'm just so thankful that he is okay, but I can't get the image out of my head of his and my parents' faces scratched out of that photo. I loved that photo of the four of us as well.

About a half hour later, my grandfather and Calvin walk into the cottage. Wilbur sweeps his eyes over me, almost as if he's checking that I am okay, and he frowns when he spots the gauze on my hand.

"I spilt tea on my hand," I offer in explanation.

He takes a seat opposite us, and Kit stirs from his sleep and sits up. "The police are up at the house, dusting for fingerprints. I'm going to increase the security around the house and there will be extra security around you both when you are going to and from school. We'll get all your things moved to another room, Eliza."

"I want to stay near my brother's room. I need to know he's nearby and safe."

My grandfather smiles. His shrewd eyes lose some of their harshness from a few seconds ago. "We'll put you in the room next door to your brothers. Calvin is going to move into the house for the time being and stay in the East Wing."

I nod my head and give Calvin a smile of thanks.

"The police want to speak with you, but I've insisted that it wait until morning. I will not have the Alderman family threatened in this way and I will get to the bottom of who is responsible," he vows in an unyielding tone.

My phone buzzes in my coat, and I pull it out to see it's a message. Frowning at who could be texting me at this time of night, I open it. My intake of breath pulls everyone's attention.

It's a photo of the writing on my wall in my bedroom and the message says, *'leave or next time someone will get hurt'.* I shudder as I hold the phone out to Wilbur. He takes it from me, and he swears under his breath. "Calvin, take this over to Detective Boyd now, please." He hands the phone to Calvin, who glances over at me in worry before he strides out of the room.

"I want you to know that I will protect you with every breath in my body. You are my blood, my legacy, and your safety is my paramount concern. Now, both of you try to get some sleep. You have school tomorrow, and we need to show the Bay that no one keeps us down."

Kit nods his head, looking spurred on by our grandfathers' words.

"Thank you, Wilbur," I reply.

"Grandfather, please. After all, we are family." He offers us a final tight smile before he rises to his feet and leaves us, Edith seeing him out.

"I'm beat. Do you want to take Calvin's bed and I'll take the sofa?"

"No," I shake my head. "I don't think I'm going to get any sleep for a bit. You go crash out; I'm going to watch some television for a bit."

Kit gives me a hug and takes himself off to get some sleep. Edith makes sure I'm settled, before she takes herself back to bed. It's already four in the morning. It's playing on my mind about the Aces. Last night I felt a part of their close-knit group and as much as I hate to admit it, it felt nice to belong. Was it all an act to draw me in, make me feel secure and then tear me down? As they say, keep your friends close and your enemies closer. I really need to get to the bottom of what I have done to Archer. Sometimes I catch him looking at me like he hates me with every breath in his body, and then other times he looks at me with such heat in his eyes.

Edith wakes me at seven-thirty in the morning. I've had about two hours' sleep and I'm exhausted. Calvin accompanies me back over to the house, to my new temporary room next to Kit's. I actually prefer this room. It's painted in a mid-grey with a white carpet and white furniture. It has that New England vibe going on. They have already moved my clothes into the walk-in wardrobe in here. I shower quickly and change into my uniform. My phone has been left on the dressing table and I can't resist looking at the message again from my mystery stalker. When I enter the kitchen, Chester and his mum are already in here eating breakfast. Alexis gestures for me to sit next to her. Her face is full of concern and worry.

"How are you, Eliza? It must have been such a shock walking into your room and seeing it like that." She studies my face with those big, expressive eyes of hers.

"Yeah, it was quite a shock," I agree, as I bite into my toast.

"It's one way of getting moved from the pink bedroom," Chester chips in, observing me with a cold smirk.

"Are you implying I did that to my own room?" I ask him, a brow arched.

He shrugs. "I'm just saying at least it gets you out of the barbie pink bedroom." He dismisses my accusation with smug nonchalance. It's then that I notice he is wearing the Hawk Bay uniform. "You're starting at Hawk Bay?"

He nods, looking bored with our company. "No. I just like the uniform," Chester says, his tone dripping with sarcasm. He climbs to his feet. "I'm off," he tells his mum without a glance in mine or Kit's direction.

"How come he is joining Hawk Bay?" I ask Alexis.

She looks up from her phone and sighs. "He outstayed his welcome at his last school."

In other words, they kicked him out. Interesting. Maybe I do need to keep a close eye on Chester. Could he be the one who trashed my room? But then what would he have to gain? I am getting paranoid about everyone now, seeing them all as a potential suspect.

CARA E. HOLT

The three Aces are holding court under the arches to the entranceway at school when we pull up outside. Their group of hangers-on surround them, including Georgie and her bitch twins. Vee waves at me when she sees me, all smiles and light. It's a stark contrast to the three cold egos beside her. Vee bounces down the steps and meets me halfway, linking her arm through mine.

"Girl, you were amazing last night in that ring," she tells me with a smile and a wink.

"Thanks," I reply, stifling a yawn. I feel her steering me towards the boys and I push her towards the main doors. "I can't deal with those three this morning. My head is fucked up enough as it is."

Verity frowns, but she doesn't protest when we move past the Aces and through the main doors. I won't look Archer's way, even if it kills me. He reminded me last night that his business was his own. As we head inside, I can feel his eyes burning into the back of my head.

We reach my locker and I load in my books for my afternoon classes. I am fighting wanting to ignore Archer and wanting to walk over and demand to know if I have him to thank for last night. My curiosity wins out in the end.

By now, the boys have sauntered into the hallway and are heading our way. I slam my locker shut and storm over to meet them. I need to look him in the eye and ask him.

"We need to talk," I announce when I come to a stop in front of them, stopping them in their tracks. Archer stands there, hands in his pockets, glaring at me.

Seb grins. "Are you ready to admit you want me, baby girl?"

I roll my eyes at him. "In your dreams." I gesture with my head at Archer. "It's this idiot I need to speak with. A word please," I say, turning my focus back to him.

He continues to glare at me; with an irritated expression, he

130

gestures with his head towards the classroom door closest to us. I don't wait for him; I stride inside and lean against one of the desks and he comes in behind me and closes us in.

"What is it, Scarlet?"

I eye him for a second, looking for any signs of guilt, but let's be honest, Archer's face never displays much emotion.

"Was it you?" I sigh "Is this just some sick and twisted game for you?"

He shrugs. "Am I supposed to know what you're talking about here?"

I scoff. "The message your little cronies left me in my bedroom."

The look he gives me makes me doubt my suspicions that it's him. Am I way off the mark here?

"What message, Scarlet?" Archer asks me. Right now, he looks deadly. Like he could murder someone with his bare hands.

I pull my phone out of my blazer pocket and pull up the photo of my trashed bedroom and hold it out to him. His frown deepens as he snatches the phone from me.

"When did this happen?"

"Last night," I sigh, "after you dropped me off. The message is in animal blood, just for effect," I say with a nervous laugh.

I yelp when Archer grabs my wrist and pulls me against his chest. "Why didn't you call me straight away?"

I pull at my wrist, but he holds me firmly in place and I raise my chin to meet his angry glare. "Because, Savage, we aren't friends. I've never needed anybody and I sure as hell don't need anyone to rescue me."

"Have you any thoughts about who it could be?" he asks me as he taps the screen of my phone.

"What are you doing with my phone? And no, I have no clue. Have I pissed people off in my life? Hell yes. I've stolen a few cars, robbed from shops, but have I pissed anyone off enough to follow me to this goddamn weird-arse Bay to write in blood on my walls and trash my room? No!" I huff out a breath after my tirade of words.

"You done?" he asks me with a scowl. "I've forwarded the photo to Seb. Are the police involved?"

I nod my head. "I have to go straight home tonight as Detective Boyd is coming over to speak with me."

"Boyd," Archer sneers, "he's fucking useless. Scarlet, if anything happens like this again, you'll ring me, you hear me?"

"Right," I snigger, "because you three have given me good reason to trust you. You've tried to alienate me since I arrived. Verity is my only friend, and no one will talk to me after you sent out the orders that I was to be ostracised. Which is it, Archer? Am I one of you or am I the enemy? You can't expect me to trust you when everything you do tells me to do the opposite."

Archer releases a breath and nods his head. "You're right. We've given you no reason to trust us, but you are an Ace now and we always protect our own. Promise me, Scarlet, you'll call next time."

"I'll call, but it doesn't mean I like or trust you, Archer Savage."

He grins a grin of pure wickedness and I'm not going to lie, it sends my heart into a gallop. "You don't have to like me to trust me."

What he does next comes as a complete shock. He grabs me by the back of my neck and pulls my lips against his. He kisses me like he wants to devour me until I'm nothing but dust. His kiss lights me up inside and I respond, pressing myself closer to him. The kiss is frenzied. It's like nothing I've ever experienced before. No boy has ever made me feel the things that Archer does, and it scares the ever-loving shit out of me.

I yank my lips away from his and before I can stop myself, my hand makes contact with his cheek, the sound ringing through the empty classroom.

"You fucking kissed me," I hiss, trying to steady my erratic breathing.

He rubs at his cheek, his eyes lit with fire. "Slap me again, Scarlet, and I'll bend you over my knee and smack that pert little arse of yours until it's red raw."

"Just try it," I spit. I grab my bag and storm from the classroom, right into the hard bodies of Seb and Rafe. "Get out my fucking way, arseholes," I snipe as I shoulder my way between them and storm off down the corridor. I'm going the wrong way for class, but so long as I put distance between myself and Savage, I don't really care.

I find the nearest toilets and I lean my hands on the basin, taking in my flushed cheeks. I'm rocking that just been kissed look. I turn on the tap and splash my face with cold water. I can't let him get to me. I can't trust him. The only person I can trust in this world is my brother. Archer looked shocked by the photo though, but maybe he's just a talented actor. But, if it wasn't him or any of his little clubs, then that means I have another enemy out there.

CHAPTER SIXTEEN

ARCHER

I stalk out of the classroom after Scarlet, but she's halfway down the corridor. Her hips swaying as she walks, anger radiating from her. I hadn't planned on kissing her, but she makes me lose my senses when she's in front of me, being all sassy and disobedient.

"What did you do to upset Little Red this time?" Seb asks with a wry grin. His eyes follow mine and lock on her retreating figure. "You know she'd be easier to control if we publicly claimed her."

"Check your phone," I tell him. "Scarlet had a visitor last night. Someone is fucking with her and I'm the only one allowed to fuck with her."

Seb pulls out his phone, and he whistles when he sees the photo. Rafe leans over his shoulder to get a look.

"Is that blood?"

I nod. "Her room was like this when I dropped her off last night. This hasn't come from us, so who else might not want her around?"

Seb shrugs his shoulders. "Maybe the grandfather's woman. I mean, Little Red and her brother are his heirs now."

I frown. He has a point. Maybe she has hopes to marry Wilbur and produce an heir of her own, but Scarlet and her brother's arrival could ruin things for her.

"What do we have on her?"

"I'll pull the file we have on Alexis. There's also her son. Silver seems to think she needs to be careful around him."

I nod. It looks like I need to have a word with Silver and find out what he knows. "We need to have eyes on her all the time. Send out the order. They report anything back to us."

Rafe nods his head and pulls out his phone to send out the message to all our Clubs. The benefit of having Clubs is that they answer to the call and don't ask any questions. "You know whoever it is might back off if we brought her in. We need to publicly declare her an Ace at some point. No one would dare mess with her then."

This isn't what I had planned for her. When she first arrived, I wanted her to feel alone here. I wanted her to hate it here, so much so that she would wish she had never set foot in Hawk Bay. My mind flits back to that kiss. Fuck. Her lips. She tastes like heaven and hell. I've never felt more out of control than I do when my lips are tasting hers.

"Okay, we bring her in."

Seb cocks a brow. "How far are we bringing her in? What about your original plan?"

"I can still bring her in and destroy her when I'm ready, but no one fucks with something that belongs to me," I growl as we walk towards class.

"I don't know, man. She fits with us. She's not afraid of violence. In fact, I think she craves it. She's loyal. She'd die for that brother of hers. Little Red is everything an Ace should be."

"She is." He's right. "But her father destroyed my family, and I can't let that go unpunished. Scarlet will pay for the sins of her family."

"Talking about the Alderman's. Our contact has the info we requested on Chester," Rafe tells me. He beckons us back into the empty classroom and we both follow him in. Rafe perches on the edge of a desk. "Chester was involved in the bullying of a girl at school that led to her suicide. Wilbur pulled him out of the school, deciding he needed to keep a closer eye on him."

"Fuck," Seb exclaims. "The bullying must have been bad for her to end things."

"We monitor him," I order. "I don't trust the cocky shit or the way he looks at Scarlet."

CHAPTER
SEVENTEEN

ELIZA

Come lunchtime I'm feeling exhausted. The events of last night and the lack of sleep are catching up on me and I'm contemplating skipping my next class and taking a power nap in the library. I enter the cafeteria and grab my tray to queue for food.

"I'll get your food, Eliza. What would you like?" I blink and look at the small boy who has just taken my tray out of my hand.

"I can get my own food, thanks," I say with a chuckle. I mean he is cute, but a few years too young for my tastes.

He swears under his breath, and he looks nervously across the cafeteria. "Look, please just let me get your food. They're watching and it's the first order they've given me. I don't want to mess up."

I follow his gaze to where the three Aceholes sit holding court at their table. Turning my attention back to the boy in front of me, I ask what is on my mind. "Why do you worship them? I mean, they're treating you like a skivvy."

He shrugs his shoulders. "Being a Club opens doors. It gets you the popular girls and gives you status. You don't get it because you haven't grown up in this town, but please just let me get your food."

I nod my head, giving into his plea. "I want the quiche and chips. No salad. I need carbs today. Get me a diet coke too, please."

He nods his head, breathing a sigh of relief, and he rushes off to join the queue.

I pivot on my feet and lock eyes with Archer. Straightening my shoulders, I head over to their table.

"What's going on?" I ask, arms folding as I stand before them, noticing the calculating look in his eyes. Seb is also grinning like he's in on some big secret.

Archer leans back in his seat. His eyes move up my body in leisurely perusal until his dark eyes fix on mine. "Watch and see." He nods his head and Seb rises from his seat and jumps on the table.

"Listen up peeps. Eliza Alderman is an Ace now. You look at her the wrong way, you touch her or upset her, and you'll have us to answer to."

Seb winks at me as he jumps down off the table and retakes his seat. That's when I notice the empty seat beside Archer.

"So that's it. Suddenly I'm accepted into the fold?"

Archer rolls his eyes. "Just sit your arse down Scarlet, before I make you."

I snigger, and he cocks a brow, daring me to defy him. "What If I don't want to sit with you three?"

Seb shakes his head, smiling. "Not an option, Red. Take a seat or face the consequences."

The rebel in me wants to tell them to fuck off and take a seat at my normal table, but I'm tired and I have no fight left in me today. Huffing and puffing, I stomp around the table and drop into the seat beside Archer.

I can feel Archer's eyes studying me and I turn and glare at him. "What?"

"I like it when you're obedient." The look he gives me melts my panties. Jesus, I hate how he affects me.

"Yeah," I reply, reaching over and taking a piece of chicken off his plate and popping it in my mouth. "Well, don't get used to it, Savage."

He half smiles, before he buries it under a frown, but I saw it.

"Here you go," the small boy from earlier says as he comes

rushing up and places my tray down in front of me. "Quiche and chips, lots of salt and vinegar."

I smile at him. "Thanks. What's your name?"

He flushes red in the cheeks and looks at the three arseholes beside me, as if unsure if he's allowed to answer.

"She asked you a question," Archer growls.

"It's Hugo," he tells me with a nervous smile. He picks nervously at his fingernails, sweating under the heat of Archers glares.

I beckon him with my finger, and gulping, he leans over the table to me. I drop a kiss on his cheek. "Thank you, Hugo." I give him a wink and his face turns bright red, adjusting his tie as he straightens.

"Anytime. I can carry your bag to class if you like?"

"Go," Archer orders coldly.

Hugo's eyes go wide, and he nods his head before scuttling off back to his own table.

Seb chuckles as he pops a chip in his mouth. "Are you trying to give little Hugo a heart attack, Red? He'll be jerking off to memories of that kiss tonight in bed. You're a tease, Little Red."

I roll my eyes and turn my focus to my food. I spot Vee entering the cafeteria and I see her look for me at our table before she spots me sitting with the Aces. She blinks, and I lip read her say 'OMG' before she heads over to us.

"So, this new seating arrangement is permanent?" She takes a seat opposite me, and Rafe whistles to the Club's table and points at Vee. One of them jumps to their feet and rushes over to us.

"Get her food," Rafe orders and the poor boy nods his head, gripping at the tray Rafe shoves his way.

"I'll have chicken and avocado salad and water. Still water, not fizzy," she tells him before she returns her attention to me. "Why are you sitting with these three again?"

I shrug my shoulders. "I'm too tired to fight them today," I admit and Archer frowns at my answer.

"I'll take you home tonight. I want to be there when Boyd arrives."

I place my fork down and stare at him. "Why? And besides, Calvin is picking us up."

Archer shakes his head, looking out at the room before him. "No, he isn't. I spoke to Wilbur earlier. I'll be taking you home and Calvin will collect your brother after football practice."

I fold my arms over my chest and huff at him. "Whatever."

"Whatever?" he replies with an arched brow.

"Yes, whatever."

He shakes his head at me and actually smiles. He smiles so infrequently it's a wonder it doesn't crack his perfect face.

When I walk out of class, I find Archer leaning against the wall, his bag flung over his shoulder. As girls from my class pass him, they all eye him like candy and one girl waves at him, winking. Jesus.

He doesn't even look their way, though. His eyes firmly fixed on me. "Ready to go?"

"Are you?" I sass. "Are you sure you don't want to soak in the adoring crowd?"

He smirks and leans over and takes my bag from my hand, placing it over his shoulder. "You jealous Scarlet? No need to be. We both know you're not my type."

I mock snigger, but in truth his comment stabs at my heart. "Well, thank the lord for small mercies, real and natural aren't your type."

He chuckles as we move towards the exit. "I think your lips liked me earlier."

I scowl at him. Fucker. He has a point, though. I didn't exactly push him away. Well, not at first. "I'm a girl, and you were there and offering it."

He smirks again, making me want to punch him in the face. It's no surprise that when we head outside, his car is there waiting for him. It's not his usual car. This is a Taycan, and I know for a fact that they retail at over eighty grand. No doubt one of his little Clubs brought it round for him. I walk around the bonnet and climb inside. I sigh and stroke the leather seat but pause when I find Archer's eyes on me.

"You like cars, Scarlet?"

I nod, chewing on my lip. I'm slightly annoyed at myself for letting him know his car impresses me. "I know how to appreciate a good car. I bet she drives like a dream."

He starts the engine and nods his head. "You really crave speed and danger, don't you?"

I meet his eyes as he pulls out on to the winding driveway. "Nearly dying can have that effect."

He swallows, frowning, and I regret that I changed the mood in the car. I quite like playful and teasing Archer. "Do you remember much from the accident?"

I clear my throat and look out in front of me, not trusting myself to look into his eyes. "I relive it every night. The sounds, the feeling of the car flying through the air. The pain when the tree branch went through my leg. The cold. I remember my father's eyes as he looked back at me. The pain in knowing that if I hadn't been late out of netball practice that night that we'd have missed the drunk driver and they'd be here today." I cough. Fuck, I didn't mean to share so much with him.

"What was your dad like?"

I risk a glance at him and see genuine interest there. "He was the best dad. He was always there for me. Dad always made time to play with us when we were younger, and I knew I could always turn to him for anything. He was kind and caring and loving, and every day I look at my brother and watch as he grows; he gets more and more like him, which is kind of comforting and kind of painful at the same time."

He doesn't speak, he just nods his head. I give myself a mental shake. Why am I sharing things like this with him? I don't want to give him any information that he can use against me.

We pull up at the Alderman mansion and I climb out of the

car, and he follows me inside. I throw my bag down in the hallway and head straight through to the kitchen. Edith is there singing along to the radio.

"Hey Edith," I say, announcing our presence. She jumps and puts a hand to her chest.

"Gosh, is it that time already?" She smiles at me and dries her hand on a towel. "Mr Savage, it's been a while since I last saw you. My, you've grown into a fine young man."

Archer grins warmly. "Hello Edith. You don't look a day older."

Edith flushes and bats his comment away with her hand. "A charmer, just like your grandfather. How is he?"

Archer gives me a side-glance. "He's good. You should pop by and say hello sometime."

I watch their interaction with interest. A polite and chatty Archer is something new. When he sees me watching him, he winks at me and smiles, and it does funny things to my stomach.

"Is Boyd here yet?" I ask Edith, changing my focus to her. I don't know what to do with a winking and smiling Archer.

"Not yet, Lovely. Why don't you both have a seat and I'll make you a drink. Redbush for you, and Archer, what would you like to drink?"

"Coffee please. Black."

"Like your soul," I comment with a snigger, and he cocks a brow at me.

"Eliza, that isn't very nice," Edith chastises me as she brews my tea. From behind her back, Archer grins in delight at her chastising me.

"Ah, he can take it," I reassure her. "Besides, he gives me as good back, trust me."

Edith looks from me to Archer and smiles. "It's lovely to see the two of you getting on so well."

I chuckle into my cup. "I wouldn't go that far; we barely tolerate each other."

"Mm," Edith comments, looking over the top of her glasses

at me.

The buzzer for the main gate goes and Edith rushes over to answer it. The screen reveals its Boyd. I cup my tea in my hands. I'm not sure why he wants to speak to me. I didn't see anything or hear anyone.

"We'll meet him in the main lounge, Edith," Archer announces as he stands and ushers for me to follow him. With a curious frown, I fall into step beside him, bringing my drink with me.

"You seem to know your way around here," I say to him as we walk through to the other room.

He shrugs his shoulder as he sits down on the large three-seater sofa. "I spent time here as a child. The four families have always been close. Edith used to watch me sometimes when my nanny had errands to run."

I snigger. "Nanny, typical."

He scowls at me as I sit down on the sofa, leaving a good gap between us. I didn't trust myself near him. He was like a beacon luring me in.

"My father was always busy with work, so someone had to be employed to look after me."

"What about your mum?" I ask, as I take off my shoes and tuck my legs underneath me on the sofa.

"My mum died when I was eight." His eyes turn as cold as ice and as he glares at me, it's like he's looking through me, lost in a terrible memory.

"I'm sorry to hear that. I know how it feels to grow up without a mum. It's hard." I blow on my drink before I take a sip, and he pops his shoulder looking away from me. Okay, so that conversation was over.

I'm pulled from my thoughts when I hear Edith opening the front door and chatting with, who I presume to be, Boyd.

"I thought Wilbur would be here," I say. I thought he would have wanted to see what Boyd wanted to ask me, but I don't even know if he is home.

"He has some business to attend to," Archer shares, surprising me. "I assured him I'd be here with you."

"Well, look at that," I cock my brow. "You and Wilbur, besties."

He rolls his eyes and shakes his head, dismissing me just as Boyd walks into the room tailed by another man, in grey cords and a battered leather jacket. Boyd, however, is in a tailored suit, looking the part.

"Miss Alderman," he says, offering his hand out to me.

"It's Miss Holton," I correct him, but he ignores me, shaking my hand, and he takes a seat opposite us. "I'd like to go through the events of last night. Where were you last night before you arrived home?"

I hesitate and look at Archer. I couldn't exactly tell the detective we were all at an illegal fighting ring.

"She was with me," Archer says. "We were at my house hanging with Seb, Rafe and Verity. I drove her home."

Boyd nods. "Are you two dating?"

My brow wrinkles at his question and before I can reply with a firm no and ask him why that question has any relevance, Archer answers for me again.

"Eliza is with me."

Boyd nods his head and looks down at his notepad. "Have you had crossed words with anyone since you arrived in town, or can you think of anyone with a vendetta against you?"

I shake my head as I place my drink down on the coffee table before me. "Well, there is one person."

Boyd looks at me, pen poised, waiting for me to continue.

"Georgia Hamilton." I pause when I feel Archer tense beside me. "She made it clear that she thinks I'm trash and I don't belong here. Plus, her and Archer used to be a thing."

Archer clears his throat. "It isn't Georgie. I've known her all my life. She might mouth off, but she isn't the type to do this."

I turn and stare at him in exasperation. I want to point out that she pushed me off a flipping cliff, but then I'd have to divulge what we were all doing on the cliff in the first place. I can't believe he's defending her? I should have known. They all protect their own when it comes down to it.

Boyd chews on the end of his pen. "Regardless, we'll pay a visit to speak with Georgie and find out where she was yesterday evening. We have reviewed the security footage and whoever did this, they covered their tracks. They hacked into your grandfather's security and deleted any footage from around the hour or so before you arrived home."

"Wilbur's arranging for tighter security to be put in place. There will be guards patrolling at night," Archer tells him.

Boyd nods and, popping his notepad in his jacket pocket, he stands to his feet. "Well, we'll be in touch. If you see or hear anything that might help, please get in touch." He holds out his card to me and Archer takes it and pops it down on the table.

"Have you considered the Silver's?"

Boyd pauses where he is standing. "The Silver's. What makes you think we need to look at them?"

Archer places an arm over my shoulder. Looking like the doting boyfriend. "Let's just say Damon Silver has his eye on Eliza. He might be seeking revenge because she rejected him."

I shake my head, holding my hand out. "This wasn't Silver. There's no animosity between us."

"I think you should check him out," Archer insists, and Boyd nods his head.

"We'll pay the Silver residence a visit." He holds his hand out to Archer, who grasps it firmly.

"Thank you, Detective. I know I don't need to tell you that this case needs the full attention of our local force."

"Of course," he replies with a nod of his head as he follows his partner to the door. It's weird the respect Archer gets from men twice his age.

As soon as the door closes behind them, I spin on my heels and glare at Archer. "What the fuck was that?"

Archer sighs, and ignoring me, he heads for the stairs. Where the hell is he going? I race up behind him. "Why did you defend Georgie? And why did you suggest they speak with Silver? You know they were both at the meet last night?"

"They were, but it doesn't mean they didn't get one of their gang to do it."

"It's not Silver," I insist as I chase him up the stairs, trying to keep my calm "He wouldn't do this to me."

I frown when I follow Archer to my room. How the hell does he know which room mine is? I follow in behind him and watch as he sits himself on the end of my bed and leans back on his hands, watching me.

"You're so quick to defend him. Should I be concerned that the photo of that kiss wasn't all that occurred between you two?"

What the? I cross my arms and tap my foot. "How dare you! You sat there and defended Georgie when you know she pushed me off that cliff and publicly threatened me at school! Or is she that good at sucking your cock that you can't see past her pumped up lips?"

He chuckles, and it makes me see red. I storm towards him, so that I'm standing right in front of him. "You think is funny? So, because Georgie comes from money, it can't possibly be her, but a boy from the wrong side of the tracks with new money. Of course, it could be him! Your kind are so predictable. Protect your own no matter what."

"How can you be so sure it wasn't the Silver's? What if they discovered you stole the horse statue?"

I falter. Could they have? "They haven't. Silver would have spoken to me about it if he knew."Archer just continues watching me. Having him sitting on my bed is all kinds of distracting, even when I am hopping mad at him. He reaches out and runs his finger slowly up my right leg, stopping where my skirt starts.

"You need to unwind. You're all tense."

I scowl at him and try to ignore the erratic way my heart beats as his finger slowly travels further up my thigh. "You can stop trying to distract me. It won't work. Admit it. It could have been Georgie."

He reaches out with his other hand and cups the back of my other thigh, pulling me further in between his legs. "It wasn't Georgie. She can be a vindictive bitch, but this isn't her style."

I scoff, trying to keep my composure as he softly runs his fingers up and down the backs of my thighs. "We're not having sex," I tell him. I try to sound firm, but it comes out all breathy. Damn my traitorous libido.

"I don't want to fuck you, Scarlet. I want to help you unwind." He reaches under my skirt and tugs at my knickers, pulling them down my legs. I know I should tell him to stop, but I don't. I just stand before him in silence, waiting for his next move. Archer smirks as he lifts my left leg and places it on the bed beside his leg. He lifts my skirt and bunches it up around my waist with one hand, exposing me to him. He chews on his lip as he takes me in. Archer looks up at me with knowing eyes. The bastard knows he is turning me on, and I hate him for it. Leaning down, he blows on my sex, making me shudder and then his mouth is on me, and I tip my head back and moan. God, his lips on me feel so good. I grasp at his head, pushing him closer. He nips and licks and sucks me and I whimper as I feel my orgasm building. I might hate him, but he sure knows how to make me forget. His other hand reaches up and covers my mouth as he brings me crashing over the edge within minutes and I moan into his hand as I find my release.

When he leans up, his eyes burn into mine. I lean down and place my lips on his, tasting myself on him. He returns my kiss as I sit myself on his lap. His phone rings and he pulls away from me to answer it.

"Yes," he says as he keeps his eyes on me. He needs to put the phone down and finish what he started. "I understand. I think it's best if Eliza stays at my house until the extra security is in place."

I arch a brow and try to grab the phone from him. Is that my grandfather? With his other hand, Archer grabs both of mine and holds them on my lap, despite my efforts to free them. I hate that he is so much stronger than me.

"I'm not leaving Kit," I insist. There is no way I am leaving my brother to sleep here if I'm not. He can think again.

"She's concerned about Kit. I'll stay over here tonight then, but Wilbur, the security detail needs to be in place tomorrow. I won't have her unprotected." He puts the phone down beside him on the bed. He talks to my grandfather like he has some say in my safety.

"Why are you doing this?" I ask him as I remove myself from his lap and pull my skirt down. Searching my bedroom floor for where he flung my underwear. "Don't make out like you care."

"You're one of us now, Scarlet. There's no escape."

I take a step back, needing to put distance between us. I can't think rationally when he's close. He distracts me with those eyes and lips and that perfectly toned body. "You're not sleeping in my room. You can take one of the spares."

He rises to his feet and takes a step towards me, and I take another one back. "You sure about that, Scarlet? Because five minutes ago you were kissing me like you wanted me to finish what we started."

I scowl. Hating that he is right. "Having sex with you would be a mistake."

"Is that so?" he says with a smirk. He looks so calm and confident as he takes another step towards me and my back hits my bedroom door, allowing him to cage me in. His hand cups my naked sex underneath my skirt. "This belongs to me. If I give the order that you are untouchable, no one at school will even sniff in your direction."

I cock a brow. "Silver would."

He grabs at my chin and yanks my face up to meet his eyes. He looks at me with a rage that could burn down the world. "If you let Silver touch you, I will personally make sure that he has no hands to touch you with ever again."

I gulp. I'd like to say he is bluffing, but this is Archer Savage we are talking about here. "You hate me. You made that clear. So why do you want me? Do you hope to make me fall in love with you Archer Savage? Because if you do, you'll be waiting for an eternity. The only people I have ever loved have been my family."

He leans in so that his lips are a breath away from mine. "I don't want your love, sweetheart. I want to break you into tiny pieces that can't be put back together again. I want to ruin you for any other man."

"You're a sick fucker," I hiss. "What happened to you to make you so cold and broken?"

His stony stare turns positively frosty. "You know nothing about my life. Don't try to get inside my head, Scarlet. You won't like what you find." He places a brutal kiss on my lips before he yanks me away from the door and storms out of it. "I'll be back in an hour. I have business to attend to."

"Yeah, yeah. Run to Georgie and get her to suck you off!" I shout after him, wrapping my arms around myself and placing my hand to my lips. I slam my door shut and scream in frustration. God, he infuriates me. One minute he's making me feel pure ecstasy, and the next he's threatening to destroy me. I hate that I still want him. I angrily stomp to the ensuite, and strip off and climb under the showerhead. Fuck Archer Savage and the sports car he drove in on.

An hour later I've changed into my pyjamas and I'm sitting with Kit and Edith on the floor in the informal lounge, looking at old photo albums of my dad.

"Look at this one," Kit says, laughing as he points to a particular photo in the album. It's a photo of our dad dressed as a knight complete with a plastic sword. "Who is the little girl that is with him?"

"Oh, that is Libby Savage. Those two doted on each other. They were inseparable."

"Savage," I repeat, leaning in closer to look at the photo. I see a pair of dark brown eyes that remind me of the set that were burning into me earlier as he promised to break me.

"Yes, Libby was Archer's mother," Edith pauses and releases a sad sigh. "It is so sad to think that she is no longer with us."

"Archer mentioned she died when he was eight," I comment, hoping Edith will reveal more.

"It was a terrible thing. Her father found her. She'd jumped off the roof at the back of the house. That poor boy without a mother at such a young age."

I look up from the photo, and look at Edith, taking in her teary expression. "She killed herself?"

Edith nods her head to me. "So very sad."

I hear a door open and close and then Archer appears in the doorway. He pauses when he finds us all sitting on the floor. "What are you all doing?"

I slam the photo album shut. "Nothing. Just looking at old family photos."

He bobs his head, looking from me to the photo albums spread out on the floor. He has an overnight bag thrown over his shoulder. "Is there a room made up for me, Edith?"

Edith collects the albums together. "There is. I've put fresh sheets on the bed in the room opposite Eliza's. Now, who'd like cheese on toast for supper?"

Kit's eyes flash up to hers and he grins. "Oh, Edith, you're the best, you know that?"

Edith laughs at his enthusiastic reaction, and she places a hand on Archer's hand as she passes him. "Are you having some?"

He smiles down at her in a way I've never seen him smile at anyone before. With genuine warmth and affection. "I'll not say no to anything you cook, Edith." He turns his attention to Kit. "Want to show me how good you are on FIFA?"

Kit's eyes light up. "You're on." He jumps to his feet. "I'll get the X-box set up in my room." He speeds out of the room, leaving me alone with Archer.

"You're going to play FIFA with my brother?" I ask in both

surprise and sarcasm.

He leans against the door frame, hands in his pockets, and nods his head. He's changed into navy joggers and a fitted grey sports jumper. Even dressed casually, he still looks like he's stepped off of a photoshoot.

"You got a problem with that?" he challenges me.

I shake my head as I get to my feet. "Nope."

"Good," he says as he swivels and turns to leave the room. "Oh, and nice PJs. Snoopy is cute."

I feel my cheeks flush red at his comment, and I look down at my pyjamas, suddenly feeling like I look like a silly little girl. I hate how he gets under my skin so easily.

ALONE, I OPEN THE PHOTO ALBUM BACK UP AND FLIP THROUGH some more pages. More photos of my dad and Libby and a few other children. Always the same group together and I realise that the blonde kids are likely Seb and Verity's parents. The other boy is likely Rafe's father. It's strange to think that they all grew up together, and that their parents before them did the same. Like a tight-knit community. I run my finger over a photo of my dad and Libby; they look about fourteen and Libby is gazing up at my dad like he hung the moon. I can't help but wonder if my dad and Libby became more than just friends at some point.

It's strange seeing my dad as a young boy. Until now, I've never seen any photos of him as a boy. He really reminded me of Kit. He looked happy in these photos. He didn't look like a boy who wanted to leave the life he had behind and never have any more contact with his family. I wish I could ask him why he turned his back on his family. Why he changed his surname and gave up this life of affluence. Surely there must be someone in this town that holds the answers. It is time to start digging into my father's past.

CHAPTER EIGHTEEN

ARCHER

Kit and I play on FIFA for a good hour before Edith announces it's time for him to go to bed. He protests, so I tell him I have some calls to make now anyway and Edith smiles at me in thanks. Kit leaves, but not before I promise him a rematch. He is a good kid. One thing for sure is that he adores his sister. He literally beamed when he spoke about her before. I get it. They only had each other to rely on, so they were close. Spending time here is playing with my conscience. My plan was to destroy Alderman's daughter, but when she is around me, I like it.

My curiosity gets the better of me and I seek her out. She isn't in her room, so I head down to the den, thinking maybe she's curled up watching a movie, but as I head back out into the basement corridor, I hear the sound of a punchbag, and shaking my head I smile to myself, of course she is in the gym, punching the shit out of the bag. I chuckle to myself, thinking it's probably my face she is imagining as that punchbag. I pause in the doorway, taking a second to watch her without her knowing. Hell, she is perfect. She's wearing a sports bra and little navy gym shorts that mould to her tiny waist and rounded hips. My cock hardens instantly in my pants. Jesus, what am I? A twelve-year-old boy that can't control his urges?

"You're not punching from your waist," I comment, making her jump, and she turns to face me. Sweat drips down her chest in-between the crevice of her tits and I find I want to follow it with my tongue.

She arches a brow at me, wiping the sweat from her forehead. "Did I ask you for tips?"

"No," I reply, walking into the room and coming up behind her. I place one hand on her waist and hold the other just below her wrist. "When you pull back, bring it back like this and then swing at the waist."

I release her and for a beat she stands there in silence before she adjusts her stance and does as I have instructed her to. She hits the bag with far more force than her last punch.

"You want to spar?" I ask her, pulling my hoodie over my head and heading over for a pair of gloves.

"Me and you, spar?" she says incredulously, likes it the most stupid idea she has heard come from my lips yet.

"Unless you're chicken?" I challenge, walking towards her as I secure the gloves. I'm a bastard. I know she can't turn down a challenge and as she glares at me, she knows that I know it.

"Okay, Let's see what you've got Savage." She bounces on the balls of her feet, spritely and tiny.

She might be small, but it means she can move quickly, duck and dive, and surprise her opponent.

I hold my wrists up and watch her intently as we size each other up. I study her, looking for clues as to which way she'll go, where she will try to hit first. She makes her move, trying to get a jab in to my side, but I block her and get one in under her right breast. I don't hit her hard; I know how forcefully my punches can land, and the last thing I want is to explain to Wilbur why his granddaughter has a few broken ribs. She bounces on her feet and gets a punch under my arms and into my abdomen. She can throw a mean punch. I mean, it doesn't wind me, but I feel it. As we spar, I can't help but think whether fate is fucking with me. It's as if this girl is made for me. She is everything I'd look for in a partner. Feisty, strong, stubborn as fuck and as sexy as sin. She gives me as good as I dish out. I make my move when she tries to duck away from me. With an arm to her waist, I slam her down into the mat, winding her somewhat and I quickly climb over her, my thighs holding her prisoner.

"Are we wrestling now?" she asks, her breathing unsteady.

Gods, how I crave her. I want to taste her again. I want to hear those breathy little moans she makes when she is close to orgasm. I want to hear her whisper my name and beg me to take her. I want to own every inch of her delectable body and know my mouth has touched every part of her. It's while I'm distracted thinking of all the dirty and wicked things I want to do to her that she catches me off guard. She boxes me on the chin, sending me rearing backwards on to my backside and off of her. Scarlet springs up onto her feet like a coil and chuckles to herself in delight. She shakes her head at me, grinning as she pulls her gloves off.

"Oh dear, Archer. Everyone knows the number one rule. Never get distracted, as your opponent will take that as an opportunity." She leans down and ruffles my hair, throwing her gloves in the tub by the door as she waltzes out of here. Those sexy little hips swaying as she goes.

I shake my head at myself and laugh. Scarlett just played me like a fiddle.

I WAKE UP BOLT UPRIGHT IN BED WHEN I HEAR SOMEONE CALL out. Immediately on high alert, I jump from my bed and reach for my knife. I listen out and move into action when I realise it's Eliza. She's crying for help. I exit my room and check the corridor before I quietly open her bedroom door and enter the room, my hand holding the knife out in front of me, ready to take out whoever is in here.

She's lying in her bed, tossing and turning in her sleep. "Please help them," she begs in her sleep. Her face is twisted in anguish and desperation. "Save them," she screams. Taking a breath, I place my knife down on top of the drawers by the door and softly pad over to her bed. Pulling back the covers, I climb in behind her and finding her waist, I pull her into me. "Shush, Scarlet," I whisper. "It's just a nightmare. I got you." I feel her still in my arms.

"Archer," she says, her voice barely a whisper, as she comes to.

"It's me. I got you. Get some sleep." She relaxes in my arms and curls her body into me. She places her hand over mine, and sighs before she stills and falls back asleep.

I lie still, listening to her steady breathing. Why am I here? Why am I comforting her in the middle of the night? I should revel in her fear, thinking of ways I can use it to manipulate her and destroy her. She turns in my arms and I still as she wraps an arm around my neck and nuzzles in against my shoulder. She doesn't wake, instinct drawing her to me. The urge to protect her roars inside of me. I need to remember why I hated her and her family. I need to remember that she is a means to an end and that when I have what I want; I need to destroy that spirit in her. So why does it feel like the last thing in the world I want right now?

CHAPTER NINETEEN

ELIZA

I still when I wake up and feel warm flesh under my cheek. The Ace tattoo stares at me as I open my eyes. I search my brain, trying to figure out why he's in my bed and, more importantly, why I am wrapped around him like a cobra. I ever so carefully lift myself up and lean on my elbow so that I can take this opportunity to observe him while he sleeps. My eyes sweep over his dark lashes, stubble lines his jaw, and those lips that speak words that make me want to punch him, look soft and tempting. I greedily sweep my gaze down his body, down past his chiselled chest and that fucking ace card tattoo, down to that dark hair that disappears into his boxers. Oh my, he's definitely got everything working down there. His dick tents his pants and I bite my lip as thoughts of slipping my hand in and having a feel flicker through my mind. I mean, I don't have to like a guy to sleep with him. Sex is just sex. My hand snakes down his chest and I carefully lift the elastic on his boxers. I yelp when his hand reaches out and snares mine at the wrist.

"Don't start something if you're not willing to see it through the entire way, Scarlet," he warns me, his voice dry and husky from just waking up. One dark eye opens and meets mine.

"Who says I don't want to see it through?" I ask him, chewing on my bottom lip. His dark eyes flash to mine at my admittance. I can't deny it. I want him. I've tried fighting it.

"You did yesterday, when you said us having sex would be a

mistake," he reminds me, still holding my wrist prisoner, half inside his pants.

"It will be a mistake, but it doesn't mean I don't want to do it," I tell him, twisting my wrist in his grip.

He surprises me when he releases my hand and places his behind his head, watching me with lazy interest. He is challenging me, seeing if I'm gutsy enough to take what I want. Keeping my eyes on him, I free him from his boxers and wrap my hand around him. He takes a sharp intake of breath, his eyes never leaving mine. Rubbing my thumb over the head of his dick, I smile when I find his pre-cum on my fingers. I move my body down until I line my mouth up with him, then wrap my lips over him. He hisses and his hips buck upwards, pushing him further into my mouth. It's no surprise that Archer is packing down here. Everything about him is big and obnoxious. I lick, suck and kiss him, until he grips my hair at the base of my head and pulls me away. Grabbing my waist, he flips us, and I end up under him. Archer grabs my left leg and lifts it up to his shoulder as he enters me in one quick hard thrust, making me moan aloud. He fills me perfectly. He smirks down at me. Placing a finger to his lips.

"Quiet, Scarlet. We don't want to wake Kit."

He pistons his hips and moves in and out, thrusting his hips in a circular motion and hitting all the right places. I reach out for him, and he leans down and captures my lips with his. His tongue explores my mouth and I kiss him back as my need for him grows, dominating all my thoughts.

"Are you going to come for me, Scarlet? Are you going to come undone for me?" he asks, his eyes burning into mine as he owns me from the inside out. You can say what you like about Archer Savage, but he knows how to take me to a high like no other. He covers my mouth with his as I come like a rocket, moaning against his mouth as I'm hit by my release. He moves quicker and harder and the bed squeaks in protests as he takes me hard and fast, and I watch in fascination as his features tense and then he moans out my name as he comes.

He leans his head against mine as we both catch our breath and our hearts steady. This is bad. Have I started something I can't turn away from? He is addictive. The way he makes me feel when it's just the two of us, with nothing else between us. He pulls out of me and my greedy vagina whimpers at the loss of him, already planning how she can tempt him back inside of her. Archer rolls onto his back and stares up at the ceiling.

"I still don't like you," I tell him, earning me a throaty laugh from him; one I can't help but smile at.

"I like that you can't backchat me when your mouth is filled with my cock," he says, laughing to himself and I jab him in the chest.

He wraps an arm around my waist, and we lie there in silence.

"Archer, were our parents ever a thing?"

I feel him tense at my question. He immediately withdraws from me, and he swings and sits up, giving me his back.

"You're right, Scarlet. This was a mistake." He rises to his feet and without a backward glance, he collects his boxers from the floor and stalks out of my room across to his, as naked as the day he was born.

I stare at the closed bedroom door. Fuck him. How dare he just walk out of here like that? I throw my covers back and stomp over to his room as naked as the day I was born and throw his door open. He's sitting on the end of his bed, still naked, with his head in his hands.

"You don't get to walk away from me, Archer Savage," I hiss as I storm over to him and shove him in his chest.

He rises to his feet and glares down at me. "Can't you take the hint, Scarlet? We fucked. I got what I needed and now you need to take the hint and fuck off."

I clench my fists. He was fine until I asked about our parents, and I know there is more to this than he is letting on. "I clearly touched a nerve with my question. What do you know about our parents that you aren't telling me?"

"Nothing," he growls. He stands and moves to go past me, but I step into his space, stopping him.

"There is something. I can tell by the way your jaw is tense as fuck. Were our parents dating?"

He smirks, and his stare is hateful and angry. "No, they weren't dating."

"But they were something," I insist, stepping further into his space, crowding him and not letting this go.

"Back off, Scarlet," he orders, gritting his teeth.

"No, tell me," I insist, holding my own.

He leans down right into my face, his expression filled with aggression and pure rage. "They were engaged."

I step back in shock as if someone has just slapped me. "Engaged?"

"Engaged," he repeats as he grabs me by both my wrists and manhandles me towards the door. "Now get the fuck out of my room." He opens his bedroom door and shoves me out, slamming the door in my face.

Reeling from what he has just told me, I retreat to my bedroom. In a daze, I sit myself down on my bed and I tuck my knees up to my chest as I struggle to come to terms with this revelation. What the hell? Our parents were engaged.

The tension in the car is palpable. I tried to insist that Calvin was driving us, but Archer firmly informed me that Wilbur has agreed it was best we ride with him. I stare straight ahead as we drive to school. Kit seems oblivious to the tension and chats away about football and United's latest signing, and Archer smiles and listens to him. I want to punch that smile off his face. Annoying fucker. First, how dare he walk away from me after sex, and second, he can't just drop a bombshell like that and not expect me to have questions.

We pull up at school and Kit jumps out of the car with a quick farewell to me, leaving Archer and I alone in the car.

"You know I will not let this go, right?"

He sighs as he kills the engine. "There's nothing to tell. They were engaged and then they weren't."

"Were they in love?"

He sniggers. "Oh, Scarlet. You think there's any room for love in families like ours? We marry for power, to strengthen mergers and deals."

A cold shiver runs through me. "Wait. Was it an arranged engagement like with Verity and Rafe?"

His jaw tightens. "I'm done with this conversation," he barks as he climbs out of the car.

Oh, we are so not done here. I jump out and rush around to him, blocking his path. "I have a right to know. He's my father."

Archer grasps me by my chin. "You have no right to anything. You want answers, ask your dead father's ghost for them."

I flinch and take a step away from him. "Fuck you, Archer-fucking-Savage," I hiss, turning on my heels and running smack into Seb's chest.

"Woah, Little Red. Slow down," he jests, his voice relaxed with that signature humour.

I shove him in the chest and storm around him, and somewhere behind me I think I hear Archer call after me but fuck him and the arrogant fucking ship he sailed in on. I find the nearest girl's bathroom and lock myself away in a cubicle. I rest my head in my hands. Reeling from the news that my dad and Archer's mum were once engaged. A thousand questions race around my mind. I'll ask Edith tonight; she will tell me the truth.

AT LUNCHTIME I THROW MYSELF DOWN IN THE SEAT BESIDE Archer. Seb and Vee both cock a brow in question at each other and shrug as if to say they don't have a clue what's going on. Archer leans back in his seat and flicks continually at the ring pull on his drink.

"Can you quit doing that?" I bark in annoyance.

He flicks it louder and more persistent.

Rafe chuckles, looking at us. "I think mum and dad are fighting."

I glare at him from over my sandwich. "Fuck off, Rafe."

Rafe whistles and turns his attention to Archer, but he doesn't get to ask anything further as Hugo appears at our table clutching a white box with a red ribbon tied around it.

"What the fuck do you want?" Archer growls at him and he tenses and looks from Archer to me with wide eyes.

"Ignore the moody bastard, Hugo," I say with a warm smile. "What have you got there?"

He holds the box out to me, smiling nervously. "A guy gave it to me outside and he asked me to give it to you."

I frown as I take the box from him. "A guy. What guy?" It's a red box tied with a black silk ribbon.

Hugo shrugs his shoulders. "I didn't get a good look at him. He was wearing shades and a cap."

I nod my head and smile at him. "Well, thanks for bringing it to me Hugo."

He beams at my thanks. "Anytime. Can I get you anything?"

"Do one, Kid," Archer barks, making poor Hugo jump out of his skin. Hugo gives me one last smile before he turns and retreats to his table.

"Did you have to be so mean?" I ask him as I pull the bow apart and lift the lid on the box.

"Holy fuck," Archer says pulling my attention from him to the box. I look down and cry out when I look and see what is inside.

"Is that a fucking dead bird?" Seb asks, leaning over the table and looking inside the box.

I shiver as I take in the dead bird.

Archer leans over me, his breath on my face. "It's a raven. A red raven."

An icy chill travels through me when I understand the meaning. The dead bird has been spray painted red. Whoever sent this knows that I fought recently under my alias.

Archer leans in and pulls out a white piece of card. Written in beautiful red calligraphy, it says: 'Final warning. Leave.'

"This is fucking sick," Verity exclaims, covering her mouth as the smell of the decaying bird hits her senses.

ARCHER CLOSES THE LID ON THE BOX AND PUSHES IT TOWARDS Seb. "Take it. I need a word with Hugo." He rises to his feet and strides across to Hugo's table. He grabs the poor kid by his blazer and drags him towards the cafeteria exit. I quickly collect my bag and run out after them, and the others follow suit. Archer drags Hugo into an empty classroom, and we all follow inside.

"Archer, don't hurt him. It's not his fault," I protest, wanting to protect my little admirer.

"I need to know exactly what the guy looked like that gave you this parcel."

Hugo looks like he's two seconds away from pissing in his pants. "I don' know. He had shades and a hat on. He was wearing blue overalls. I think he was a courier, maybe."

"I need more," Archer insists, gripping him by his blazer. I step up and, ducking under Archer's arms, I stand in between him and Hugo.

"You need to back up," I tell him softly but firmly. The anger is radiating off him. I turn to Hugo and smile, trying to reassure him. "Don't worry, you're not in trouble Hugo. Is there anything you can remember about this guy? Could you see his hair under his hat? How tall was he? Anything?"

Hugo scrunches his forehead. "No, sorry. He might have had dark hair. I wasn't really paying much attention to what he looked like. I'm sorry."

I nod my head and smile again. "That's okay Hugo. You head

off now and enjoy your lunch. I apologise for Archer going all Incredible Hulk on you."

"That's okay," Hugo insists, looking over my shoulder with wary eyes and a tight smile as he grabs his bag and walks backward out of the room. As soon as he's at the door, he takes off like his arse in on fire. Poor boy. Archer has scared him half to death.

"You scared the poor boy," I say to Archer as I close the door again.

Archer ignores my comment. "We need to check the school security cameras."

Seb nods and pulls his phone from his pocket. "On it. I'll sweet talk Miss Reed," he says with a cheeky wink before leaving the room.

"Do I want to know how he plans to sweet talk the school receptionist?" I ask them all, and Rafe chuckles and winks at me. "Use your imagination."

"Ugh," Vee exclaims. "My brother is such a dog. Miss Reed is at least thirty."

"Thirty-two actually," Rafe informs her, and Verity puts her fingers in her mouth and mimics being sick.

I sit there quietly, my eyes fixated on the dead bird. Who is the sick fucker trying to mess with my mind?

Vee comes up beside me and places her arm around my shoulders, looking at me with concern etched across her face. "Are you okay? You look pale. Maybe we should ditch classes today and do something fun."

I smile at my friend. She wants me to feel better, and I love that she cares so much. "I have to admit, I'm not really in the mood for school right now."

"Then let's ditch. We could go for some retail therapy? Buying clothes always makes me feel better," she tells me with a wink.

Archer sniggers and Vee serves him a haughty glare. He holds his hands up in mock surrender. "I have a better idea of what might help Scarlet de-stress."

Verity rolls her eyes. "Any excuse for sex."

"Actually, I wasn't thinking of sex, although I agree; it's a great way to unwind. My idea doesn't involve getting naked."

I arch a brow, curiosity getting the better of me. I'm intrigued to see what Archer has in mind.

"You game Scarlet?" he challenges me, his eyes asking me to trust that he knows what I need.

I nod my head. I needed to get out of here and do something fun.

Rafe whistles. "Road trip."

No doubt Wilbur will receive a call about me missing college, but right now, I don't care. I pull out my phone and send a text to Kit to tell him I'm cutting classes for the afternoon and that I'll meet him at home. Probably not the best role-model behaviour to show my brother, but he will understand.

We head out to the car park and as we leave the main entrance; we walk straight into the deputy head, Mr Spencer.

He frowns, pushing his glasses up his nose. "And where do you lot think you are going?"

Archer doesn't look worried as he takes a step towards him, and I see him gulp in response. "We're leaving for the afternoon, and you're going to mark us as being in school this afternoon. Isn't that right, Mr Spencer?"

I see his jaw tighten in anger as he looks from Archer to Seb, who is smirking as if he's in on some secret. "How is your wife these days Mr Spencer?"

"Now listen..."

Archer steps further into his space, crowding him.

"Go on, go," he hisses in frustration and as soon as Archer steps back, he rushes around him and heads into school like he can't get away from us quick enough.

"What was that?" I ask as I watch our teacher's hasty exit in shock.

Rafe winks at me. "Leverage, Little Red. Always make sure you have leverage...you never know when you might need it."

I shake my head. This really is a world away from anything I am used to. How is it possible that three seventeen-year-old boys can control the teachers?

Verity links her arm with mine and urges me forward as Archer strides towards the SUV "It's best not to ask," Verity advises me with a sigh. This is old news to her, she's used to how these boys operate.

Seb joins us a few minutes later and from the frustrated look on his face I can tell he doesn't bring good news.

"Well?" Archer asks him when he silently climbs in the front passenger seat, a deep frown marring his face.

"Nothing on the cameras. They mysteriously went offline for fifteen minutes, right around the time the parcel was delivered."

Archer releases a frustrated sigh and looks at me through his rear mirror. "We'll find out who's doing this Scarlet, I promise you."

Chewing on my lip I bob my head in response. Whoever is trying to scare me, they have resources, this isn't some amateur kid here and this makes me wonder if my suspicions about Georgie are wrong. I mean, yes, she's rich but she doesn't strike me as overly smart.

CHAPTER
TWENTY

W e drive for about thirty minutes and Seb lets out a whoop of excitement when we turn off the motorway and head down a dirt road.

"Any idea where we are?" I ask Vee. She shakes her head in response, looking as clueless as me right now.

Seb turns in his seat and waggles his eyebrows. "Oh, you are going to love this Little Red."

I search the scenery ahead of us to get some sign as to where Archer is taking us, but I have no clue. We pull into a car park and Archer smirks at me through his mirror before he climbs out. He knows the suspense is killing me. I'm not good with surprises; they make me feel out of control.

We all climb out and follow Archer up the hill to where a large wooden warehouse sits. Maybe we were go-kart racing?

As we pass through the gated entrance, a guy comes forward. He's in his late twenties and has tattoo's all up both arms and on his neck.

"Arch, long time no see," he says grinning from ear-to-ear as he takes Archer's hand.

"Hey, Logan. Yeah, it's been a while. I've had a lot going on lately."

Logan nods his head as he takes in the rest of us. His eyes rest a while longer on me though, as he recognises the stranger in the group.

"You brought a girl?" He smirks. "Well, this is new."

Archer rolls his eyes in response. He doesn't do well with teasing. "Logan, this is Wilbur's granddaughter, Scarlet."

Logan blinks in surprise. "I heard he is back in the Bay. Nice to meet you Scarlet," he tells me with a warm smile.

"Thanks. My name's actually Eliza. This arse just thinks he has a right to re-name me."

Logan chuckles. "Oh, I like you." His gaze flits to Archers. "Now I see why you brought her. Come on, let's get you all set up."

"Set up with what?" I ask as I stride to keep up with the boys.

"Shooting. You're going to learn how to shoot today."

My eyes widen in surprise as I look over at Archer and he gives me a half-smile as if to say, 'you're welcome.'

"Can we do this without parental permission?" I ask him. I am excited to have a go, but we're under eighteen.

"Already sorted it with Wilbur. He signed the permission slip and emailed it over as we were on our way here."

I shake my head in disbelief. How is he always one step ahead of everything?

🐾

THE AFTERNOON TURNS OUT TO BE A BLAST. AFTER GOING through all the safety and checks, we hit the range and I'm not going to lie, the adrenaline rush I got when firing a gun for the first time is amazing. I picture my mystery stalker when I focus on the target and aim for right between the eyes. I hit wide the first few shots, but then Archer comes up behind me and shows me how to stand better. With him guiding my arms and encouraging me, I hit the target straight dead in the head. Placing the gun down, I whizz round to face Archer and throw my arms around his neck.

"Did you see that? I hit the target?"

I pause when I realise, I have just thrown myself over him in my need to share my excitement. His arms wrap around my waist, and he looks down at me. "You did good." He leans closer and places a kiss on my forehead before he lets me go and I find three sets of eyes on us.

"What?" I ask, feeling my cheeks redden.

Seb winks at me as he glances at his sister. "Nothing, Red."

Feeling self-conscious, I turn my attention back to shooting as Logan reloads the gun for me. We shoot for another hour before Logan informs us he has a shooting party arriving soon and we're going to have to call it a day. My disappointment must show on my face because Archer reaches for my hand to get my attention.

"We'll come again, Scarlet."

I nod my head in response. Shooting has got me on an adrenaline high and all I can think about is how kissable his lips look right now. I clear my throat, trying to clear my head, as Archer closes his hand around mine, guiding us to the exit.

"Thanks again, Logan."

"Anytime, especially you Eliza. You come by anytime," he grins, winking at Archer, who grunts under his breath and pulls me towards the exit.

"That was so much fun," I say as we reach the Land Rover and when Seb climbs in the back, I realise it looks like I'm upfront with Archer.

"You are a weird girl," Vee states with a shake of her head. "I mean, who would choose shooting over shopping?"

Rafe wraps his arm around her, and chuckling, he kisses her head. "You make shopping look like an Olympic sport, Vee."

I watch them through Archer's mirror. It's strange to think they'll be married one day and despite me still trying to get my head around this arranged marriage shit, I can see that they are so well matched. Pulling my gaze from them when they lean in for a kiss, Archer's eyes meet mine. He's looking at me like he is in some kind of internal war with himself. "You, okay?"

He clears his throat and nods, pulling his hypnotic eyes away from me as he starts the car and pulls back on to the road. "Let's go eat. I'm starving."

We eat at a cosy-looking place a few towns out from the Bay. It's set back along a small country lane, and you would likely miss it if you didn't know it was there. The restaurant itself is in a large barn with huge wooden beams on the inside. There is an enormous fireplace with a burning fire that heats the space and gives it that cosy ambience that just makes you want to curl up with a hot chocolate and watch the flames. I order a hot chocolate with cream and a chicken pie with chips. Verity orders a chicken salad — obsessed with watching her weight even though she's already tiny.

Seb and Vee muck around play-fighting, and Rafe ignores them, scrolling on his phone. As I sit here watching them, it's clear to see they are all close. That they are there for each other and I can't help but crave being a part of it. To feel like I belong and am accepted. To know that someone will have my back should I need them. For the last four years it's been just me and Kit, but it's been hard having to always be the strong one and not having anyone that I can rely on.

"What's running around in that mysterious mind of yours Scarlet?" Archer asks me from where he sits opposite me. While I have been busy observing his friends, he has been busy watching me.

"Is there just the four of you? Do any of you have other siblings?"

Archer leans back in his seat and continues studying me. "I'm an only child. Rafe has an old sister, Octavia. She's married to my cousin, Gabe."

"Wow," I comment, "you guys really like to keep it in the founding families."

"Our family ties are strong. We know and trust each family, and what better way to strengthen that trust than with marriage?" Rafe pipes up, not taking his attention from his phone but clearly listening in on the conversation.

CARA E. HOLT

"Was your sister's marriage pre-arranged?"

He lifts his eyes from his phone to look at me and I hope I haven't pissed him off with my questions. "They were, shall we say, steered towards each other. They're happy. My sister's first child is due this December."

I nod my head, stirring the cream on my hot chocolate and return my attention to Archer. "What about you? What are your thoughts on the Aces tendency towards marriages of alliance?"

He takes a drink of his coffee before he answers me, like he has all the time in the world. I have to wonder if anything fazes this guy. He's always so in control. "I think I will do my duty to my family and if that means marrying someone they believe will strengthen us, then so be it."

"But what about love? What if you meet someone and fall in love?"

His response is a dismissive snigger. "Love has no place in our world. Love makes you weak, vulnerable to others who want to have leverage over us."

I can see from his expression that this is what he truly believes, and to be fair, I agree to some extent. Love can cause pain and regret, and it makes you vulnerable. That is why I have shut myself off to ever letting myself care about anyone other than Kit. That way, I've remained strong and never felt that feeling of disappointment when someone let me down. But then I remember the love my parents shared. The way my dad used to look at my mum like she was the centre of his universe.

"Do you believe in love, Eliza?" Vee asks me, and again I hadn't realised that she had been listening in, thinking she was too busy trying to wind her brother up.

I shrug my shoulders as I feel the weight of everyone's stares. "I've never been in love, so I can't comment, and I have no intention of ever finding out."

Verity sighs. "Love, lust, hate, they're all closely interlinked."

"Which ones do you feel for me, Vee?" Rafe asks her, grinning and placing an arm around her shoulder, pulling her into his side.

"Why all three of the previous babes," she tells him, dropping a quick kiss to his lips. Rafe's response is to nuzzle into her neck and whisper something in her ear that brings a blush to Vee's cheeks.

"Don't talk dirty to my sister when I'm in the same room," Seb groans, throwing a salt sachet at Rafe. Rafe grins a wicked grin at him before he grabs a hold of Vee by the back of her neck and pulls her in for a toe-curling kiss.

Seb groans and jumps to his feet, muttering about needing some air. I avert my gaze from Verity and Rafe, who pull apart and whisper to each other. Archer has remained quiet, and I find his eyes on me again. I shuffle under his scrutiny. Is he listing all my flaws in his head right now?

The waitress arrives with our food and Seb returns to his seat and normal conversation resumes. It has been one heck of a strange day. Starting with dead birds, to shooting, to talking about arranged marriage and love. One thing I can say about today though, is Archer knew exactly what I needed today in order to let off some steam, and that fact alone scares the shit out of me.

When Archer pulls up in the drive at the Alderman mansion, the place is a hive of activity. Two large vans sit in the driveway with A1 Security services written across the side.

"It looks like Wilbur has taken my advice on tighter security."

I frown as I watch a guy go round the side of the house with a ladder over his shoulder. "Great. No sneaking out for me anymore."

"What do you need to sneak out for, anyway?" Archer asks me with a frown.

I lean over the central console in his car, leaving my face a hair's breadth away from his, and I wink. "Wouldn't you like to know Archer Savage?"

Before I have a chance to pull away, he grips the back of my neck and holds me there, half balanced over the gear stick. "You can't take this lightly, Scarlet. Someone is out for you. Promise me you won't put yourself in harm's way."

"Why do you care?" I ask him. He's so close I can feel his breath on my mouth.

"You're an Ace and no one messes with one of us," he explains, his eyes not moving from mine. He runs his thumb across my bottom lip. "I'd like to take you upstairs and fuck you senseless right now, but I need to take this fucked up gift down to the station."

"Oh," I reply, gulping and my cheeks heating. He smirks at my reaction.

"Have I rendered you speechless, Scarlet? That's a first."

I dart my eyes to outside checking that there is no one around and then I climb over the central console and drop myself onto his lap. He says nothing, he just waits as if he's curious to see what I'll do next. I unzip the zipper on his school trousers and push my hand inside.

"Scarlet," he warns me, his voice husky and unstable. "There are cameras everywhere. You'll give Wilbur a heart attack."

I sigh, pulling my hand from his trousers, realising he has a point, but as I go to climb off him, but he holds my head in place with his hands and leans in and kisses me. Making my toes curl and my body want more.

"Later," he promises me. "Let Edith fuss over you. I'll be back shortly."

Flushed and unsatisfied, I climb off his lap and grab my schoolbag, I climb out of the car and watch as he drives back down the drive. Later couldn't come quick enough.

When I walk into the house, I falter in my steps when I come face to face with my grandfather. He's dressed in an expensive navy suit, looking like he's just come out of a business meeting, and I have to wonder if he dresses like this every day.

"Eliza," he greets me with a slight curve in his mouth. "How are you?"

"I'm okay, all things considered," I reply, fidgeting with the strap of my bag. I can't help but feel nervous under his scrutiny.

"Good," he replies, offering me a tight smile. "We have a charity function coming up soon. Alexis's designer friend will call by later this evening with some dresses for you both to try."

"Oh, I was planning on hanging out with Archer this evening,"

His approval is apparent from his expression. "I'm pleased to see you are spending time with Archer. He would be a good match for you."

I let out a nervous laugh. "We're just friends. I'm a little young for finding my match."

He doesn't laugh along with me. He just gives me that tight smile again, the one that makes me wonder if he has ever really smiled. "The designer won't take up more than an hour of your time. That should leave you plenty of time to spend with your friend."

The way he says friend makes me think he doesn't believe for one second that Archer and I are friends.

"Oh, and Eliza, I've asked my lawyer to get your surname legally changed to your true family name. I can't have my heirs not using the Alderman name."

I want to tell him I have a surname and that it is the one my parents chose for me and Kit, but then I remember that if it wasn't for him, we would still be in foster care. We'd still be wondering each day if they would move us again and I can't let my brother go back to that life. "Of course." I turn on my heels and walk away from him at a measured pace when really, I want to run from there as quick as I can.

When I come down for dinner, I falter in my steps when I see Archer is here. He's standing over by the window, a drink in his hand, chatting with my grandfather like they are old friends. I guess in some ways they are. I am the stranger here.

"Ah, here she is. My beautiful granddaughter," Wilbur says when he spots me loitering in the doorway. "Archer was just telling me about your plans for October half term."

"Plans?" I repeat as a maid offers me a glass of non-alcoholic squash. It grates on me that Archer gets alcohol, but I get juice. Sexism is alive and well in Hawk Bay.

"The ski-trip. Edward has a beautiful chalet with a magnificent view of the slopes."

"Ah, the ski-trip," I say, making out as if I know what the hell he's talking about. "Yeah. Can't wait, though I've never been skiing before, so it could be an interesting experience."

Wilbur pats Archer on his shoulder. "I'm sure Archer here will teach you and guide you."

I smile tightly and nod. I can't help feeling like there is a double connotation to his words. Chester strolls in at that point, a cigarette hanging out of his mouth, and Wilbur's attention thankfully turns to him as he tells him coldly that there is no smoking in the house.

Dinner is painful. Archer takes the seat beside me, and this has Chester smirking like the Cheshire Cat. What is his problem?

Wilbur asks Kit about his football practice, and he listens to Kit's avid chatter and seems genuinely interested in him. I jerk slightly when I feel Archer's hand on my thigh as it snakes under the spilt in my dress and climbs slowly and tantalisingly up. I reach under the table and grip his hand with mine, stopping him in his tracks, and he fights a smirk, squeezing my hand in his before he returns to his meal. Two can play that game, arsehole. So, when my grandfather turns his attention to Archer and asks him more about his plans for when he finishes college, I move my hand up his leg and I see the muscle in his cheek tighten.

Keeping my eye on Alexis, who is droning on about some charity ladies evening she is helping to organise, I creep my hand up higher until I feel the bulge in his pants. Bingo! I rub my hand over him and feel him grow and harden under my touch. His poker face remains on point, but I can see be the way he grips at his knife that he is struggling to hold his composure. I purposefully clear my throat and squeeze his thigh before pulling my hand away.

"What do you think, Eliza?" Alexis asks me and I look at her blankly. I was totally not listening to a word she has been saying.

"Sorry, what did you say?"

"I said you could be one of our auction dates," she repeats, giving me a hopeful smile.

"Ah, I'm not sure anyone would pay to date me."

"Nonsense. I'm sure Archer here would bid," Alexis suggests, with an encouraging wink at Archer.

"Of course," he says. "Anything for charity." No one else notices the undertone to his voice when he says the word charity, but I don't miss the double connotation he aims at me, and I glare at him from over my glass as I take a drink.

Dinner is painful, but having Kit and Archer there makes it bearable. Kit loves it when Wilbur pays an interest in his football training, and he clearly wants to impress him. It pains me how desperate he is to belong here, to have that sense of a place to call home.

"Well, gentleman, shall we retire the lounge for drinks and leave the ladies to fuss over dresses," Wilbur suggests, standing to his feet and waiting for the others to follow suit.

"I have homework," Kit announces, looking apologetic.

Chester gestures to his phone. "I've already made plans with friends."

I didn't know Chester had any friends here in the Bay. Considering he's only just started at school, he has moved fast.

Wilbur sighs and looks at Archer. "It looks like it's just the two of us."

Archer stands and smiles warmly at my grandfather. "Lead the way, Wilbur." He can really turn on the pleasantries when it suits him.

Alexis claps her hands in excitement and comes round to my seat, ushering me up and linking her arm through mine. "I can't wait to see what Christian has picked out for us. He has such an eye, you know. He knows what suits my body better than I do."

"Can't wait," I say with a forced smile. I look over my shoulder as we climb the stairs just as Archer looks back before he enters the lounge and I give him a pleading look that has him grinning, as if he knows that this is not my idea of fun.

"Ah, beautiful ladies," greets a man with a goatee beard manicured to perfection, as he rushes towards Alexis and kisses her on both cheeks. He's wearing grey tailored trousers and a fitted white shirt with a pair of designer shades resting on his black, smoothed back hair. "You must be Eliza." He leans in and kisses my cheeks and then stands back and circles me a few times as he looks me up and down. "We need to emphasise that tiny waist and show off the girls, I think." He taps his chin with his finger, looking deep in thought. "Size eight, yes, and a c-cup?"

"Yes," I answer, looking at him in amazement.

He reaches out and runs a piece of my hair through his fingers. "Darling, I love your hair. I am thinking a deep burgundy dress or maybe purple."

"Actually, I am thinking black. It's kind of my go-to colour."

Christian shakes his head, the silver chain at his wrist jangling as he waggles a finger at me. "No black. We want you to shine, not blend into the background. You have a face and a body that needs to be seen."

He dismisses my protestations and heads over to a clothing rack that has many dresses in garment bags. He lifts one down and holds it with such delicateness, like he is holding a new-born baby. "Alexis, darling, as soon as I saw this dress, I thought of you. It's by Lola Rose, an up-and-coming designer. The pale pink will complement your hair perfectly."

Alexis unzips the bag and pulls the dress out, holding it against her. It's full length but fitted at the body with loose chiffon that falls to the floor with a deep split on one side to show off a bit of leg. Alexis gushes over the dress and rushes behind the dressing screen to try it on.

"Now, my little jewel. How about this one? It's purple silk, simple but so elegant, and will accentuate those curves." He holds out a dress and I have to admit when I unzip it, it is beautiful in a classic and elegant way. "We'll need to use titty tape as it hangs too low at the back for a bra."

I study the dress, but I'm unsure and he must see my hesitation as he takes it from my arms and pulls out another one. "How about this stunner?"

The dress is a deep burgundy. Its satin like the previous dress, with simple straps it drops into a low 'v' showing some cleavage without being too revealing. I lift it out of the bag and take a look at the back. It's more or less backless and drops into a ruched 'v' towards the top of my backside. It clings to the body and hips area but then finishes with a floaty fish-tail, giving room to walk comfortably. Christian can see that I like this one, so he ushers me towards the other dressing screen to try it on.

As I am undressing and climbing into the dress, I hear him gushing and fussing over Alexis. She asks him if he can take the hem up slightly on the dress for her. I come out from behind the screen and Christian turns his full attention to me.

"You are a vision, Eliza," he tells me, placing his hand over his heart. "That dress is perfection on you. No panties when you wear it, though, my dear. I think my work here is done," he states, clapping his hands together. "Okay, Eliza, dress off and zipped away safely. Alexis, my dear, let me help you up onto the stool whilst we pin the hem."

I undress and slip back into my black jumper dress. I don't think Wilbur had been too enamoured with my clothing choice for dinner, but I liked to be comfortable and didn't see the need to dress up for a family dinner at home. I thank Christian for his time, and he showers me with air kisses and tells me he can't wait to see a photo of me in the dress.

I head over to the East Wing, ready to throw myself down on my bed and catch up on my latest Netflix binge watch. I swing my temporary bedroom door open and falter when I find Archer lying on my bed, shoes off, with his legs crossed, looking very at home.

"Comfy?" I ask, arching a brow and leaning my hip against the door frame.

He doesn't answer me he just does a slow scan of my body from head to toe. It feels like he is undressing me with the heat from his eyes. "Close the door."

Rolling my eyes and acting as if my heart isn't in fact going at a hundred miles an hour, I close the door behind me and take my time walking over to my bed. His jaw tics in annoyance. I climb onto the bottom of the bed and crawl on all fours towards him, settling myself on his lap, my thighs straddling him.

"Did you enjoy teasing me at dinner earlier?" he asks me as his fingers stroke my thighs in small circles that send shivers down my spine.

"You started it," I argue.

He leans up, his eyes sparkling with promise, and he lifts my dress up over my hips and up over my body. "Then I better finish it."

CHAPTER
TWENTY·ONE

ARCHER

I wake up with her scent surrounding me, that mix of her favourite perfume and her strawberry body wash. She is fast asleep, lying on her side with one leg draped over me. Her scarlet curls frame her face, contrasting beautifully with her pale complexion. If I was ever asked what my ideal woman would look like, it would be her. She is slim, but with curves in all the right areas. Her tits are the perfect handful. I never sleep with a girl. I take what I need and send them on their way, but with her I find I enjoy waking up with her beside me. When my grandfather informed me that Wilbur had discovered an estranged granddaughter, I'd envisioned her in my head. Nothing could have prepared me for her beauty. Those big expressive chestnut eyes that burn with fire and defiance, but there's a vulnerability hidden there that she doesn't allow anyone to see. The large scar on her right thigh is a reminder of what a warrior she is. She cheated death and came back stronger. My plan had always been to claim her and then destroy her, to chip away at her self-esteem until she became a shell of her former self. To destroy her the way her father destroyed my mother. What I hadn't planned for though, is how well she fits with us. Vee adores her and even Seb and Rafe like having her around. My cock stands to attention, desperate to have her again. She is becoming addictive, but I have to remember my endgame. She must pay for her father's sins.

Her eyes flutter open and meet mine, with a lazy smile on her face as she stretches out that delectable body. "Morning."

"Morning," I reply. I reach for her waist and roll us over until she is underneath me.

Her eyes widen as she feels my cock against her stomach, and she bites her bottom lip and looks over at her bedside clock. "We'll have to be quick," she says, wrapping her legs around me, giggling when I throw the covers over us and rub my stubble along her cheek.

DRIVING TO SCHOOL, I TAP THE STEERING WHEEL TO THE SONG on the radio. I'm in a top mood. Morning sex and a shower with Scarlet is the best way to start the day. I pull into my spot at school and climb out. I spot Georgie deep in conversation with Alexis's son, Chester. I didn't know they were friends. Georgie spots me from across the school grounds and hastily throws her hair over her shoulder and rushes off to the main entrance.

"Did you see that?" I ask Scarlet, and she looks up from her phone with a blank look on her face. "Never mind."

"Hey, hey, hey, Familia," Seb greets as he throws his arms around both our shoulders. "How are we this morning?"

I side eye my best friend. He is awfully chipper this morning. "Who were you with last night?" I ask, knowing for sure that a girl has put him in this good mood.

Seb shrugs, tapping the side of his nose with his finger. "Ah, a gentleman never tells."

Scarlet sniggers and Seb's eyes jump to hers with mock upset. "You wound me, little red. Speaking of, are you responsible for the upbeat mood I detect from Archer?"

Scarlet pops her phone in her pocket and, winking at him, says, "A lady never tells."

Seb pulls his tongue out at her but drops a kiss on her cheek. If it was anyone else, I'd likely tell him to back the fuck away, but he's my brother and I know he would never hit on any girl I am involved with.

"Any news from the police about the creepy dead bird in a box?"

I see Scarlet's face change from a look of amusement to anxiety. Whoever this fucker is, he is messing with her head.

"Nothing," I tell him. "They are going to test for prints and DNA."

Seb nods as he walks along beside us into school. "It must have been someone who saw her fight that night, right?"

I nod my head, resting against the lockers as Scarlet stops and grabs her books from her locker. "There must have been at least seventy to eighty people there that night. It is like looking for a needle in a haystack."

"It creeps me out to think they are watching me," Scarlet shares. "I hate not knowing who this is or why they are targeting me."

I lift her chin with my finger, getting her to look at me. "We'll find them Scarlet and when we do, they will pay for daring to threaten one of our own."

She nods her head. "Oh, when we find them, I'll be the one making them pay."

"See," Seb grins, nudging me with his shoulder, "she's fucking perfect for our world."

Seb is right. She is tough and can fight her own corner, but like it or not, we rule the Bay and whoever dares to think they can get away with this will answer to us and pay the price.

CHAPTER
TWENTY-TWO

ELIZA

I t's during second period that I notice the stares and whispers. I'd forgotten how it feels to have everyone looking at you and talking about you. Since the Aces had publicly declared me one of them, no one has bothered me. Don't get me wrong, some girls still give me bitch glares, and some look at me with respect for turning up out of the blue and sliding into position as an Ace. I try to switch off from the stares and whispers and concentrate on my Business Studies teacher who is talking us through our project brief. When the bell rings, I grab my bag and high tail out of there, feeling like all eyes are on me and like I am missing out on some great secret.

I'm heading to my locker when I spot Vee rushing towards me from the other direction. Her face is twisted in anxiety.

She grabs a hold of my wrist and without a word she pulls me into the nearest classroom and closes the door. "Look, don't stress, okay? The boys will get it shut down in no time."

I scrunch my face. What on earth is she jabbering on about? "You've lost me."

Verity's expression changes from one of reassurance to discomfort and she chews vehemently on her bottom lip. "Okay, you haven't looked at your phone this morning?"

I shake my head and rest my bum against the desk behind me. "No, I've been in class. What's going on Verity?"

With a sigh, she pulls out her phone and moves to stand beside me. "See for yourself."

She presses play on a video, and I take a second to process what I am seeing. Is that? Fuck no, it isn't. I lean in closer, the video now having my full attention. There's no doubt the couple having sex are me and Archer. You can see everything, as the camera angle has a great side-on view of the bed.

My cheeks flush and a roll of nausea washes over me. Vee presses pause and stands herself in front of me, searching my face with concern.

"Are you okay?"

I stare blankly at her for a beat. "Am I okay? No, I'm not fucking okay. There's a goddamn sex tape of me and Archer!! I'm naked." I stand and begin to pace up and down the classroom. "I'm going to kill that fucker," I hiss. I am livid, shaking in anger. "I should have known he was reeling me in to play with me."

"Wait, what?" Vee stops me in my tracks, holding out her hand to interrupt. "You don't seriously think this was Archer?"

"Yes, of course I fucking do!" My voice raises a decibel as my anxiety increases. I turn on my heels and yank open the door, hearing it bounce back off the wall with force. I step back out into the main corridor, and everyone stops and stares.

One boy whistles at me and winks. "Nice tits, Eliza."

I glare at him and turn my attention down the corridor until I spot exactly who I am looking for. The three of them are huddled over by their lockers, heads bent and deep in conversation. I march over there like a woman on a mission. When I reach them, I shove Archer from behind, making him stumble into the other two. He turns with a growl, looking like he is ready to take someone's head off.

"Scarlet. What the fuck?"

I glare at him, folding my arms across my chest and tapping my foot, too agitated to keep still. "Exactly! What the fuck? It was you, right?"

Archer grabs my arm and pulls me towards a classroom; I resist and try to remain where I am, but he is a lot stronger than me and as much as I fight him, he manages to get me inside the empty room and pins me against the wall. I roll my eyes when the other two follow in behind us with Verity at the back and she closes the door, shutting out the avid crowd that has gathered.

"Get the fuck off me." I try to knee him in the balls, but he blocks me, holding me in place.

"Will you calm the fuck down," he exclaims, holding my wrists at either side of my body.

I scoff. "Calm down. The entire school has seen me naked and bouncing on your dick, Archer! I won't calm down. I'm fuming. Did you have this planned all along?"

"Will you shut up for two pissing seconds and let me get a word in, love?"

I scrunch my eyes and scowl. "Don't call me love. I'm not your love."

Archer sighs and leans into my face. "Read my lips, Scarlet. I didn't post that video. I didn't film us. That's not the way I operate. This is someone amateur, it's juvenile. If I wanted to destroy you, I would come up with much better ways than a sex tape."

I glare at him, my chest heaving with pent up rage. "You expect me to believe the bullshit coming out of your mouth?"

"Yes," he growls, "I do. Because it's the truth. I swear on the lives of my two brothers here."

"He's telling the truth, Red," Seb pipes in from behind. "I'm telling you; he didn't do this."

"Well, if you didn't do it, then who the fuck did?"

My phone chooses that moment to start persistently buzzing in my blazer pocket and I pull it out and grimace when I see my grandfather's name on the screen.

"Hey Gramps," I say, wincing in anticipation.

"Eliza. Care to explain why someone has sent me a very graphic video of you and Archer?"

Before I can reply, Archer takes my phone from out of my hand. "Wilbur. Someone planted a camera in your granddaughter's bedroom. Did the security company not do a full sweep of the house?"

Archer's frown deepens as he listens. "This isn't good enough. Someone has waltzed into your home and planted a camera and videoed your granddaughter and now half the Bay have seen it." He nods, listening. "I'll leave it in your hands." Sighing, he holds my phone out to me. "Wilbur's getting his legal team on it. The video will be down in no time."

I snigger. "A bit too fucking late. I imagine most people have watched it and probably even saved it to their phones!" I rub a hand over my face. "Ugh, some sicko will probably use it as wank material."

Archer cups my face with his hands. "We will take the video down and I will instruct every fucker in this school to delete it."

"What must Wilbur think?" I ask him. "He probably thinks his granddaughter's some easy whore now. Oh god," I exclaim. "Kit. Oh, my poor brother."

The thought of my brother seeing me in a sex tape makes me want to curl up in a ball and die. He will be so embarrassed. Here he is trying to settle in at a new school and all his classmates have seen me naked.

"Listen to me, Scarlet," Archer commands me, pulling my eyes back to his. "Wilbur won't think anything less of you. People have sex, it's perfectly normal. What isn't normal is someone thinking it's okay to film someone without their knowledge and invade their privacy."

"It's got to be the stalker, surely," Verity says from where she has been quietly listening, sitting on top of one of the desks.

"Seb, Rafe, go spread the word. Every fucker in this building will delete the video, and if they mention it or say anything at all, they'll be dealt with."

Rafe winks at me and pats my arm as he passes. "We'll sort it, Eliza."

"I need to go home. I can't face classes this afternoon, but I need to speak to my brother first."

Verity hops down off the desk. "I'll go find him and fetch him here."

I smile at her in thanks. It is nice having people have my back. It's not something I've had much experience with since my parents died. Verity closes the door behind her, leaving Archer and I alone.

"I'll kill whoever did this. No one messes with the Aces," he promises me firmly, with burning rage behind his eyes. I feel this overwhelming need to bury myself in his arms, to feel protected, but I fight the shit out of these strange feelings, pushing them right down out of sight. Relying on someone else is a weakness and allowing yourself to be vulnerable to that feeling just brings on a world of hurt when that person lets you down.

"You're quiet, Scarlet. You doing okay?"

I push back my shoulders and lift my head high, meeting his intense stare. "I'm fine. You think something like this will break me? I've told you, I'm fucking stronger than I look."

He nods his head as he continues to assess me, and I try not to squirm under his eyes. I feel like he sees past my walls and sees what's hiding behind there and it unnerves me to no end.

I breathe a sigh of relief when the door opens, and Vee walks in with my brother trailing behind her.

"Hey, Kit," I say with a grimace, standing to my feet.

My brother throws his bag down on the floor and throws a deep frown Archer's way before he turns his full attention to me. "You okay?"

I nod and fold my arms over my body. "I'll live," I tell him with a shrug. "Are you? It can't have been easy having all your friends see that?"

He snorts. "I can deal, sis. Besides, most of them just want an invitation to the house so that they can see my 'hot' sister." He air quotes the hot part and rolls his eyes.

"I'm sorry."

He holds out a hand to silence me. "Did he do this?" He

gestures with his head towards Archer, and I can't help but grin, seeing my brother not wither in Archer's presence. "Because if he did, I don't care if he runs the Aces or all that shit. I'll hit him for you, sis."

I watch Archer's eyes widen in surprise as he tries to fight a smile. I think we all know there's no way my brother could ever lay a finger on him.

"He didn't, but I'll find out who did and when I do, I'll take care of them myself," I vow.

Kit nods his head and looks over to Archer. "So, are you two like dating or some shit now? Because I kind of thought you hated each other."

I chuckle and look over at Archer. "Oh, I still hate him, but well, you know, sometimes shit happens." I feel my cheeks flush slightly when I realise I am standing in a room talking about sex with my brother.

"I get it," he tells me with a shrug of his shoulders. "I mean, every girl in this school fawns over him, so why should you be any different?"

"I don't fucking fawn over him," I protest, my brows crinkling in annoyance.

"Okay, you just fawn over his dick then," Kit says laughing, and Archer clears his throat.

"Okay, junior, this conversation is over," Archer orders him, giving him a playful push towards the door. "Get back to class and if anyone talks shit about your sister or gives you shit over the video, you tell me or the others, you hear me?"

"I hear you." Kit raises his fist to Archer, and I watch in shock as Archer places his fist against his. Kit grabs his bag from the floor and with a quick smile my way, he leaves.

"What the hell was that?" I ask, looking from the door my brother has just exited through and back to Archer in bewilderment.

"So, you're mesmerised by my dick, Scarlet?" Archer smirks

as he stalks towards me. I try to take a step back as he crowds into my space.

"Don't flatter yourself, Savage. A dick is a dick."

He moves closer, causing my back to hit the classroom wall. "Oh, is that so? That's not what you were saying when you rode me last night, Scarlett."

I blush as I remember how I told him his cock was heaven when that god-damn video was taken. Of all the times to tell a guy his cock was like heaven, I had to do it when we were secretly being filmed.

"Everyone says shit when they're in the throes of passion. I'm pretty sure you've called my pussy magic a few times."

He cocks a brow as his hand glides up my thigh. "It is magic." His hand cups my sex and he grins when he feels I'm wet. Fucker. "You want me to make you feel good, Scarlet? You only have to ask?"

I glare at him as he rubs the heel of his hand against my sex, stirring a rush of desire through my body. I place my hand on his chest. "I am not doing anything with you in this school, where all the pupils and teaching staff have already seen us going at it."

"And here I thought you liked to live dangerously." He pulls his hand away from my sex and I almost whimper at the loss.

He grabs my hand in his, stopping to pick up our bags as he pulls me from the classroom. "Where are you dragging me to, now?"

He looks back over his shoulder at me and grins, a sexy, bad grin that makes my core flutter. "I'm taking you somewhere nice and secluded, where no one will hear your moans of pleasure."

"Oh," I reply, my body heating with anticipation as I allow him to take me out of school and towards his car.

When we pull up at his house, I look over at him in surprise. I haven't been back here since that first night. During the day, it looks even more imposing. How is this my life these days? Archer steers the car towards the side of the house and drives into the garage that is bigger than the entire square foot of my last foster home. Parked inside, there is a Porsche and an Audi, and I chuckle out loud.

"What?" he asks me, clueless, as we both exit the car.

I shake my head. "Nothing." I move towards the door but yelp when he pulls me back and lifts me and drops me on the bonnet of the shiny red Porsche.

He cocks a brow at me when I wait for an explanation. "The staff will be in the house. So, I'm going to feast on you out here so you can moan for me to your heart's content."

"Oh, really?" I ask, sitting up on my elbows as he grabs my legs and pulls them apart, pulling my panties down my legs. He doesn't waste any time. He goes straight to town, and I'm bucking my hips and begging for more within seconds. Fuck him and his delicious tongue for having this power over me. I moan his name and beg him not to stop as he sucks and licks and sends my body into a frenzy. I explode like a rocket shouting his name and right now, I don't care if half the gated estate hears me. I've no sooner come down from my high when he turns me over and pushes me down, stomach first, onto the bonnet. When he pushes himself inside me in one quick thrust, I release a long, pleasured moan. He wraps my hair around his wrist to hold me in place, owning me and taking what he needs, and I love every second.

"Tell me, Scarlet, does my cock feel like heaven?"

I growl at him as I push my hips up to meet his thrusts. He stops still above me, and I wriggle my hips, needing him to move and give me what I need.

"Ah-ah, princess. Say the words and I'll give you what you need."

I hate him right now. He knows he has me where he wants me. I hate that he has the power to own me like this. I want to tell him to take his cock and use his hand, but right now I need him to finish what he started, so with an annoyed growl I give him what he wants. "Please, Archer, fuck me."

I can't see his face, but I know there's a shit-eating grin on his face. "Good girl." He moves again with punishing force. The sound of flesh slapping against flesh thunders through this space. He pounds into my sex, taking all he can and giving me everything I need. You can say what you like about this situation between us, but the sex is on fire.

"Let go, Scarlet. Give it to me," he demands and like the obedient girl he commands, I shatter around him, moaning his name and possibly Gods. He releases my hair and I lean up, so my back ends up against his chest and he grasps my chin and turns my head sideways. "Look at us," he orders, and through the glass wall that separates the two sections of the garage, I can see our reflection. "I'll kill the fucker who got to see you like this. Only I get to see you this way, Scarlet. The thought that some of those horny little shits at school will get off to the image of you riding my cock makes me rage." His thrusts become harder and deeper as he speaks. "You're fucking mine."

A part of me wants to protest that I'm not his, but I'm too transfixed on our reflection, watching us as he fucks me. I feel him tense, and he growls and pants in my ear as he finds his release deep inside of me.

For a beat, we remain still, catching our breaths. He clears his throat as he pulls out and he hands me my skirt and knickers. We get dressed in silence. I don't like how vulnerable I feel after we have had sex. I mean, it's not like I want post-sex cuddles and pillow talk, right? It's not, right?

"Are you okay?" he asks me as he straightens his school tie.

I smile probably a little too enthusiastically in my bid to hide my weak emotions. "I'm peachy."

"You hungry?" he asks me as I follow him through the side door and into the house.

"Always," I state, following him through the house and into a large open-plan kitchen-diner.

"Hello Archer, I didn't realise you were home." A lady with kind blue eyes stands at the kitchen island chopping carrots. She looks to be in her late sixties and has white hair that is tied at the base of her neck with a blue ribbon.

"Early finish today," he offers in explanation as he passes her and heads to the large fridge.

"Introduce me to your friend, then?" she insists as she looks at me with a curious but friendly smile.

He ignores her and pulls a carton of juice from the fridge and grabs two glasses.

"Hi, I'm Eliza Holton," I say, doing a little finger wave. I suddenly wonder if my hair is a mess in that telltale just been ravaged in the garage way and stroke my hair to ensure it's okay.

"Ah, Wilbur's granddaughter. I've heard all about you from Edith. She is pleased as punch to have young ones in the house again. I'm Jenny, the Savage's housekeeper."

"Nice to meet you, Jenny," I tell her. She has the same warmth in her that Edith does. Maybe it is a housekeeper thing, not that I had ever come across any before I moved here.

Archer walks towards me and holds out a glass of orange juice, which I take and cup with my hands. "We'll be in my room."

"Dinner will be at six sharp tonight," she shouts after us as I scuttle to catch up with him. I have my foot on the first step of the marble staircase when a door to the left opens and an elderly man of similar age to my grandfather comes into the hallway. He blinks when he spots me and then glances at Archer.

"Jesus, you're the image of her," he exclaims, studying my face.

"Grandfather," Archer says flatly as he pauses on the stairs.

"I'm Eliza," I announce, and he nods his head, smiling at me.

"Oh, I know who you are, my lovely. You are the image of your grandmother. Same eyes and her cheekbones."

I nod my head and blush. "Yeah, I noticed there's a family resemblance from her picture in my grandfather's house."

He places his hands in his pockets and smiles, staring at me like he is seeing a ghost. "The video is down," he informs Archer and I flush when I realise he's talking about the sex tape. Has everyone seen it? "Wilbur's lawyers have dealt with it swiftly."

Archer nods his head. "Good to know. I hope he's having the house cleared for anymore hidden surprises?"

"I believe that is all in hand. Today's events might need us to bring forward certain plans," he tells Archer, and I see his jaw tense in response.

"I don't see why."

His grandfather arches a brow at him. "Oh, I think we both know that's not true. Where are you two off to?" he asks, turning his question to me.

"Oh, we're studying," I offer in explanation. In truth, I'm not sure what I am doing here.

He smirks, and it reminds me so much of Archer. "Studying? Is that what we're calling it?" he replies. "It is good to see the two of you getting close," he says to Archer before he turns on his heels and retreats into the room he came from, closing the door behind him.

"Come on," Archer growls, continuing up the stairs and leaving me standing there puzzled by the interaction. I hurriedly follow behind him until we reach his room.

"What did he mean about bringing plans forward?" I ask as I leave my shoes at the door and take a seat on the end of his bed.

Archer ignores my question as he unbuttons his shirt and then undoes his trousers and pulls them down, along with his boxers. My train of thought disappears as I ogle a very naked Archer. I mean, he has a glorious body,

He smirks at me as my eyes meet his. "I need a shower. Remotes there." He gestures with his head to where the remote sits on a chest of drawers before disappearing into his ensuite. I groan and throw myself back on his bed. Why did such an arrogant arsehole have to look like an Adonis? I breathe in his scent which is all around me on his bed. What am I doing here? I mean seriously I am lying here smelling his sheets. Unease settles in my stomach. Am I getting used to having him around? I jump up off the bed and spot a pad and a pen over by his desk. I quickly scribble on it that I needed to head home and I hightail out of there like my arse is on fire. There is no way on earth am I catching feelings for Archer Savage.

CHAPTER
TWENTY-THREE

ELIZA

An hour later I'm in some bar on the edge of the bay. I'm in my trusty black ripped jeans, and a tight cropped t-shirt and Doc Martens and I feel like the old me again. Not the girl who swans around in fancy cars in a private school uniform. I sit at the bar with my drink in hand and stare off into the distance.

"Do you play?" I look up and find a guy with a mop of dark curly hair standing beside me and I realise he's talking to me. He's wearing blue overalls, like the type a mechanic wears.

"Trust me, you don't want to play me. I'm good."

He grins, the smile lighting up his grey coloured eyes. This was the kind of guy I usually went for — rough and rugged. There would be no Porsche on his drive, and I doubt he ever set foot near a private school.

"Oh, fighting talk. I like it. It's just words though, beautiful." He leans his elbow on the bar beside me and winks.

I pick up my drink and down the remains in one go. "Okay, but don't say I didn't warn you."

I follow him over to the pool table, where his friend watches me with interest. Mechanic guy hands me a cue. "What's your name?"

"I don't think we're at the name sharing stage yet," I say as I take my first shot and pocket the ball.

"I see." He grins as he walks around to the other side of the table and studies the balls. "I have to earn it, do I?"

I smile back. "Sure do."

For the next half an hour I have fun. We banter back and forth as I beat his arse at pool. It's fun and light-hearted, and there are no thoughts about stalkers or elite secret clubs. I am just Eliza Holton, a normal girl.

I'm watching him take his shot when a voice behind me and their breath at my ear makes me jump a mile.

"What are you doing here, princess?"

I swivel on my feet and find Silver standing before me. He's in jeans and a blue t-shirt that shows off his tattoo sleeves. "I'm baking a cake," I reply as I turn my back on him and study the table before I take my next shot.

"Hey, Silver. She a friend of yours?" My mechanic friend asks him, curiosity in his eyes.

"She's a girl that's on the wrong side of the Bay, Cole."

Cole's eyebrows rise in surprise. "That so? You slumming it for the afternoon, beautiful?"

I glower at Silver. "I'm not slumming it, thank you. I'm right where I should be."

"Look, Silver. If the girl wants some rough and ready, I'm more than happy to oblige her." He winks across the table at me, and I smile back at him.

"I'd think twice about that, Cole. Especially if you don't want to find yourself with a bullet in the back of your head," Silver warns him, and Cole pauses just as he's about to take his shot. "This one belongs to an Ace."

"Fuck you, Damon," I hiss as I slam my cue against the floor. "I don't belong to no fucker."

Silver walks around the table to me and pry's the cue out of my hand. "If that video that was doing the rounds tells me anything, it's that you are in denial if you believe that. You're his, princess."

I cock a brow as I wrap my arms around Silver's neck, and I lean into his ear. "Want me to show you just how much I don't belong to him?"

Silver chuckles as he rests his hands on my hips. "Jim, how much have you let this one drink?"

Jim, the bartender, looks across from the bar at me and shrugs his shoulders. "She's knocked a fair few back."

"Games over, Cole, and if I were you, I'd head home before the shit hits the fan," Silver warns him as he stabilises me when I sway on my feet.

"What are you talking about?" I ask him frowning, and Silver gestures my attention over to the security camera over by the bar. "Looks like it's time for you to go home, princess."

I swear under my breath when I see Archer climbing from his car, with Rafe and Seb behind him.

"Fuck," I hiss. How the hell did the fuckers find me?

Cole puts down his cue and makes a quick exit out of the back door just as the main door bangs open and Archer's furious eyes find me. I stop dead still when I realise I am currently standing with my arms around the back of Daimon's neck.

"Want to tell me why you have your hands on something that doesn't belong to you, Silver?"

Silver holds up his hands and steps away from me. "I think your princess here just needed to cross over to the side she feels more at home on, but you knew where to find her anyway, with that tracker you have on her phone."

I clear my throat and unwind my arms from around Silver's neck and glare across the room at Archer. A god-damn tracker?

"Is this how you want to play it Scarlet?" he asks me, his eyes burning into mine. "There's nowhere to escape. Now get your annoying arse over here. We're leaving."

I fold my arms over my chest and glare at him. "Like fuck I am." I see the thunder in his eyes and turn on my heel to make for the back exit, but I've barely taken a step when his arm is around my waist, and I'm thrown over his shoulder.

Seb leans down and grinning he waves at me. "Bad kitty."

Scowling at him, I give him the finger. "Put me the fuck down Archer!" I demand, pummelling his back with my fists.

"Tell your staff, Silver, that the next time he serves her drinks, he'll have me to deal with."

Silver chuckles. "If she hadn't have got served here, she would have only gone somewhere else."

"Put me down this fucking instance, Archer," I order him, feeling beyond pissed off. His answer is to smack me hard on my arse, the sound echoing around the empty bar.

"Quiet, Scarlet. You're in enough trouble as it is," he barks at me as he turns and exits the bar with me dangling down his back.

I glower back at Damon. "Traitor," I shout, and he raises his hands in front of him as if to say he did what he had to.

Archer throws me in the passenger seat and, snapping my belt tightly in place, he slams the door shut. Seb chuckles from the back seat and I twist round to glare at him just as Archer climbs in the driver's seat.

"I fucking hate the three of you," I snipe as I fold my arms and stare out of the window.

"Were you planning to fuck him?" Archer spits as he drives like a maniac down the tight winding roads.

"Can you not drive like a lunatic?" I ask him, clutching to the sides of my seat.

"Answer my fucking question," he orders, and I jump at the dark bite in his tone.

"So, what if I was? This," I say, pointing between the two of us, "this is just sex. We are not good together."

Seb sniggers again from the back seat, and I whip round and glare at him. "You got something to say?"

Seb leans back in his seat and grinning, he looks over at Rafe. "Mum and Dad are fighting again."

"Fuck you," I hiss as I turn back around and face the front.

"You even think about letting another guy touch you and I'll cut off his dick and leave it on your pillow."

"Little Red's just scared Arch," Rafe pipes up from the back. "She's scared she's catching the feels. Isn't that so, Eliza?"

A cold chill runs through my body as he hits the nail on the head. I can feel Archer's eyes on me. "Is that what today was about? Are you falling for me, Scarlet?" he asks, the humour clear in his voice. "I know you think my dick is heavenly, but it's just sex, Scarlet."

I try not to visibly wince at his words, but I can't deny the stab my heart feels. I snigger and look over at him. "Don't flatter yourself Archer Savage. It will be a cold day in hell before I ever fall for you. We have good sex. It's nothing more than that."

"Is that so?" he asks me, brows cocked.

"Yep," I answer, tilting my chin in the air. He hits the brakes suddenly and I hold out my hand to steady myself. "What the hell?" He puts the car into reverse and heads back the way we just came.

"Where are we going?" I ask him as he speeds down the road, his jaw tense and his grip on the steering wheel making his knuckles whiten.

"You have a stalker out there who is filming you and sending you dead fucking birds, and you think it's a good idea to go AWOL on your own to a seedy bar?"

I blanch. When I went to that bar, I didn't even think about my stalker. "I wasn't thinking about that at the time."

"No. You weren't thinking at all, Scarlet. Your behaviour was pure fucking stupid today."

I frown when I realise we are pulling up at the fighting ring. "Why are we here?"

He kills the engine, and he leans across the car's console, his face an inch away from mine. "Because I'm feeling the need to fight and fuck. Hopefully, pretty little Freya is here tonight."

"Fuck you," I hiss, and grinning at me he climbs out of the car leaving me sitting there fuming.

"Oh, Little Red. You really poked the bear tonight, honey," Seb says with a long whistle.

I climb out of the car and stalk after Archer, and I hear Seb and Rafe follow behind us. I struggle to keep up with Archer when we get inside, but I catch up to him when he reaches Dev and leans in and talks in his ear.

"Come on, Little Red," Seb says, swinging an arm over my shoulder. "Time to sit back and watch the fallout from your unacceptable behaviour."

I sigh as Seb guides me to the side of the ring. "I don't know why he is so mad."

"You don't? You leave a note saying you're going home but you're not there and no one has seen you or heard from you and you have a psychotic stalker out there. He thought something bad had happened to you and instead he finds you in a bar, drunk, flirting with Silver."

I chew on my lip. Okay, when he puts it like that, I can kind of see where he's coming from. Seb nods his head as he sees the cogs turning in my head. A roar goes up in the crowd when Archer steps in the ring. He looks all kinds of deadly as he glares at his opponent. The poor guy fighting him has no idea that I'm to blame for the beating he is going to get tonight. I watch in morbid fascination as Archer goes to town on this guy. He doesn't stand a chance. His opponent puts up a good fight, but it's a forgone conclusion and as he hits the floor out cold, the crowd goes wild, chanting Archer's name. He ducks under the ring and leaves with no acknowledgement to the crowd, heading straight to a room at the back. I'm chewing on my lip, eyeing the door he went through, debating whether I should go speak to him. I know deep down he is right. My behaviour tonight has been stupid and reckless. I do have a stalker out there and I put myself at risk tonight.

I go to take a step towards the room I saw him go into when I see Freya, the girl who propositioned him the last time we were here, step into the room.

Seb tsks behind me. "Will you never learn, Little Red? You poke the bear, and you pay the consequences." He leans in close behind me. "How does it feel knowing she's in there with her lips on him?"

"Okay, fuck this!" I exclaim and I stride towards that room like my arse is on fire and I can hear Seb's mocking laugh behind me. I fly through the door and find the two of them sitting on a bench chatting and laughing like old friends. I hate that I feel so insecure.

"What the fuck do you want?" Archer hisses, his cold eyes staring deadly into mine.

"Can we talk, please?"

I feel Freya's eyes on me, but I don't give her my attention, focusing entirely on him. He scowls at me, not giving me an answer and, feeling bold, I walk towards him and drop myself down on his lap and wrap my arms around his neck. I drop soft kisses down his neck. "I'm sorry," I whisper into his ear. "I was an idiot and I'm sorry, okay?"

I hear the girl clear her throat from behind me. "I'll take that as my cue to leave. See you around, Savage." I hear her footsteps as she leaves the room, and then I dare to raise my head and meet his face.

I press my lips against his. "I'm sorry, Archer."

He grabs a hold of my chin between his fingers and squeezing tightly, he lifts my face so that my eyes are in line with his. "Say the words, Scarlet."

I hesitate. I don't want to say the words he demands from me, because to do so goes against everything I stand for, against everything I have spent the last four years building. "I belong to you."

He nods his head, his cold glare giving nothing away. "If I ever see you letting another guy touch you, I will make you watch as I cut him. You ever do that again and I'll chain you up in my room and keep you there for days. Understand?"

I nod my head as he releases his tight grasp on my face. "You are coming home with me tonight. Text granddaddy and tell you are spending the weekend in my bed."

The car journey away from the warehouse back to the rolling, opulent gated community on the clifftops is quiet. Rafe has his headphones in, and Seb is watching some shit on YouTube on his phone. I'm sitting up front with Archer, who has remained silent since he grabbed me by the hand and dragged me behind him from the warehouse and into his car. He pulls up at Rafe's house and with a quick farewell from him we pull away and drive along to the next mansion on the hill and drop Seb at his doorstep.

"See you tomorrow mum and dad," he says grinning as he walks off towards the side of his house and suddenly, I'm all alone with my dark boy. We remain silent as we drive up the driveway of the Savage mansion grounds. Archer doesn't bother parking the car in the garage, he leaves it outside the front of the house. I follow him as he climbs out of the car and heads inside the house. He drops his keys into a bowl near the door and he makes for the stairs. He doesn't tell me to follow him, but I do anyway. He holds the door of his bedroom open, and I pass him and step inside.

"Strip," he orders, as he closes and locks his bedroom door.

"Pardon?" I ask him, pretty sure I hear him tell me to strip.

"Take your clothes off and get on the bed," he barks coldly.

Rolling my eyes, I turn and face him. He stands with his arms folded, waiting for me to undress. I slowly lift my top off and unclasp my bra and let it slide down my arms and fall to the floor. I pull the zipper down on my jeans and tug them down over my hips and onto the floor. Keeping my eyes on him as I strip, and I see his jaw clench when I hook my fingers in my panties and shimmy out of them.

"On the bed," he orders me as he lifts his t-shirt over his head and throws it on the floor. I silently obey him, sitting myself down at the bottom of the bed. "Further back and spread your legs and bend your knees."

It's on the tip of my tongue to tell him to fuck off, but I resist and shuffle my bum slightly further up the bed and spread my legs, bending them at the knee. He walks over to a set of drawers and pulls something out, and then turns back around and walks towards me. I swallow when I see he holds some rope in his hands. My heart beats faster with apprehension and excitement. Archer takes one of my ankles in his hands and, wrapping the string in a loop around it, he secures it to the bedpost. He then takes my other ankle and secures that one to the opposite post, leaving me lying wide open and exposed to him. He takes one wrist and then the other and he ties them together at my front. Grabbing a hold of my hips, he pulls me as near to the edge of the bed as he can, spreading my legs. He walks across the room and picks up a small black leather footstool and brings it over to the bed and drops it at the bottom and sitting down; leaning in, he licks between my folds, making me gasp in pleasure. He goes to town on my pussy. Licking, sucking and teasing me until I'm whimpering and calling out his name as I build towards that crescendo and just as I am about to come, he pulls away and slaps my thigh with a sharp slap that echoes around the room. Yelping, I look up in confusion when he stands and steps away from me. He walks away and pours himself a glass of bourbon and silently takes me in.

I sigh in frustration. I am so close, and he has denied me. "You're not going to let me come tonight, are you?" This was his way of teaching me a lesson. Of teaching me not to disobey him.

"You're right, Scarlet. I'm going to bring you to the edge repeatedly tonight, until you writhe in pain with the need to come." Putting his drink down, he unzips his jeans and pulls them down with his boxers until he is standing naked before me. I groan as I drink him in. Those washboard abs that beg to be kissed and explored. I follow the trail of hairs down to his erect cock that begs to be licked. He wraps his hand around himself and smirks at me. "You don't get to have this tonight. You don't get to feel the pleasure I can give you as I bury myself deep in your greedy pussy and fuck you hard and long." His hand moves up and down his cock, pleasuring himself, and I watch with rapt attention. He walks back towards the end of the bed, and I watch as he continues to get himself off, his hand moving faster and his jaw clenching as he gets closer. "Fuck," he groans as he finds his release and he leans over me and comes all over my stomach. "You don't get to have my come in your pussy tonight, Scarlet."

He sits back down on the stool, and he dives back in between my legs, making me writhe beneath him with need. This continues for the next hour. He brings me so close to my release and then he pulls back and leaves me unsatiated and wanting. As he pulls away again, just when I am so close, I sob. I fight the tears that are threatening to fall "Please," I beg him. Desperate to feel some relief.

"What is it you want, Scarlet?" he asks me with a cold smirk. As he walks up the side of the bed, running his finger along my body, from between my legs, across my stomach and up between my breasts.

"I want you," I moan, writhing on the bed with need.

"What do you want from me?" he goads me, knowing full well just what I need and want.

"I want you inside of me," I beg, hating him for making me need him so badly.

"Are you mine?"

"Yes."

"Do you belong to me and to me only?"

"Yes."

"Are you going to let another guy anywhere near this pussy?"

"No. Never."

Grinning coldly, he leans over my face. "I want to hear you beg."

"Please. Please Archer. I need to come. I want your cock in me now. Please fuck me."

I hate the smug expression on his face as he walks back down to the bottom of the bed and he lifts my hips with his hands and pushes me further up the bed, untying my ankles. He climbs on the bed and smirking, he leans over me, his dark eyes holding mine captive as he lines himself up at my entrance and enters me in one quick hard thrust, making me gasp.

He feels good inside of me. I hate that when I'm with him like this that all my fears and insecurities disappear. I hate that no one has made me feel like he has. He makes me vulnerable, and that scares the living shit out of me. Archer lives up to his name. He takes me slow and hard until I shatter apart calling out his name like he is a god. I lie there in post-coital bliss, feeling exhausted from his cruel torture earlier.

I yawn loudly, and he cocks a brow, leaning on his elbows. "Don't tell me you're tired because I am far from done with you tonight."

"Oh," I exclaim as he moves down my body and his warm breath blows against my sex. If this is my punishment, at least I'll die with a smile on my face tonight.

CHAPTER
TWENTY-FOUR

ARCHER

I'm leaning against the kitchen worktop drinking my coffee when my dad strolls into the room. He's breathless after his morning jog. To look at him, you wouldn't think he was forty-four; he exercises for at least an hour every day and he runs every morning.

"Son," he greets as he reaches in the fridge for some juice. "I've been meaning to ask, how is it going with the Alderman girl?"

"Well, she's in my bed upstairs."

He nods his head. "Has Wilbur said anything to her yet?" He comes and takes a seat opposite me.

"No, but when he does, I don't think she's going to like it. She's not very good at doing what she's told." I smirk to myself. Scarlet likes to defy. It's in her very nature.

"Well then, you'll have to bring her into line and make sure she knows who's in charge."

I frown and nod my head. "I know what my duty is."

"Let's hope she isn't as ungrateful as her father was, and she takes the opportunity afforded to her." I don't miss the bite in my father's words. I'm under no illusion of his feelings towards Scarlet's family. His hatred for her father is something he has never been good at hiding. My dad had been a Club. He came from a wealthy family, and he'd always been ambitious. He'd hidden nothing from me when he'd told me about how Andrew Alderman had seduced my mum and made her fall for him before he devastated her by choosing some poor girl from a neighbouring town, leaving my mother devastated. She never recovered, becoming a shell of the fun-loving, vivacious girl everyone knew and loved. "Never forget what her family has done to ours. They are the reason I wake up without your mother every day and the reason you have grown up without a mother in your life. Don't be fooled by her, son. Remember, emotions cloud your judgement."

"I never get emotionally involved with anyone," I calmly remind him. After all, I'm my father's son. If there is one thing he has taught me it's that love makes you weak. It gives your enemies a target, and in our world, we have plenty of people who want to knock us off our spot at the top. I don't think my dad has ever told me he loves me or given me a hug. We're just not that kind of family.

My dad claps me on my shoulder as he passes me on my way to the sink. "Make me proud, son."

I finish my coffee and I think about the girl curled up in my bed upstairs. My dick stirs to attention at the thought of her. The sex is amazing. Every time I have her, I crave more. I've explored every inch of her delectable body and it is still not enough. Scarlet would be my wife one day soon. She will be mine in every sense of the word and once she is, I'll enjoy breaking her down, bringing her in line. Her family will rue the day they ever destroyed mine.

I pour her some orange juice and head back up to my room. When I enter, the bed is empty, and I can hear the shower running. My need for revenge goes out the window when I think of her naked in my shower. Pulling my joggers down, I enter the bathroom and find her with her back to me swaying those hips as she sings to herself. Fuck, she is beautiful. The dangerous kind of beautiful, that makes a man forget who he was before her. I stalk her from behind and she jumps slightly when my arm wraps around her waist and I pull her back against my chest.

"Morning, Scarlet."

"Savage," she replies. She shivers when I run my finger down her side.

"What are you doing today?"

Scarlet turns and faces me, and I struggle to pull my eyes from those perfect tits that fit so perfectly in my hands. She wraps her arms around my neck and smiles up at me and fuck if I don't like it when she smiles at me like that. She's always so busy scowling at everyone, giving them that look that says come any closer and I'll gut you, so when she smiles at you it is mesmerising.

"I am going to find myself a job," she announces, and I blink, thinking I've misheard her.

"A job?"

She chuckles as her hand wraps itself around my dick. "Yes, you know, one of those things that you go to, and you earn money." She drops to her knees before me, and I arch a brow in surprise.

"You don't need a job, Scarlet. Wilbur will give you whatever you need."

"Ah," she replies as she licks the tip, making me hiss. "But I don't want my grandfather's money. I want to earn my own."

I look down at her, intrigued, as she wraps her warm lips around me. She is a puzzle. Most girls would take whatever they could get if they were presented with a rich family, but not Scarlet. She wants to make her own way. I close my eyes and tip my head back as she worships my cock. I could get used to her on her knees before me.

"Come on, I'll run you home," I announce as I put on my trainers. The shower lasted a lot longer than expected. I took her hard and fast up against the tiles and she took it like the vixen she is. The thought of owning her, of her having my ring on her finger and the world knowing she is mine and mine only causes a roaring sense of satisfaction in me.

She scoffs at me as she grabs her phone off the bedside table. "I live next door, remember? I think I can manage the walk."

"You sure about that?" I grin and give her a wink. She should be sore from the number of times I've taken her.

"I'm sure, Savage." Returning my wink, she heads towards my door. "I'll see you Monday at school."

Once again, she surprises me. Most other girls would beg to know when they would see me again but not her. She dismisses me like I am a welcome distraction and nothing more and damn if it doesn't make me want her even more.

CHAPTER
TWENTY-FIVE

ELIZA

"Eliza, is that you?"

I pause at the bottom step. So much for hoping to sneak in without being seen. "Yeah, it's me," I reply as I cross the hallway and enter my grandfather's office. He's standing at the window, dressed in a pale blue shirt and grey tailored trousers. I'm beginning to wonder if he sleeps in a suit.

"You're working on the weekend?" I ask him as I drop myself down into the armchair opposite his desk.

"Business doesn't stop because it's the weekend. Were you with Archer last night?"

I nod my head, my cheeks colouring slightly.

"You like him?" he asks me, studying my face as he awaits my reply.

"I wouldn't say like. Like is a strong word."

He nods his head and offers me a tight smile. "I didn't particularly like your grandmother that much when we first met, either. You know she was supposed to marry Edward Savage? I thought she was a real nerd; she always had her head in a book. She would always look down her nose at me like I wasn't good enough for her attention and it used to drive me insane."

I smile and sit up straighter. This conversation is unexpected, but I'm eager to know more about my late grandmother. "So, what changed?"

He laughs to himself and shakes his head. "I was driving home from practice one night. It had been pouring with rain for hours and she was biking it home from the library. I helped her after she skidded off her bike. She'd cut her leg, so despite her protests, I swept her up and put her in my car and brought her here. Catherine protested all the way that she was fine and that I could just take her home, but I found myself not ready to let her go yet and by the time I dropped her off at home I was already planning how I could get more time with her."

I watch him as he talks about her, and I can see that he genuinely loved her. It's fascinating to see, given all he presents to the world is this hard-edged businessman. "Weren't you and Edward Savage friends, though?"

My grandfather grimaces. "We were. We grew up together, like every generation of the four founding families before us and since. He was like a brother to me, but she became more important. I had to have her. To make her mine, no matter the cost, and in the end, she defied her family, and we married in secret at eighteen."

I nod my head, chewing on my lip. "Did you know Verity is promised to Rafe?"

"I did." He takes a seat at his desk, keeping his eyes on me. "They will make a fine match."

"You don' think it's wrong to force two people together at such a young age for the sole purpose of strengthening family ties and business."

He studies me for a beat before he replies. "For generations our families have made advantageous marriages. The four families have remained loyal to each other through the Aces and through marriage. Besides, do Verity or Rafe object?"

"No," I reply with a shake of my head. "I just can't get my head around it. I can never imagine getting married at such a young age."

"They feel a duty to their family. They understand the years of trust and power built by the strong connection between the four families." He leans forward in his seat. "I am looking forward to introducing you to everyone at the dinner dance."

"Oh, you really don't need to," I protest. The last thing I wanted was an evening full of the rich and elite of Hawk Bay.

"I insist. I want to show off my beautiful granddaughter."

"What about your grandson?" I ask him. "Don't you want to show him off, too?"

He half smiles and clears his throat. "Of course. He has a few years of growing up to do yet before he becomes of part of our society."

"And by society, you mean the Aces?"

He bobs his head side-to-side. "That and other things."

I lean forward, putting my elbows on my knees. "What if I don't want him to be a part of the Aces?"

Wilbur's eyes narrow for a second before he schools his expression. "It's his legacy, as it is yours. You are a part of this family. It's in your blood."

I nod my head and toy with the ring on my finger. It's my mum's wedding ring. I've worn it ever since she died. "Why did my dad leave here? He never once mentioned you or this town?"

Wilbur sighs and straightens his tie. "Your father and I had a complicated relationship." He looks down at his watch. "I have a conference call; we'll have to finish this conversation another time." He gets to his feet, effectively ending our conversation.

"Sure, no worries," I reply, as I rise from my seat and clear my throat. "I'll see you later."

"Oh, and Eliza, perhaps you should start dressing more like a young lady of your social standing."

I pivot on my heels to reply that I like the way I dress, but before I get the chance, the door is closed behind me. I stand there for a second and shake my head. Wilbur really has a knack for getting his message across. At times he displays a slither of warmth and then in a split second he can change and be almost cruel, but he does it politely. Clever, really. Can I trust him? No. There's only one person I trust in this world, and that is Kit.

I head up to my room, still reeling from my conversation with Wilbur. I head over to my bedside table to take my contraceptive. Opening my top drawer, I frown when I can't see my tablets. That's odd. They are always in my top drawer. I open the next drawer down and there they are. I must have put them in the wrong drawer when I was half asleep the other night. I pop my tablet in my mouth just as my phone rings.

"Hey Vee," I greet my best friend.

"Hey yourself. What are you up to today? I'm bored."

I laugh. Verity is one of those types of people who can't stay still, she always has to be on the go. She isn't very good at sitting still and doing nothing.

"Actually, I'm going to head down to the Marina and see if I can find myself a job."

"A job? What do you need one of those for?"

I laugh. "You're as bad as Savage. I want to earn my own money."

"Eliza. You know that Grandaddy Wilbur is super rich, right? Just spend his money. Call it time paid back for all the years he wasn't in your life."

I tsk her. "Such a rich girl attitude Vee, I'm disappointed. Well, as strange as it may be, I am going to get myself a job, so are you going to come and help me?"

She sighs down the phone at me. "Well, I'd rather go shopping but I guess I can help you, so long as we end the day at Sam's champagne bar."

"You do know we're underage, right?" I chuckle. Anyone would think that round here, the legal drinking age didn't exist with the way my fellow college peers drink.

Verity scoffs. "Oh, sweetheart, our families own half the bars and shops in the bay. You really don't have to worry about looking eighteen. I am going to introduce you to rosé champagne today."

I'VE TRIED MOST OF THE PLACES IN THE BAY WITHOUT SUCCESS, when Verity suggests we try a little café up near the nature trail. It's popular with the kids at school and gets quite a bit of business at the weekend with tourists and day-trippers. We enter and the place is busy. It has an American diner feel with leather seat booths and a juke box over in the corner. I can't say I'm keen on the uniform, its pale pink and short and fitted with a white piny, but it fits the feel of the place.

We head over to the counter and an Asian girl with glossy dark hair meets us at the counter. "Hey, what can I get you both?"

"Actually, I'm looking for a job. Do you have any vacancies?"

The friendly girl taps her cheek. "Actually, I think we might. Angie gave her notice in last week. Let me grab Jess for you. She's the manager."

A few seconds later, the server and who I presume is the owner comes from out the back. Jess looks to be in her early thirties with mid-brown hair that is held in place under a hairnet. She smiles warmly at both Verity and I.

"So, which one of you girls is looking for a job?"

"That would be me," I reply, pointing at myself like an idiot.

She nods her head, and I can feel her giving me the once over. "Do you have any experience?"

"I do," I say with a firm nod. "I've had a few weekend and evening jobs. I've worked in a small café before, and I've also done waitressing at an Italian restaurant."

She seems happy with my response, and she holds her hand out, offering me some papers. "Fill this in and get it back to me as soon as you can. You need to do Saturdays and a couple of evenings a week."

"That's fine. I'm used to balancing school and work. Do you have a pen? I'll fill it in now for you."

She seems impressed by my eagerness and, nodding her head, she offers me a black biro.

We head for a quiet booth in the corner, and I concentrate

on filling in the form whilst Verity sips on a Vanilla milkshake and scrolls on her phone. It takes me a while to fill it all in as I have to reference my phone for details of my previous employers for references, but eventually I get it done. We head back over to the counter and Holly, the server, shouts Jess for me.

"All done?" she asks me, wiping her hands on her apron and holding her hand out for the form.

"All done."

She takes it from me and scans the document. "Well, Eliza, I'll have a good read through this later this evening and if I think you're what we're looking for, I'll invite you over for an interview and a test shift."

"That would be great, thank you. I promise I'm a hard worker."

We head back out to Vee's car, and she convinces me to hang out at her house for a bit. I immediately regret my decision when she pulls up outside the house and I can see both Archer's and Rafe's cars are here.

"Great," I groan, frowning at the black golf on the drive.

Vee chuckles as she undoes her seatbelt. "Oh, honey, let's not pretend like you aren't addicted to his penis."

I roll my eyes at her. "Are you like ninety? Who calls it a penis these days? And I'm not addicted."

"Uh-huh," she teases as we both climb out and head to the door.

"Can we head to, like, the opposite side of the house to them, please? I can't be dealing with Archer's brooding ego today."

"Movie afternoon? We can head to the theatre room and hide in there."

I breathe a sigh of relief. "That sounds perfect, but please tell me you have popcorn."

"Girl, this is the Collings house. We have a popcorn machine."

Shaking my head, I follow her inside. "Of course you do. I keep forgetting my new bestie is a rich bitch."

The cinema room is out of this world cosy. It's painted in a dark purple, giving it that cosy vibe with plush black velvet chairs that recline. The kind you sink into and never want to leave. She isn't kidding about the popcorn machine. There's even a shelf full of jars of sweets and cookies. It's insane!

We decide we want to watch a re-run of my favourite vampire show and we settle down with our bowls of popcorn and get lost in the vampire brothers.

"Who would you choose?"

I eyeball her. "Are you serious? There's no contest. It's Damon every day, all day long."

She bobs her head from side to side. "Yeah, but Stefan has some morals. Plus, he's super romantic and caring."

I snigger. "Give me dark and dangerous over romantic any day. Romance is for idiots."

"You're so cynical. One day, some guy is going to capture your heart and you'll eat the very words that just came out of your mouth."

I shake my head, laughing. "Never. Love is a weakness. Do you love Rafe?"

As she thinks over her answer, I cock my head and observe her. "I think so, maybe. There is a great sexual attraction between me and him and I care about him. I think in time, when we're properly together then, yeah, I'll love him."

I twist in my seat to interrogate her further. I'm still super intrigued by this whole arranged engagement shit. "But what if the two of you marry and you discover that actually you don't love him? That, yes, you care about him, but it's not love."

She shrugs her shoulder as she digs in the jar of sweets at the side of her. "I think I love him a bit. I guess if he called off our engagement and told me he'd met someone else, I would be hurt."

"And is that an option? Could either one of you call it off?"

"Don't be silly," she says, scrunching up her nose as she thinks about it. "It's what's expected of us. The two of us have known this was the plan for years."

I put my popcorn down on the floor, needing to dig deeper on this subject. "But what if one day you bump into a guy and boom! You're smitten. He's the one, your soulmate, the person put on this earth just for you."

She sighs and cocks a well-groomed brow. "I thought you didn't believe in soulmates and love at first sight?"

"Well," I bristle, "I don't for me, but for other people I do. I mean, take my mum and dad, for example. They were so in love. Even after all their years together, they were still deeply in love."

"Why isn't it for you? Why should other people have that and not you?"

Great, now she's back to grilling me. "Because I'm just not made for love. "

She tilts her head. "Because you don't think you deserve it?"

"Jesus, is this a therapy session?" I ask, smiling at her, but inside I feel uneasy at her scrutiny.

She smiles back at me, but it's a sad smile. "You deserve love, Eliza. You might have this hard-shell exterior, but you're loyal and caring and you'd do anything for those in your inner circle. You have a big heart that is capable of a life-long, deep burning love."

I roll my eyes and throw a sweet at her. "Okay, enough with the deep shit. Let's concentrate on drooling over our vampire boys. You can keep Stefan and I'll keep Damon."

"Deal." she grins as she picks up her bowl and we return our attention to the screen.

I should have known they'd find us. Our peace only lasts another twenty minutes when the door opens, and Rafe sticks his head in and looks at the screen.

"Not this shit again, Vee," he groans and shakes his head at her. He pushes the door open wider and comes and drops himself down in the seat beside her. Reaching into her bowl, he takes a handful of popcorn before looking over at me. "Does Arch know you're here?"

I frown, pausing my hand that is mid-way to my mouth and full of peanuts. "No. He's not my fucking keeper."

Rafe chuckles to himself and returns his attention to Verity's bowl. "I never understood your obsession with sweet. Salty is the best."

"Actually, salty with a bit of sweet is the best," I add, as I chuck a peanut in the air and capture it in my mouth.

"Can you do any other tricks with that mouth?"

I jump at the sound of his voice and turn to find him leaning in the doorway. He has a five o'clock shadow today and his hair is a little unruly. He's wearing shorts and a t-shirt that clings to his biceps. Why did he have to look so flipping edible all the time?

"Wouldn't you like to know?" I snipe, pulling my greedy eyes away from him and back on the screen.

"Ready for tonight then, ladies?" Seb asks us with a waggle of his eyebrows.

I groan. Did he have to remind me? Tonight, is the charity gala ball and my official introduction to the well-to-do of Hawk Bay. "Can't wait," I reply, my tone hinting at my lack of excitement. It's hard to believe we've been here two months already.

"Are you going to save your last dance for me, Little Red?" Seb asks me, winking my way and blowing me a kiss. "What?" he asks, looking over the top of my head to where Archer loiters in the doorway.

"I'll have to check my dance card," I tell him. "Think it might already be full."

Seb snorts. "I don't doubt it after that sex tape. They'll be lining up to dance with you."

Verity throws popcorn at him, and he holds his hands up to defend himself. "Hey, quit it, sis."

"Do you have to remind her about the tape? I've spent all day trying to help her forget about her weird arse stalker and you ruin all my hard work."

"I think I may have got myself a job today," I announce, effectively changing the subject. I didn't want to waste any more of my energy on my stalker today, because if I did, then he was succeeding in interfering with my life.

"A job?" Archer sniggers. "Why do you need a job, Scarlet? Is Wilbur not giving you enough of an allowance because I can have a word?"

I roll my eyes. What it is with everyone and their shock at me wanting to earn my own money. "Wilbur is more than generous, but I don't like spending his money. Besides, I enjoy working. It gives me a purpose."

Seb chuckles as he chews on a mouthful of popcorn. "I'm sure Archer can find something to give you a purpose if you ask him nicely."

I shake my head and offer him a pointed stare. "Is everything about sex with you?"

"Who said I was talking about sex?" he asks holding his hands up in the air and grinning at me. Those hazel eyes of his sparkle with mischief and humour.

"Where's the job?" Archer asks, striding further into the room and sitting casually down on the carpeted floor in front of us, resting his weight on his arms behind him.

"The Bay Café, and I haven't even had an interview yet, so I might not even get it."

"You think that is a good idea with your stalker out there?" Archer asks me, a frown marring his perfect face. I'm distracted with thoughts of kissing my way along his jawline. "Scarlet, are you listening?"

I blink and pull myself away from my lusty thoughts. "I can't hide away. If I do, then I'm letting him or her win."

"It's definitely a guy," Seb states with certainty. He sits down beside Archer and lies flat out on his back.

"How so?" Verity asks him, tilting her head in intrigue at his comment. I too turn my full attention on him, pulling my eyes away from the delectable specimen before me.

"He put a camera in your room. It is definitely a guy. He wanted to see you naked."

Verity raises a finger. "A girl might want to see her naked as well," she challenges.

Seb dramatically rolls his eyes. "Not everyone wants a mixed grill like you, sis."

She fake laughs at him and gives him the finger. I love watching them being siblings together. They remind me so much of Kit and me.

"I think the stalker is female," pipes up Rafe, who has remained relatively quiet up until now. He's the quieter one of the three, but I'm under no illusion that he isn't just as deadly as his two friends.

I turn to him, curious about what he has to say. When Rafe speaks up, it is normally something worth listening to.

"If he had an obsession with you, then he wouldn't want other guys seeing your body or seeing you in a sexual act. Whereas a girl, she'd think it would make you look easy and damage your reputation."

I nod my head. He has a point. "Someone like Georgie, for example."

I hear Archer tut and I swing my eyes to meet his. "Defending her again. Was she that good at oral sex that you won't see reason?"

Archer sighs and glares at me. "It isn't her. I asked her."

This brings a snigger from both Verity and me. "That girl tells lies like it's going out of fashion," I say, shaking my head in annoyance at him. It really bugs me when he defends her.

"Don't get jealous, Little Red," Seb says. "Archer hasn't let her ride the Savage train since well before you arrived in town."

"Jealous," I snigger, "yeah, right." I cringe inside at how unconvincing I sound and when I chance a glance at Archer, he's studying me with an intense look on his face.

"Come on," he says, standing to his feet and stretching,

revealing those delicious abs that I love to ogle. "I'll run you home."

I kind of want to protest that I live three houses down, but then I remember there is some sick fucker out there that wants to drive me out of town, so instead I nod and grab my phone. I lean over my seat and hug Verity.

The car is silent as Archer drives down the winding driveway of the Collings mansion. I'm still mad that he defended Georgie and that he can't see that the stalker could definitely be her.

"Listen, Scarlet, you need to have your wits about you at this charity dinner tonight. The society will be sizing you up to see if you have any weaknesses they can exploit. Just remember, every fucker in that place has an agenda."

I scoff. "It sounds like tonight is going to be great fun."

Archers' fists tighten against the steering wheel. "You need to take my warning seriously. I know you think this society is some pathetic gentleman's club, but it's so much more than that." He pauses, "People have mysteriously disappeared when they have disobeyed the society's orders and don't think because you're an Ace they'll go easy on you, because they won't. If anything, they expect more from us as we set the example for everyone else."

I cross my arms and shift in my seat so I can study his face. "You really are a puzzle, aren't you? One minute you're telling me you hate me, and I don't belong here, and the next you're warning me like you want to protect me. You need to make your mind up Archer. Are you team Holton or team stalker?"

"Trust me, if I wanted to scare you, I wouldn't hide behind dead birds and messages on walls. If I was coming for you Scarlet, you'd know it was me."

"You don't scare me," I tell him, sniggering. "I can look after myself. It's what I've been doing for the last five years, and I've survived just fine."

Archer glares at me from across the car. "You should fear me Scarlet, because I'm going to be your destroyer."

I laugh. I can't help it, and this just makes his glare sharpen.

"See, there you go! Warning me in one breath and threatening to break me with the next. Do you have bipolar? You know I'm done with this toxic thing we have going on. If you're my enemy, then you're my enemy. This weird thing between us is over."

His answer is self-assured smirk which just makes me want to punch him in the face. God, I hate him right now.

"You'll never be free of me, Scarlet. Now are you getting out?"

Scowling at him I realise that we are parked on the drive outside Wilbur's mansion. I've been so engrossed in our war of words that I haven't even noticed we have reached our destination.

"Stay away from me tonight, Archer."

His dark gaze looks straight ahead as he says. "I'm afraid that's not an option."

With a frustrated growl I throw open the door and jump to my feet, slamming the car door behind me. He peels off the drive. His anger reflected in the speed of his retreat.

CHAPTER
TWENTY-SIX

ELIZA

Two hours later and I'm still in a foul mood thanks to that psychotic fucker. With a critical frown on my face, I take in my reflection in the floor-length mirror. Who is this girl before me? Clothed in expensive dresses and her hair professionally styled. Why do I feel like I am playing a part in a movie, and I don't even know the plot? I must admit, the dress is beautiful — I look elegant. My burgundy hair is curled in loose effortless waves and my make up really brings out the amber in my brown eyes. The dress is satin and a beautiful burgundy colour. It has spaghetti straps and a deep V-neck, but it's the back that makes this dress the showstopper that it is. The dress is backless and stops in a ruched point just at the base of my spine. Its floor-length, hugging my waist and hips and ending in a fishtail style at the bottom. Underneath the dress is a pair of killer black heels that add to my small height, making me stand taller. I pick up the small black clutch from my bed and throw my phone and the burgundy lipstick inside. I wonder if I should arm myself. Chances are, my stalker might be there tonight. I hate not knowing who they are. They could be someone I dance with tonight and that chills me to my bones.

There's a knock on my door and I can't help but break into a smile when I see my brother. He's wearing a tux, and it makes him look older and more mature. I know I'm biased, but he's a handsome boy.

"Wow, sis. That dress is a knock-out." He whistles as he strolls into my room, hands in his trouser pockets.

I wink at him as I put on a pair of diamond pear-drop earrings. A gift from Wilbur. "The tux suits you, little brother."

He comes up beside me and grins. "I'm catching up on you, sis. I'll soon be taller than you." He's not wrong, he's about my height now, although in the heels I have a bit of height on him. When did my brother go from a kid to a young man?

"Want to bail and go to the arcades instead?" I ask him, and he chuckles and shakes his head.

"No way am I missing out on this posh bash. Besides, I can't disappoint the ladies and let them miss out on this," he jokes, gesturing at himself and spinning in a circle.

I give him a playful clip around the ear. "Arrogance doesn't suit you." I take out my phone. "Come on, let's have a selfie."

Kit steps in closer and with an arm around my waist, we lean in and smile. Another one for the memory book.

We head downstairs and find Wilbur, Alexis and Chester all in the formal lounge. Wilbur and Chester are both in tuxes and Alexis is wearing the gown she picked when I was with her.

"Ah, here they are. I thought I was going to have to send Chester up to get you." He looks us both over and something like pride glistens in his eyes. "You both look perfect."

I shiver inside at his choice of word. Is that what he expects from us? To be perfect, because if it is, he is going to be sorely disappointed with me.

Edith arrives in the room at that moment and her eyes tear up as she looks at both me and Kit. "My word, look at the two of you. Eliza, you look stunning my dear, and Kit, wow where has that teenager gone?"

Kit laughs and his cheek stain red. "I'm still here, I promise. My sweaty socks are still all over my bedroom floor."

Edith beams at him. "Now, why doesn't that surprise me?" She holds up a camera. "Let's get a lovely family photo of you all."

We all gather in front of the fireplace. Wilbur and Alexis front and centre. Kit stands on Wilbur's side, and I stand next to Alexis. Chester takes up position beside me and his arm wraps around my waist, his fingers gently squeezing my skin. There is something about Chester that I find nauseating, and I can't put my finger on it. The camera clicks and Edith takes a quick look at the photo. Smiling she nods her head. "Beautiful. I'll get this one printed out and put in a frame for the fireplace."

Wilbur clears his throat and adjusts his bow tie. "Okay, we need to get going. It is time to introduce you to the good people of Hawk Bay."

Edith passes me my black shawl and, wrapping it around my shoulders, I follow everyone out to the waiting limo. Yes, that's right. Wilbur has a limo for special occasions. Obtuse or what?

When we arrive, Calvin offers me a hand as I step out of the car and I take it, not wanting to stumble in these heels. He smiles tightly at me, but it doesn't meet his eyes, and I hesitate before letting go of his hand. "Have a lovely evening, Miss."

Wilbur ushers me to catch up, and we head inside. We move through the house and into what I can only describe as a ballroom. The ceiling is decorated with beautiful painted scenes, and large floor-to-ceiling Georgian style window's frame either side of the room in perfect symmetrical order. The circular domed ceiling in the centre of the room holds one of the most beautiful chandeliers I have ever laid eyes on. I laugh at my own thoughts. Let's be honest, I'd never seen a chandelier until I moved here. The room is full of people, all dressed in their finery, conversing, with glasses of champagne in their hands. Servers dot the room with trays of drinks, and I can't help but feel like I'd be more at home with them than I am with this crowd.

I spot Kit taking a glass of champers and I eye-ball him. "What?" he asks, feigning innocence. My grandfather chuckles and tells him to take it.

"Only one," I insist to Kit, and I find Wilbur watching me

with those shrewd eyes of his. "You don't need to parent your brother anymore, Eliza. That's my job now."

I bristle inside at his comment. Just because he's rocked up in our lives, he seems to think I'm going to step back and not look after my brother. I hold in my anger and plaster a smile on my face. "Of course. I am just used to it only being the two of us."

He nods, placing his hand on my back, ushering me forward. "Well, I'm here now. Now, let's introduce you to some important people." I watch him scan the room and his eyes settle on a group of people over to the left of the room. "The man I'm going to introduce you to is the head of Hamilton Construction. He also owns the security company, who installed all the extra cameras at the house. He's a member of the society, of course, and someone we regularly do business with."

"Georgie's father," I state rather than ask.

The group of people cease talking as we arrive. I can tell straight away that the lady to my right is Georgie's mother. They have the same Bambi eyes and the little ski-jump nose.

"Ah, Wilbur, it's great to see you." The dark-haired man bellows and he shakes my grandfather's hand firmly. "Alexis," he says with a warm smile, and then his eyes fall on me. I feel his gaze work over me, and I do my best not to fidget under his stare, keeping my shoulders back and my head high. "And this must be your granddaughter? Why Wilbur, she's a beauty. The names Callum." He steps forward and into my space and drops two warm and wet kisses on my cheeks. I can smell the whisky on him and the powerful stench of tobacco smoke.

"It's a pleasure to meet you," I reply, all smiles and grace. I step to the side and let my brother step up. "This is my brother, Kit."

"Well, now. Aren't you the image of your father?" He shakes his head, doing a double take. "It's like seeing him all over again."

"You knew my dad?" Kit asks, shaking his hand.

"I sure did. We used to play cricket together. We were in the same form at school."

"Eliza, it's lovely to meet you." The blonde lady I recognise as Georgie's mother steps forward and kisses my cheeks. "I'm Felicity Hamilton. I imagine you know my daughter Georgie? She is in your year at school."

I keep the smile on my face and nod my head. "Yes, I've met Georgie. We don't socialise in the same circles, but we have met."

Callum clears his throat, a frown marring his features. "Well, we need to change that. I shall insist Georgie invites you to dinner one evening."

"That would be lovely," I reply. It will be a cold day in hell before I accept that invite.

"Where is your daughter?" Wilbur asks. "I was hoping she'd take Eliza under her wing tonight."

Callum searches the room. "Lord knows, she'll be off gossiping somewhere with her girlfriends or planning how to spend more of my money." He laughs and everyone joins in with him.

I place my hand on Wilbur's arm to get his attention. "I'm going to take Kit and see if we can find Verity." I return my attention to the Hamilton's. "It was lovely to meet you both."

As we make our escape, I hear Callum tell my grandfather what a lovely young woman I am. Job done. I've played my part as Wilbur's doting granddaughter.

"Come on, let's make our escape," I tell my brother as I guide us through the crowded room. Kit pulls me to a stop half-way across the floor and gestures to two boys standing over by two open glass doors.

"Leon and Hugh are there. I'll catch you later, sis."

And just like that, I'm dumped and left to my own devices. I scan the room looking for Verity when from behind me a hand cups my elbow, startling me. "I was hoping to meet you tonight, Eliza."

I turn to find a raven-haired man with tanned skin and dark eyes, and I instantly know this is Archer's father. "Mr Savage," I say with a polite smile, offering my hand. He surprises me by taking it in his and raises it to his lips.

"We meet at last. How did you know who I am?"

"You and Archer have the same eyes and that same dimple in your left cheek when you smile," I explain, then I become flushed when I realise that I've revealed I have studied Archer's features in far too much detail.

"And you are the image of your grandmother. Minus the coloured hair, of course." He smiles, and it sends a shiver down my spine. Now I know where Archer gets his cold demeanour from. "I hear my son has been making you feel welcome in the Bay." The look in his eye suggests he means more than just as an acquaintance, and I can't help but wonder if he's seen the video. The thought of this man seeing me in that way makes me want to vomit.

"Father. I hope you're not interrogating poor Eliza." Archer comes up beside me and places an arm around my waist and smiles down at me. I can't help but feel relieved he is here despite my earlier decision to stay the hell away from him.

His father smiles over at us, lifting his champagne glass to his lips. "Not at all. I'm just getting to know the belle of the ball that has captured everyone's attention."

I shrug off his comment and flush. "I think you flatter me. There are many beautiful women in this room tonight."

He nods. "There are, but none of them hold the allure you do. It's been the talk of the Bay, the return of Wilbur's long-lost granddaughter."

"Come, Eliza, Vee has been looking for you," Archer says, and even though I want to tell him he can get his arm from around my waist and leave me the hell alone, I take my opportunity to escape his father.

Archer's hand at my waist heats through my dress as if branding me. He looks sinfully good tonight. Archer Savage in a tux is every girl's deepest desire. As we cross the room, I watch all the females, young and old, ogle him with desire in their eyes.

"You look beautiful," he tells me as we move across the room.

"Thank you," I reply politely. "So, where's Verity?" I ask.

Archer shrugs his shoulders. "I've no idea. I could just see you weren't comfortable under my father's scrutiny, so I thought I would rescue you."

I snigger. "My hero." I hate it when he can read me so well. I always thought I was a closed book, that no one knew what I'm really thinking inside, but somehow Archer sees past the façade, like my soul is laid bare to him. "You can go now; I'll find her myself."

He snickers. "And let the vultures descend. Even I'm not that cruel, Scarlet. Trust me, I'm doing you a favour."

I scowl at him as we come to a stop in the alcove of two of the large Georgian glass doors. "You know, before you came along, I had to handle my fair share of vultures and I did just fine on my own. Now, run along and find Georgie. I'm sure she'd love to stroke your ego and much more tonight."

He shakes his head and a half-smile dances on his lips. "I think we both know you don't mean that. You don't strike me as someone who likes to share."

I cock my head as I hold his attention. "We're done, so it's not a matter of sharing."

Archer makes me jump when he steps up into my space and pushes me back against the alcove. "I say when we're done, Scarlet. And you and I are far from done. We both know it will be my face between those smooth thighs of yours tonight and it will be my name you're screaming. I intend to rip that dress off you later and remind you who owns you."

I hold my head high, even though it brings our lips dangerously close together. "Not happening."

He smiles. It's a smile that oozes confidence and certainty. "You can lie to yourself all you want, but your body tells me a different story." He runs a finger down the centre of my chest, setting it on fire as he goes. "Your breathing has quickened." He places and palm flat on the centre of my chest. "Your heart is racing." His grin widens. "And I bet if I had a feel under this dress, you'd be wet for me."

Growling in frustration, I try to push him off me, but the brute doesn't budge an inch. "Save all your dances for me tonight."

I don't get the chance to tell him he's the last person I intend to dance with as he strides off into the crowd, leaving me breathless, frustrated, and turned on. I hate how my body reacts to him. I neck my Champagne back and, composing myself, I venture into the room to find Vee.

Unfortunately for me, when I find her, she's with Rafe and Archer. The three of them huddled together like they're conspiring. "What are you three plotting?" I ask, sneaking up on them and making Vee clutch at her chest in surprise.

"Finally! I've been looking for you everywhere!" Verity pulls me into a hug. Her vanilla scent engulfing me. She's wearing a floor-length dress in a pale blue lace-overlay. It clings to her petite frame, and it looks amazing on her. "Eliza, you look fucking gorgeous. No wonder Archer's in a pissed off mood. He knows he's going to have competition for your attention tonight."

Archer snickers and swirls the amber liquid in his glass. "I think we all know that's not true."

"Anyway, enough about him. What were you three talking so seriously about?"

Verity eyes Rafe, and she thinks I don't see him shake his head. I'm not going to lie. It hurts when they exclude me. No matter how many years I live here, I'll never share the closeness that these four do. I'll always be on the outside perimeter of their tight little group. "Nothing worth your time, my girl."

"Want to go for a walk around?" I ask her, gesturing with my head to the room behind us. "You can point out who I need to avoid tonight?"

Vee laughs. "Everyone. You need to avoid everyone. Well, except us four, of course."

"Talking of you four, you're missing a musketeer. Where is Seb?" I ask, noticing his absence and looking around the room to see if I can spot him flirting with some socialite blonde.

"Uh, he's with our parents somewhere. He'll join us shortly." Is it me or does she seem cagey about me asking after Seb? I am about to ask her if she's coming with me when I'm tapped on the shoulder. I turn with a smile plastered on my face that flattens the minute I see who it is.

"Chester. What can I do for you?"

With a drink in his hand, he comes to stand beside me, placing an arm over my shoulder in a gesture that feels a little too familiar to my liking. I look across at my friends to find a stone-faced Archer fixated on his arm.

"Aren't you going to introduce me to your friends?" he asks me, pointing with his drink at the three of them.

"Oh, err, sure," I reply, giving him a puzzled look. "This is Verity, Archer and Rafe."

Chester nods his head as he silently assesses each one. "Ah, yes, the Aces of the school. I've heard a lot about you all and seen a little too much of you Archer." He grins and winks Archer's way.

"What is that supposed to mean?" Archer asks him with an icy undertone to his voice. I can see the tightness in his jaw that tells me he isn't happy.

"Oh, you know," he leans forward slightly, bringing me with him, "the sex tape. I guess Eliza here was shielding most of your body. The same can't be said for hers though, hey?"

He looks down at me and grins, and I don't miss the fact that his eyes linger on my cleavage. Creepy fucker. "I think the whole of the Bay got a good look at Eliza's bouncing tits."

I do a sharp intake of breath and react quickly, standing myself in-between Chester and Archer, who has just stepped forward into his space.

"Don't," I tell him, placing my hand on his chest. "Archer, look at me, please."

He resists for a minute, but when I clear my throat, he pulls his death stare from Chester to look at me.

"It's not worth it. Chester is trying to get a rise out of you." Seeing that Archer isn't going to cause a scene, I turn on my heels and glare up at a smirking Chester "Why don't you run along and cause trouble somewhere else? Oh, and Chester, if I were you, I wouldn't try to piss me off, otherwise I might just pay you a visit in the night and cut your balls off." I end my threat with a sickeningly sweet smile. "Now kindly fuck off."

Chester remains unfazed and smiles down at me. "I'll be seeing you later, sis."

"I am not your fucking sis," I mutter as I watch his retreating figure.

"That boy is Satan, dressed in a tux."

"You're not wrong," Vee comments, coming to stand beside me. She gives my waist a squeeze. "He makes my skin crawl. I hope you lock your bedroom door at night with him around?"

I nod my head firmly. "Trust me, I do." I'm about to ask her if she's ready to go for a wander when a bell rings throughout the room.

"Oh excellent. Dinner is served. I'm starving. Come on." She loops her other arm through Rafe's and pulls us along, leaving Archer to trail behind us.

I am disappointed to find out my neighbour at dinner is Georgie. Fuck my life. Of all the people in this room, I had to end up sitting next to her. I try to convince Vee to swap with me, but she's having none of it. Lucky bitch has been put next to Rafe's mum.

I feel Georgie sit up taller when I take my seat next to her. Even I have to admit she looks good tonight. Georgie has her blonde hair up in a stylish up-do with curled tendrils framing her face. Her dress is a pale green and is corset style, so it pushes her boobs up and gives her some serious cleavage.

The meal is painful. Georgie is all smiles and politeness, but she gets the odd dig in when she thinks no one is listening. Thankfully, we are sitting across from Archer's grandfather, who I can't help but adore. He has a funny streak and a love for one-liners that has even Georgie chuckling. He mentions more than once how much I look like my grandmother, and I see a sparkle in his eye when he talks about her. It's obvious, if you look closely enough, that he held a torch for her in his younger years.

When dinner is finally over, I make myself scarce as quickly as I can, using the need for a bathroom break as my excuse to escape and get some air. I weave through the house until I find a door to outside and take a walk around the extensive gardens whilst I have a sneaky joint that I'd hidden in my purse. What I wouldn't do now to be in my pyjamas in bed, watching my favourite show on Netflix. I put out the joint and spray myself with some perfume to hide the smell and head back inside. I enter through the same door I left and make my way along one of the many corridors in this house. I come to a stop and hide behind a large antique and expensive looking vase when I hear voices coming from a room to the left. Georgie's mum comes out into the hallway fixing her hair, with a quick look up and down the hallway before she heads off back in the ballroom's direction. I arch a brow in surprise when I see Archer's Dad exit the same room, seconds later, zipping up the flies on his trousers and running a hand through his dishevelled hair. It doesn't take a genius to work out what those two have just been up to. Who would have thought it? Archers' dad is giving it to Felicity Hamilton. Archer's dad is a free agent, but Felicity most certainly isn't.

A hand reaches around my waist, and I gasp when a firm male body presses against my back.

"What are you doing sneaking around out here?" The male voice asks me in my ear.

"I'm not sneaking around Seb. I was just admiring this vase. It looks old."

Seb snorts behind me, which tells me he doesn't believe a word of it. "Like you have a thing for old stuff. Who are you hiding from? Wilbur, or Archer and his possessive arse?"

I laugh and turn to face him. He's dressed in a tux, like every other male here. He looks very much the distinguished young gentleman tonight. "Why, look at you." I straighten his bow tie. "Don't you look dapper?"

"And don't you look good enough to eat, Little Red? That dress is sinful. Shall we hit the dancefloor and make Archer jealous?" He waggles his eyebrows at me, daring me to play along.

"I will dance with you," I reply. "But not because I want to make anyone jealous."

"Sure thing, gorgeous," Seb says, winking at me and grabbing hold of my hand as he pulls me back towards the party.

The dancefloor is bustling with couples dancing along to the live band plays over by the corner of the room. No expenses were spared here tonight. He grabs me by my waist and clasps my hand in his as we move across the floor.

"Someone has the moves," I say, impressed.

Seb shrugs but grins. "These hips can move." I don't miss that he's not referring to his dancing skills.

"Too much information, Seb," I say, laughing and shaking my head at him. He dips me, making me clutch at his arm, before he yanks me back up and holds on tightly to my waist.

As we're dancing, I catch one of the serving girls, watching us from the side-lines. Well, I say watching us but really her full focus is on Seb. She looks familiar.

"I think you have a fan," I tell him, and gesture with my head over to the girl. He follows my gaze and when his eyes meet hers, she drops her stare to her feet, her cheeks heating in colour.

"She's a little young for me," he replies, his gaze turning frosty.

I look back over at the girl. "She's not that much younger than us. She looks about fifteen. Does she go to our school?"

He shakes his head, turning his attention away from the girl and back on me. "No. If she's a server, then I imagine she attends the state school. Anyway, enough about the girl. Let's look and see if Archer is watching."

His mischievous eyes search around the room, and he grimaces. "Look who poor Savage got lumbered with?"

I follow Seb's line of sight and they land on Archer and Georgie. She is clinging tightly to him, her mouth moving non-stop as she likely chews off his ear about something inanely boring. Archer, meanwhile, has his eyes focused over her head on me. His dark eyes burn into me, branding me and claiming me.

"I couldn't think of two people more suited to each other."

Seb sniggers into my hair. "You couldn't be more wrong. You see, Georgie, she destroys and hurts people out of boredom and to make herself feel better. Archer destroys people because they deserve it."

"Did Robinson deserve it when you and your cronies filled his mouth with soil and made him think he was being buried alive?"

Seb looks down at me and gives me a firm nod. "He did. That slimy little shit had been lurking outside the houses of some of the girls at school and taking photos of them getting changed. Robinson is a little peeping tom, and he needed to be taught a lesson."

I reel from this piece of information. I had always presumed that they had punished him because he'd failed to bow down to them or he had failed to do a task they set him. It never occurred to me that maybe he was getting what he deserved.

"Have I rendered you speechless, Little Red?" Seb grins down at me.

"I think I need a drink," I announce, releasing my arms from around Seb's neck. I head towards the nearest waiter and grab a glass of champers on my way out of the room. I make my way along the hallway until I find a cosy-looking library. I escape inside, closing the door behind me. I make a beeline for the comfortable old sofa by the fire and slip my heels off, then tuck my feet under me as I sit down and, leaning my head back against the cushions, knock back the champagne. I probably shouldn't have any more tonight. I'm likely to say or do something I don't think Wilbur would approve of. Seb's revelation about Robinson has left me feeling confused. I'd made assumptions that night, just as they'd made assumptions about me. I couldn't think of Archer as someone who had a moral compass, because that would be dangerous for my heart.

"So, this is where you're hiding out?"

I yelp and nearly drop the glass in my hand when I hear his voice. I open my eyes to find the devil himself standing before me, his hands in his pocket. He studies me like I'm his favourite piece of artwork.

"Go away Archer. I'm not in the mood for this drama between us tonight."

He bends down and places his hand under the split in my dress. "I don't want any drama tonight either, Scarlet. I just want to touch you. To feel your skin against my fingers."

"No, Archer," I sigh, trying to push his hand away. "I told you; we're not doing this anymore. You hate me, remember, and I don't particularly like you."

He smirks. The self-assured fucker smirks at me.

"We both know that now we've started, we can't stop this. No matter what that head of yours is telling you. Your body is telling you a whole different thing." His hand moves up my right leg, causing goosebumps as he progresses past my knee and up to my thigh. "You see. I can't let you go now, Scarlet. I'll ruin you for any other guy. No one else can give you what you need."

"And what is it you think I need?" I snipe, trying to keep my breathing steady even as he pushes my dress up my thighs and exposes my lace thong.

He leans in and drops barely there kisses up my right thigh and then my left, and I shiver in anticipation. "You need someone to take control, so that you can just breathe and feel."

He hooks a finger around the top of my thong, and, with his other hand, he rips them apart in one quick tug. Smiling, he pops them in his jacket pocket.

"Did you have to tear them?" I hiss as he begins a tortuous trail with his finger up my leg again. He stands to his feet but remains leaning over me, his face level with mine, and I fight the urge to reach out and place my lips against his.

"Time to go face the wolves, Scarlet." He offers out his hand.

I glare up at him. Seriously? He steals my underwear, kisses my skin and makes me want things and just like that, he turns it off.

"What's the matter? I thought you said no?"

"I did say no." I deepen my scowl. He is tying me up in knots.

"So, let's go. Besides, Wilbur sent me to find you, and he insisted that you and I dance together."

I huff and fold my arms across my chest. "I don't want to dance with you."

He tilts his head, still holding his hand out for me to take. "Yes, you do Scarlet. You hate it, but you want me."

I release a long, frustrated breath and place my hand in his. "One dance and that's it."

"Why are people staring?" I ask him as he leads me on to the dancefloor and places a possessive hand at my waist.

"Because every man in this room wants it to be his hands on you, and every woman here wants to be the one in my arms."

"Wow, your arrogance knows no bounds, Archer."

"I never pretended to be anything I'm not," he replies as he tugs me closer, so our bodies are touching everywhere possible as the slow seductive beat of the music surrounds us.

I glance around the room as we dance and I spot Wilbur and Archer's grandfather standing together, watching us with a great sense of interest on their faces.

"Did I tell you? The café rang me earlier, and I had an interview over the phone. I got the job."

Archer gives me a half-smile. "Congratulations. I've no idea why you want to waste hours of your free time waiting on people, though."

"I want to earn my own money. Besides, I've always had a weekend job."

He shakes his head like he can't understand me. "Wilbur could have got you something in one of his offices in town."

"But then I'd have got the job because of who my grandfather is and not because I was the right person for the job. I want to make my own way in life and not rely on someone else."

Archer studies me in silence. "You really are unlike any other girl I've met. Most of the females in the bay here have never done a day's work in their life. What time do you start?"

"Eight in the morning."

"I'll run you," he announces.

"I can walk. I have two legs, you know?"

"Oh, I know. They look beautiful wrapped around my waist," he says with a heated look. "You have a stalker, remember? You can't walk there. It's not safe."

"Then I'll get Chester or Wilbur to run me."

He sighs in exasperation. "Chester will probably still be high off the coke he was snorting earlier and Wilbur's an old man, let him have a lie-in. We both know you'll be waking up in my bed in the morning."

My hands at the back of his neck form fists. "So presumptuous, Archer."

"It's not presumptuous, Scarlet. Its fact."

CHAPTER
TWENTY-SEVEN

ELIZA

I wake up the next morning and berate myself mentally because whose bed am I lying in? Not my own, that's for sure. I can feel Archer's warm steady breath against my ear. He spoons me, one arm draped over my waist. It's official — I have no willpower and I hate that he knows it.

"Archer," I say gently, tapping his arm. "I need to get up. I have work."

He groans and nuzzles his face into the back of my neck. "Forget the job. You don't need it."

I tap his arm harder. "Let me up. I need to get ready for work!"

I yelp when he suddenly rolls us and he's above me staring down at me, with sexy bed hair, that I may have tugged on a bit last night. "God, Scarlet, it's only six-thirty. You don't start for another hour and a half."

"I need to shower and wash my hair. So let me up, Savage."

He cocks a brow and smiles down at me. Relaxed, playful Archer is still taking some getting used to. I can handle him when he's moody and demanding, but when he's like this it really throws me off. "Who said I was done with you yet?"

I push on his chest. "Up. Now!"

With a sigh, he pulls away from me stands to his feet. He turns and offers me his hand. "Let's get you showered, then?"

"Uh-uh, I'm not going in that shower with you because we both know what will happen if I do."

He rolls his eyes at me. "We'll shower nothing more. Come on, you don't want to make yourself late."

With reluctance, I place my hand in his and let him lead me into his ensuite. Naked Archer and a shower are just too good to resist.

Needless to say, he drops me at work with minutes to spare. I give him shit for it all of the drive there and he just smirks and eyes me in my uniform like he wants to devour me.

"I'll pick you up at four." He looks me over in my uniform and sighs. "Is it supposed to be that short?"

"Yes. Besides, it's not that bad," I reply as I tug on the hem.

His response is to snigger. "Go to work Scarlet before I take you back home and lock you in my bedroom."

Sighing, I climb out of his car, and no sooner have I shut the door he's speeding off down the lane. I knock on the glass door, and I see Jess come from out the back. She gives me a friendly wave and come and lets me in.

"All ready for your first day?"

"I am." I can't wait to feel like my own person again. Archer and Vee can tease me all they want, but I will make my own way in life.

THE DAY PASSES QUICKLY, AND I SOON GET THE HANG OF things. Jess just has me waiting tables today. She tells me she'll show me how to work the till next week and I do a quiet fist bump when she turns her back as that means she's going to take me on permanently.

There's a steady flow of customers all day. Even Calvin pops in to pick up a coffee and he tells me to keep up the good work. By the time I finish, it's dark outside and I'm dead on my feet. Jess gives me my shifts for the next week and tells me to take a caramel doughnut with me when I go. She asks me if I'll take the rubbish out before I head off, so I open the side exit off the kitchen and make the short walk outside to where the bins are located and I'm that occupied on my task that I don't hear someone come up behind me and its only when a hand closes over my mouth, and I feel cold metal at my neck that I panic.

"You were told to leave town," the male's voice whispers in my ear. "You didn't take my warning seriously."

I want to tell him I do take him seriously, but all that comes out is muffled sounds as he presses his hand tightly over my mouth to stop me from screaming out for help.

"Leave. Before you ruin everything," the whispered voice demands. I whimper in protest when he removes the knife from my neck and runs it up my left leg and under my uniform. "I must admit you are a little temptress in this sexy little get-up."

I wriggle in his hold, trying to get free and the knife nicks at my thigh. "Now look what you made me do. You think the Aces can protect you? They can't. I'm always one step ahead. This is your last friendly warning. We wouldn't want you to end up in a terrible accident like your dearest parents, would we now."

My phone ringtone blasts out into the silence of the night, and I take his moment of distraction to elbow him as hard as I can in his side whilst I ram my head up and backwards into his jaw. It works, his grip loosens, and I take off like my life depends on it, running round the side of the café to the car park out front where I know Archer is waiting for me. He's out of the car when he sees me.

"What's wrong?"

"He, he..." I can't catch my breath.

Archer cups my face with his hands. "Breathe, Scarlet. You're okay. I've got you."

I nod my head as tears pour down my face. "My stalker, he was here. He held a knife to my throat."

Archer moves to leave me and seek him out, but I grasp at his coat. "No. please don't leave me alone. Please," I beg him.

He must see the distress in my face because he folds me into his arms and gently strokes the back of my head as he pulls out his phone. "Boyd. It's Savage. I need you down at the Bay café now. That fucker just held a knife to Eliza's throat."

I don't hear Boyd's replies but Archer pockets his phone and I hear the alarm on his car beep. "Come on, let's head back inside and sit you down." I let him guide me back in through the doors of the café. I hear Jess ask him what's wrong, and he tells her that someone has just attacked me at knifepoint. She ushers Archer and me through to the back, into the little staff room. Archer settles in a chair with me on his lap.

"Did he hurt you anywhere, Scarlet?" I can hear the rage in his voice that he is struggling to control.

"I think he cut my leg when he had the knife under my dress."

I hear him swear under his breath. "Can I look?"

I shake my head, keeping my arms clutched tightly around his neck. "Please, just hold me."

He releases a deep sigh and strokes up and down my back. "I've got you, Scarlet. I'll keep you safe, I promise."

Jess quietly returns with a warm cup of tea, and I lift my face from the nook of Archer's neck to thank her. She says she'll leave us alone and will let us know when the police arrive. When she's gone, Archer lifts my face and examines it, wiping my tears away with his thumb.

"I forgot what it feels like to cry," I tell him. "I haven't cried since the day we buried our parents."

He offers me a sad smile. "I haven't cried since the day my mum died, either." He leans in and kisses the top of my head. "I swear we'll find this fucker and when we do, I'll kill him with my bare hands, Scarlet."

Archer reaches between us and pulls his phone out of his jacket pocket. "Seb, it's me. Can you guys get down to the diner? The fucking stalker attacked Scarlet tonight with a knife."

I hear an expletive of swear words down the phone before

the call ends. "How did he know I'd be here tonight? How did he know about my job?"

"I don't know Scarlet, but we'll find him, I promise."

CHAPTER
TWENTY-EIGHT

ARCHER

I'm raging. I feel an urgent need to punch and destroy something or someone, but she clings to me like I'm her lifeline. The police arrive and do a sweep of the area and ask Scarlet some questions, but she's in shock. Jess closed the café early before the police arrived, so the place is quiet. Wilbur's away in the city, but he calls me straight back after he gets my voicemail, and he speaks for a minute on the phone with Eliza, who assures him she's okay and that he doesn't need to come straight home. If the fucker gave a shit about her, he'd get his arse in that private helicopter of his and come home to look after his granddaughter. She eventually lets me look at her thigh. Luckily, it's just a small nick. It doesn't need stitches. Jess offers to clean it up for her, but Scarlet shakes her head and says no. With some persuasion she lets detective Boyd take a photo of the injury and then when everyone leaves the room, she lets me clean the cut with an antiseptic wipe. There are cameras on the side of the building, so Boyd should be able to find footage of the fucker. He tries to push her to go down to the station, but I can see she's in no fit state, so I tell him it can wait until tomorrow and he leaves, promising to keep us updated on what they find on the camera recordings.

Shortly after, Seb, Rafe and Vee all rush into the small staff room and hover around us. Vee has tears in her eyes as she sees her friend huddled in my arms with tear stains on her face. I hate that the sick fucker has done this to her. Scarlet is one of the fiercest girls I've ever met, and she shakes on my lap in shock and fear. She won't let me take her to the hospital. She flat out refuses. Even when she's in shock, she's still a stubborn thing.

"I want to go home," she tells me as she sits up on my lap and lifts her eyes to mine.

"Okay. I'll take you home now," I agree. I gently cup her face and kiss her forehead. It's killing me seeing her like this and I wouldn't even dare begin to examine the emotions I'm feeling right now.

"Will you stay with me?" she asks me, her voice uncertain and shy.

"That's a given and from now on you don't go anywhere without one of us four with you. Anywhere, Scarlet, okay?"

She nods her head, putting up no argument and whilst part of me is relieved, part of me is gutted that she doesn't fight me on it, because that's what she would have done before that bastard put the fear of God in her.

Jess accompanies us to my car, her eyes full of concern for her newest employee. She pushes a bag into my hand and tells me it's a caramel doughnut for Eliza as they're her favourite.

"You come back to work when you're ready, okay Eliza? This job will still be here for you whenever you're ready."

There's no fucking way she's returning to work here, but that's a conversation we'll save for later because right now I need to get her home and in bed.

"Oh Eliza," Edith clucks as she opens the front door and ushers us inside. Rory and Calvin are both here and it is clear from the look on all their faces that Scarlet has woven her way into their hearts in the short time that she has been here. I'm carrying her in my arms, her legs wrapped tightly around me as if she's afraid I'm going to let her go.

"Can I get you a hot chocolate, Eliza? I have the caramel syrup you like?"

"No thanks," she says with an appreciative smile for Edith. "I just want to go to my room if that's okay? Is Kit home? Does he know?"

"He's stopping over at a friend's house, but I can ring him and fetch him home?" Calvin offers, already reaching for the car keys in his pocket.

"No. Let him enjoy his night. I'd rather he didn't know. He'll only worry."

I don't want to point out to her that he'll find out anyway, as the café had been pretty full when I'd burst in there carrying her.

We head upstairs and into her new room. I have a feeling that Scarlet has no intention of moving back into her old room, where her privacy was invaded in the worst possible way.

I sit her down on the bed and untie her white trainers and take off her socks. She sits there in silence and watches me. At least she's letting me take care of her and not fighting me and insisting she can do it herself, but then is that a bad thing that she isn't?

I leave her for a second while I head into her ensuite and start her a warm, soapy bath. When it's ready, she lets me guide her in there and she stands silently in front of me whilst I undress her. She puts a hand on my arm when I go to leave her to it.

"Will you get in with me?"

I nod my head and immediately pull my t-shirt over my head and strip my bottom half. I get in first and then she steps in and sits herself down between my legs. I coax her back until she is resting her head on my chest. I lather up some of her signature strawberry soap on a sponge and wash her.

"Archer. He wasn't someone our age, he was older. I could tell by his hands." She sighs. "I can't shake the feeling that I knew his voice from somewhere, but I can't place it."

It isn't much but at least now I know it's not some little fucker from the academy or that weasel fucker, Chester, who looks at her with hungry eyes that make me want to cut his heart out.

We settle on the bed after the bath, and she falls asleep curled up against my chest. I stroke up and down her back and tell her I'll keep her safe but even as I say the words I feel like the biggest liar because it's always been my goal to strip her of her strength and leave her a broken shell, the way her father left my mother. So broken that not even marriage and a son could ease her heartbreak until one day she ended it all and left me alone, with an emotionally void father and a grandfather who hankered after the past. So why does the thought of hurting her in any way feel wrong? What the fuck is this girl doing to me?

I will find out who is doing this to her because she's mine. It's like he's flaunting it in my face that he can get to her — and it has me raging. When I find out who he is, he'll suffer in ways he never thought possible. Being an Ace isn't all charity balls and initiation games. Me and my two brothers, have been tasked with doing some terrible things. We know how to break a man's will down, we're experts at it. I'll make him beg for death.

CHAPTER
TWENTY-NINE

ELIZA

I wake up and for a minute I feel fine and then the events of last night hit me and a cold sense of dread runs through my body. Maybe I should leave. Kit and I could just pack our bags and go. I'm seventeen, so I could get a full-time job and pack in college. Things would be tight, but we'd manage.

Archer sleeps with his arms around me. When I needed him, he was there for me. He made me feel safe. He looked after me and he was so gentle with me. I've never leaned on anyone else since my parents died, and I can't lie, it felt good just to let him hold me up instead of trying to do it myself. I shift so that I can look at him while he sleeps, and I can't resist leaning closer to press a kiss to his lips. He jumps slightly at the feel of my mouth on his, but he stays still and holds back when I try to deepen the kiss.

"Scarlet, you need to rest," he tells me as I roll on top of him and straddle him. His eyes drop to my thigh, and he runs his thumb over the cut, a deep frown crossing over his face.

"I don't want to rest," I insist. "I want to feel your hands on my body, to replace where he touched me."

I feel his fists clench at my waist. "Touch me, Archer, make me forget last night."

He cups the back of my neck and kisses me like he's never kissed me before. It's a kiss that sears my soul and knits me back together from the inside. He spends the next half an hour kissing every inch of my body, making me quiver in need. He kisses the cut on my leg before his mouth moves between my legs and I tip my head back and close my eyes and just feel the euphoria that he creates in me. When he lines up at my entrance, his eyes hold mine as he enters me. He's gentle. He strokes my face as he moves in me, and rains kisses over my cheeks and nose. It's never been like this between us before. It's always been frenzied, but this, this feels a lot like making love. Afterwards he holds me in his arms and pops on the television and we just sit quietly in my bed, cuddled together in this little cocoon.

"Archer. Tell me what happened between our parents. I need to know."

He's quiet for a second before he speaks. "They grew up together, like me, Seb, Rafe and Vee. They were best friends as children and then, when they became teenagers, they became more than friends. My mum adored him. I have one of her diaries and the way she idolised him, well it was intense.

"The two families had hoped they'd become more than friends and the two families expected them to get engaged one day and marry. She talks in her diary about how he suddenly became distant and would make excuses for why he couldn't see her. Then one day she got home from college to a note shoved under her bedroom door." He pauses and I wait with bated breath. "It was a letter from your father telling her he'd left the Bay that afternoon. That he hadn't been in love with her the way she loved him, but he had felt a sense of duty to his family to be with her. He told her he was in love with someone else and that they were eloping together and starting a new life. He wrote that he hoped one day she'd find someone who could love her the way she deserved."

I sit up and look down at Archer. I need to see his face and see what he's thinking. "He broke her heart?"

Archer nods, playing with a strand of my hair between his fingers. "Two weeks after he left, she found out she was pregnant."

"Wait, what?"

Archer puts a finger to my lips to shush me. "She lost the baby. She went on a drinking binge and crashed into the bridge over by the park in the bay. It left her with a limp as her leg was badly broken and had to be pinned in several places." Archer runs a finger down my chest, trailing it up and down between my breasts. He looks like he's miles away as he tells me their story. "She was never the same. She eventually married my father. It was an arranged marriage. A business merger for the two families. I don't think she ever loved him. I remember I'd watch her sometimes when she thought I was busy playing and she'd have this far-away, haunted look in her eye. Now I know that at the times she was like that, she was thinking of your father. I don't think she ever stopped loving him." He sighs, running his hands up and down my thighs. "She was never really present as a mother. It was like she didn't see me. She drank more and more and self-medicated. Then one morning my grandfather found her. She'd jumped off the roof of the mansion and taken her own life."

"That's why you hate me. Because of what my dad did to your mum," I state rather than ask, because I don't need his confirmation. He blames my father for his mother's suicide. "I'm sorry he did that to her. Knowing the man he was, he would have stayed with her if he'd known she was pregnant."

Archer's face hardens, and he pulls his hands away from me. "You don't know that. Besides he loved someone else. Your mum."

I hadn't really processed that part of this story. "The person he ran away with was my mum?"

He nods his head.

"But I don't understand. Was she from the Bay too?"

Archer fondles one of my breasts in his hands, stroking over my nipple with his thumb and it instantly hardens. "She lived in the next village. She went to the state school there. A fisherman's daughter, they say." Archer offers me a tight smile. "You can imagine the scandal when your dad left with her. It was the talk of the town. The Alderman heir and the poor fisherman's daughter."

I shake my head, trying to process everything he's told me. This was my mum's home, too. I feel an overwhelming need to find out more about her life here and how they met.

"We should get dressed and head down to the police station," he tells me, his tone closed off and matter of fact.

I grab his face in my hands and force him to look at me. "I'm sorry my dad hurt your mum, but that isn't on me, Archer. My father made mistakes I can't atone for.

"I'm not asking you to," he replies, but the tone of his voice tells me a different story. He heads into my bathroom, leaving me to process everything he has just told me.

Once he's done in the shower, he leaves me to shower and dress. I throw on my clothes and head downstairs to find coffee and toast. As I reach for the kitchen door, I hear Archer's voice coming from the library.

"It's too soon!" I hear him bellow. He sounds angry and I wonder who it is he is talking to in there.

"You knew this day was coming, Archer," a voice that I recognise as his grandfather's replies with a forceful tone of authority. He must have his phone on speaker.

"Maybe we should wait a while longer," the third voice belongs to Archer's dad. I can't help it. I lean closer and listen in.

"I'm not ready," Archers insists.

"You'll do as you're told if you want to get your hands on your legacy, boy. You want your inheritance, then do your duty to this family," his grandfather orders him. "The Alderman's are having all four families over for dinner this evening and we'll make the announcement then."

"And what if this is the last thing I want? Does what I want have any bearing on the matter?" Archer growls. I can't see him, but I can imagine his jaw tightening.

"What you want is irrelevant. You'll do as you're told. Now this conversation is over. I have business to attend to."

I panic when I hear footsteps nearing the door, so I quickly but quietly take off down the corridor into the kitchen and throw myself down on one of the barstools.

"Hey," I say smiling and waving when Archer walks into the room. He falters in his stride and gives me a funny look. Yeah, way to play it cool, Eliza.

"What are you doing sitting there?" he asks me with a frown as he comes to a stop on the other side of the kitchen island.

"I'm waiting for you to make me a coffee."

He cocks a brow as he folds his arms and studies me. "Are you okay? Is this odd behaviour some sort of delayed shock from last night?"

A cold shudder snakes down my spine at the mention of the last night. The memory of the coolness of the knife against my throat and the man's breath against my ear has me hugging my arms. The heat from his palm over my mouth. I jump when I feel Archer's breath against my ear. I have been so lost in my own head that I haven't even noticed him walk around the island to me. He places my coffee down and surprises me when he kisses my head before he leaves me to make his own coffee. I hug the cup in my hands and take a drink. Just how I like it, black.

"Are you feeling up to giving your statement today?"

"I have to be. I can't get his voice out of my head."

He frowns in response. "Don't tie yourself up in knots thinking about it, Scarlet."

I feel so frustrated. The fucker had been right behind me, talking in my ear, and I have nothing to give the police to help identify him.

He leans on the island, his cup in his hands. His shirt sleeves are rolled up to the elbow, showing off those muscular arms that held me last night and made me feel safe. He is so beautiful it makes my heart twinge in my chest.

"What's on your mind, Scarlet?"

"I just wanted to say, you know, thank you for last night. For being there for me when I needed someone." I gulp and look down at my cup. It's hard for me to admit that I needed him last night. I'm so used to relying on only myself, but last night it felt good to let him take control of the situation.

"You're an Ace, Scarlet. You're one of us now."

"Is that the only reason?" I ask him. "Because I'm an Ace?"

He doesn't answer me for a second, he just frowns and, placing his drink down, he rubs at the back of his neck.

Is he nervous? No, surely not. Nothing ruffles Archer's feathers.

He reaches into his blazer pocket and pulls out a clenched fist.

"I have something for you," he tells me as he walks around to where I'm sitting. He spins the bar stool so that I'm facing him and, holding out his fist, he opens it. "I planned to give it to you to wear at the charity dinner, but you were being particularly difficult that day, so I didn't."

I look down into his open palm to find a necklace. Its silver, or possibly white gold, and the pendant is a playing card. I look up into Archer's unreadable expression and lift it out of his hand to take a closer look. The playing card is the queen of diamonds.

"Archer, it's beautiful." I look up at him and smile. "Why are you giving me jewellery?"

He looks at me, conflicted. Like he is warring with a battle inside him. "All the females get a necklace. Theirs is usually a club card. You wear an Ace like Vee."

"Oh, okay." What a stupid idiot I am. Thinking that he got this especially for me. I'm just his fuck buddy, nothing more. "Well, it's cute. Thanks." I move my hair to the side and undo the clasp.

"Here, I'll do it," he says, taking it from me and turning my chair until I have my back to him again. His fingers brush my neck as he places it around me and fiddles with the clasp. I place my hand over the pendant and whisper a thank you. "We should get going," he announces, clearing his throat and walking away from me towards the front of the house.

I sit there for a beat, running my fingers over the pendant. The revelation hits me like a dagger in the chest. I care about the reason for the necklace, because I have caught feelings for Archer Savage. Something shifted for me last night. "Fuck," I say to myself, as I come to terms with the fact that someone has managed to knock down the carefully constructed walls around my heart and it scares the ever-loving crap out of me.

CHAPTER THIRTY

ELIZA

I'm quiet on the drive to school. Giving my statement was harder than I'd expected it to be. When my voice had wavered, Archer had clasped my hand in his and stroked his thumb over my palm in reassurance. Seeing the CCTV from the side of the café had been even harder for me to watch. It was like watching it happen to someone else. Like I couldn't equate that the girl on the screen was me. My stalker had been all in black, his face covered by a balaclava. There was no way they could identify him from the footage they had. My stalker had been clever and covered his face and hair.

We pull up at the academy and Archer kills the engine and I shake my head, pulling myself out of my thoughts. When I realise, he isn't making a move to get out of the car either, I look over and he's sitting there just watching me.

"What?"

"Scarlet. I need to tell you something. I wish I could take it back now, do things differently. Fuck, how do I explain?" He bangs his fist on the steering wheel.

I can't get a read on his expression. Is that regret? Guilt?

"Okay. Well, spit it out Savage."

There's a loud thump on my window, making me jump sky high. "Morning mum and dad." With my hand on my chest to calm my racing heart, I turn to find Seb standing at my window, grinning at me. He opens my door and holds it open for me. "Are you two planning on coming in today, or just staying here in the car park?"

I look back at Archer as I'm about to climb out and he just lightly presses his fist to his forehead and mutters that it doesn't matter. Whatever it is he wanted to tell me, it obviously wasn't important. I climb out of the car and Vee bounds over and links arms with me.

"How are you feeling?" Her big expressive eyes look me over.

"I'm okay. I think."

She rubs her hand along my arm in comfort. "Well, you now have four bodyguards. Everywhere you go, we go. You need to pee. I will go with you. You need to go for a run... yeah, Archer will go with you. I don't do running."

I smile at my friend. She always makes me smile and lifts my mood and I love her for it.

"Eliza!" I stop in my tracks, hearing my brother's voice, then see him striding towards me with relief etched across his face. He ploughs into me and throws his arms around me. "Are you okay? Calvin told me about last night." He pulls back and does a scan of my body. "Are you okay? Are you hurt?"

I smile at him and gently pinch his cheeks. "I'm okay, I promise. Take more than some creepy arsehole with a knife to take me down." I'm doing what I always do, putting on a brave face to protect my little brother.

"Don't do that," he says with a deep sigh. "Don't pretend you're okay when you're not."

I shake my head, keeping the smile plastered on my face. "Hey. I'm okay, I promise. Yeah, it was scary, but I'm here. I'm safe." I'm not sure who I am trying to convince more — him or me.

He pulls me in for another hug. "Me and you against the world," he whispers in my ear so the others can't hear.

"Always," I tell him as we pull apart. "Now, go on. Get to class and stop worrying," I insist shooing him away with my hand and, with some reluctance, he leaves and catches up to his friends who are waiting for him near the school's main entrance.

We head inside and I falter in my steps when everyone stops what they are doing and stares at me. Great! It looks like news has got around my attack last night.

"Don't worry about them. They'll have something else to gossip about by lunchtime," Vee assures me, glaring at the people staring as we walk past them. All four of them walk me to my first class, much to my embarrassment. Archer insists he'll be here at the end of class to take me to my next one.

As I enter the room, I find Georgie glaring at me from behind her desk. "Are you banging all four of them now? It's really pathetic that you have to make up stories about being attacked to keep his attention."

"I'm pretty sure gang-bangs are your thing, not mine, George," I counter-back as I take my seat at the back of the room next to Silver.

Her cold eyes follow me as she yells at me that her name is Georgie, not George, and I can't help but grin that I got a rise out of her. I know full well what her name is, but calling her George is such fun.

"Good to see you're alive and well, princess," Silver greets, leaning back in his seat, his legs stretched out under the seat in front of him.

"Don't you start," I hiss. I pull my tablet out of my bag and dump it on my desk.

"Seriously though, are you okay?"

I look up at him and see genuine concern there. "I'm fine." I twist in my seat to face him. "Hey, could I ask a favour?"

He bobs his head side-to-side. "It depends what kind of favour, princess."

I look around the classroom to make sure Georgie or anyone else isn't listening in, and I lower my voice. "I need you to do some digging for me. I think my mum might have lived in the next village. I need to find out where she lived and if she has any living relatives."

Silver nods his head, listening. "Why can't you ask Archer? There's nothing those Aces don't know about everyone in this bay and the neighbouring villages."

"It's complicated." I pull the photograph of my parents from my schoolbag and place it on his desk. "This is my parents. I've put her date of birth on the back. She told me her maiden name was Parker, but that might not be true. I also know she was a fisherman's daughter."

Silver sits up in his seat and takes a hold of the photo, studying it. "It's not much to go off, but I'll see what I can do, but you might want to check grandaddy Wilbur's office out. I imagine if anybody has info on your mum, it would be him."

I don't get a chance to respond as the teacher walks into the room and demands everyone faces the front and stops chatting. Silver has a point. I've heard before that the Aces have files on everyone here. Their deepest, darkest secrets were on record to ensure their loyalty. It is time to have a snoop around Wilbur's office, as soon as the opportunity presents itself.

All I can think about all day is getting home and getting into his office. Archer asks me more than once if I'm okay, but he puts my distraction down to last night's events and doesn't push me.

It's finally the end of the day and I insist Archer drops me off and leaves me. Reminding him that Edith and Calvin will be there, as well as the security personnel and guard dogs now in residence at the mansion, as well as all the extra security cameras and alarms. I spend fifteen minutes with Kit and Edith in the kitchen. Edith clucks and fusses over me and I'm touched by how worried she is for me.

I announce that I have homework to do and head up to my room. I grab a kirby grip from my dressing-table drawer and, in bare feet, I tip-toe back downstairs to Wilbur's study. I fidget with the lock, whilst on high alert for the sounds of anyone heading this way. I fist bump the air when I hear the door unlock. Taking one last look to check no one is around; I enter the office and quietly close the door behind me.

I look around the room and ponder where to start. He has a wall that is floor to ceiling with bookshelves that hold many books, from Mandela's biography to books on business. I walk around to the other side of his desk and pull open the drawers. I'm disappointed to find nothing worth my time. It's just spare pens and paper. I sit down in his executive style chair and study the room. There had to be a safe in here somewhere. Or maybe he didn't keep any documents here. Maybe he kept them in a safe in his bedroom or at his offices in London. This is useless.

"Caught you."

I jump in my seat and find Chester standing in the doorway. I have been so lost in my thoughts again, I didn't even hear him open the door.

"Close the fucking door," I hiss at him, gesturing with my hand.

Taking his time, no doubt on purpose, he strolls into the room, hands in his pocket, and closes the door behind him. He drops into the seat opposite me and reaches onto the desk for a small wooden box. Opening it, he pulls out a cigar and puts his feet up on the desk. He lights it and sits back, puffing on it and smirking at me.

"What do you want, Chester?" I growl, frustrated that he has caught me in here.

"Uh-uh, I get to ask the questions here, love." He blows rings of smoke into the room, making me cough. "I'm sure Wilbur would not be happy to know you have been snooping around his home office."

"What's it to you why I'm in here?" I snipe, folding my arms across my chest and glowering at him from across the table. The shady shit is enjoying making me squirm.

"What are you looking for? I might be able to help."

This makes me laugh aloud. "Seriously? You expect me to believe that you would ever help me?"

His lips curl into a cunning smile. "You scratch my back, I'll scratch yours."

So, there it is. If I want him to keep quiet, I'll have to give him something in return. "Okay. I'm looking for files on my parents."

"Ah, I see," he replies with a nod. We stare at each other in silence across the desk. "I might know where his safe is and how to get in." He takes a puff on the cigar. "It will cost you, though."

"Name your price, Chester. Let's not play games here."

He grins, his eyes never leaving mine. "You'll owe me a favour."

"A favour." I scoff, narrowing my eyes at him. "What kind of favour?"

He smiles. It's a cold and calculating smile. "A favour of my choosing that I can call upon when I decide and you'll do it, no questions asked."

"Nothing sexual," I insist, and he chuckles, his eyes snaking down to my chest.

"As tempting as that could be, agreed. Nothing sexual."

I lean over the table and hold out my hand. "Shake on it."

Laughing, like he's humouring a child, he leans up and places his larger hand in mine. "Deal."

I have a feeling that one day in the future I'll live to regret this, but right now, I don't care. The need to find out more about my mother's past is greater than the danger of owing this weasel a favour.

He takes another puff on the cigar, showing no signs of moving, and I tap my nails on the desk and glare at him. "Today would be nice," I hiss. The longer I'm in here, the greater the chance someone finds me and then what excuse could I give for being in here?

"So impatient," he tsks, making me clench my fist on the desk. Punching him in the face is feeling really appealing right now. Slowly, he gets to his feet and meanders over to the bookshelf. He looks over his shoulder at me, blocking my view. The next second, a part of the bookshelf swings open to reveal a safe.

"Dare I ask how you know how to get into Wilbur's safe?"

He arches a brow and winks at me. "Probably best if you don't know."

I snicker. "Trust me, I don't want to know. You keep my secret and I'll keep yours."

He blocks my view again and I roll my eyes at his attempts to keep me from knowing the safe code. I get it. Knowledge is power, right? The safe beeps as the door releases and, standing back, Chester gestures to the open door. "Have at it."

Jumping up, eager to get what I came for, I stick my head inside. There are several folders in here. The first one is some kind of business contract, which I immediately dismiss. The next few files are also business papers, and my heart sinks as I move down the pile. I stop still in my search when I see my name on the next file.

"What the fuck?" I pull out the file and take a seat back at his desk. Chester's interest suddenly perks up and he walks around the desk and comes to a stop at my side.

I open the cover of the folder and my world tilts on its axis. The first item in the folder is photos of me at age thirteen in my school uniform. I turn the photos over only to find more photos of me. The next shots are a series of me when I was working at the local cinema in our last foster home.

"He knew. All this time, he knew where we were, and he never came for us. He left us in foster care."

Chester whistles in surprise at the side of me. "Always knew Wilbur was a ruthless bastard, but even this is a shocker."

I snap my gaze up at Chester and glare at him. He is enjoying this. "I wouldn't look too smug. Once he gets fed up with your mum, the two of you will be out on your ear without a second thought."

"Maybe," he replies, "or maybe to win the game you have to play the long game and always be one step ahead."

I shake my head, tired of Chester and his riddles, and concentrate back on the file. A report pulls my attention and I lift it out.

Subject currently lives with the Peterson family. Subject attends St. Cuthbert's Holy Family School. She works every Friday evening and Sunday afternoon at the local cinema. Subject was recently put on birth control.

"The bastard," I growl. "All this time. He left us to move from foster home to foster home." Which leads to the next question. Why? "Why did he wait to claim us?" I ask myself aloud.

"Well, isn't it obvious?" Chester comments, sitting on the edge of the desk and smiling down at me like he is enjoying every minute of my meltdown. "It didn't serve his purpose to claim you until now, and why is that? Why are you valuable to him now, at nearly eighteen?" Chester stares at me as if waiting for some great revelation to hit me and when it doesn't, he rolls his eyes and mutters under his breath, "And here was me thinking you were smart." He stands up and stubs the cigar out in the crystal ashtray on the desk. "I have people to see. Make sure when you've pulled your jaw from the floor that you close that safe properly and leave everything as it was, love."

When he's gone, I allow myself to freak out. I pace the office and keep looking back down at the photos in the file. What am I missing here? Why leave us in foster care all this time? Why bother coming for us at all? There's only one person I'm going to get answers from and that's my dear old grandfather. It's time for Wilbur and I to have a real honest conversation, whether he likes it or not.

CHAPTER
THIRTY-ONE

ELIZA

B y the time it comes for me to get ready for the dinner party, I'm a pent-up ball of anger and hurt. I want to scream and shout and smash things, but I store it all up for later. I laugh at myself for believing that he had found us and brought us home because we were his family and he wanted to do right by us. I'm such a fool. I let my guard down and look where it has got me. I let Archer Savage worm his way into my soul and brand it with his initials, knowing full-well that he was a cold-hearted bastard with a grudge against me. I let myself believe that we could finally build a life here and make roots. That we had a blood relative who cared for us. I feel my insides harden like steel as I rebuild that wall around me that has been slowly breaking down. Never again. Never again will I let anyone play me.

I pull out a pretty green skater dress and pause. He wants a doting, dutiful granddaughter. Well, tonight he is getting Eliza Holton. Throwing the dress in the bottom of the wardrobe, I dig around until I find my black pleather leggings. I pull them on and finish them off with my studded black biker boots. I pull on my black knitted polo neck jumper and then I sit at my dressing table and apply thick black eyeliner and do a dark grey smoky eye. I finish my outfit off with my favourite burgundy lipstick. Now I am ready to face him.

When I walk into the lounge, everyone stops what they are doing and stares at me. Wilbur is standing with Vee's father and

Archer's grandfather. Vee is in a pretty blue shift dress, and she stares at me open-mouthed with a brow arched. I offer her a confident wink as I pass her and walk further into the room. My grandfather's hand is at my elbow as he steers me back towards the door.

"I don't know what this show of defiance is, young lady, but you will go and change now," he hisses in a whisper.

I yank my elbow from his grip and step away from him just as Edith walks into the room and announces that dinner is served. Wilbur's eyes burn with rage, but he turns and smiles at his guests and escorts them across the hallway into the formal dining room.

"Scarlet, what game are you playing?" Archer asks as he comes up beside me and places his hand on my back. "I need to talk to you before we go in there."

"Not now, Savage. I have something I need to do." I stride away from him and follow the others into the room. Plastering a smile on my face, I take a seat beside Alexis and Chester sits down beside me before Archer gets a chance to. Grinning, he leans into my ear. "That new look is killer, love."

I don't respond as I survey the room. Taking in all the people sitting at this table. All members of the founding families. I wonder what they will make of my news tonight. Will they be shocked?

The first course is served, and I sit there like the quiet and good granddaughter Wilbur desires. I can feel Archer's eyes burning into me from across the table. My eyes meet his and he raises a brow in question at me and in answer I turn my gaze towards my grandfather. He knows I am up to something.

The meal continues on, and I am polite. I answer questions from Rafe's dad about my studies and when Alexis tells me about another lady's ball she is organising; I smile and say I'd be happy to help with the arrangements. Once the desert is out of the way, I'll make my move.

Wilbur derails my plan when he stands to his feet at the head of the table, holding a flute of champagne in his hand as the server brings one round for everyone.

"Now, before we enjoy desert. I have an announcement." He looks over at me and smiles at me with such warmth and affection that it makes me want to vomit. He's the perfect actor. "I have had the recent joy of welcoming my two grandchildren home." He looks from me to Kit, and Kit grins back at his grandfather and blushes when he feels everyone looking at him. "There is nothing more important than family. Our four families have stood together for the last two centuries. We stood together in business and in family union and became the power-house of this region. Our loyalty to each other is what keeps us at the top." He smiles and looks around the room. "So, with our continued unity in mind, it is my great pleasure to announce that the next union to strengthen our ties will be the engagement of my beautiful granddaughter and the grandson and heir of the Savage legacy, Archer Savage."

You can hear a pin drop as I drop my glass and it smashes on the floor. "What did you just say?"

My grandfather maintains his cool composure. "You and Archer will announce your engagement to the world when you turn eighteen. Edward and I have discussed it and we both agree that a union between our families is necessary to keep our four families strong and unified."

"No," I say firmly as I stand to my feet. "Not now, never."

Wilbur smiles apologetically at his guests before he turns his sharp eyes on me. "You will do your duty to this family and join our two families together."

I laugh, I tip my head back and I laugh. "Oh, this is hysterical. How did I not see this one coming? It all makes sense now. What a complete fucking idiot I have been!" I turn my attention to Archer, who has remained in his seat and silent. "Well, don't you have anything to say about this?"

Archers clears his throat before he meets my eyes. His face is devoid of any emotion. "Scarlet, I know it's a shock for you, but just hear him out."

I scoff and stare at him, open-mouthed. Why isn't he shocked or angry? And then my brain remembers all the time he has looked at me and told me he owned me, that there was no escaping him. "Oh, wow. You knew. You knew the day I arrived here."

"Scarlet, look—"

I hold my hand up "You played me. Was that always the plan? To seduce me and make me pliant so that when he dropped this news, I'd just smile and agree. God, no wonder you always looked so smug. Did it feel good to know I didn't have a clue this was coming?" I look over at Vee. "Can you believe this, Vee?"

Vee keeps her eyes trained on her glass and then she slowly lifts her eyes. I am still at what I see in them. Guilt. "You knew." I look over at Seb and then down the table at Rafe. "You all knew."

I turn to Chester. "Well, did you know as well?"

He shakes his head, grinning. "I'm as in the dark as you are, love."

I turn my attention back to the four people I'd trusted. The four people who told me that I am one of them now and that they'd always have my back. "You all knew. Vee, you were my friend. How could you do this?"

She looks up at me, her eyes wet with tears. "I'm sorry. It wasn't my place to tell you."

"Like hell it wasn't. Friends have each other's backs." I wipe a tear from my eye. Furious with myself that I am letting any of the people in this room see me cry.

I turn my rage back towards Wilbur. "I found your little file on me today. The photos of me and Kit. For a long time, you've known where we were. You let us think we had no one in this world. You watched us move from foster home to foster home and you did nothing." I laugh. "Well, now, I know why. I didn't serve a purpose to you three years ago, did I? But now, now you can palm me off in marriage like I'm some kind of disposable possession. I am just a means to an end to you."

I look across the room at Kit, who has been sitting beside Wilbur with his mouth hanging open, watching all of this unfold. "Come on, Kit." I hold my hand out to him, expecting him to jump up and take it straight away. When I look back at him, he looks from me to Wilbur, anxiety written all over his face.

"Would it be so bad, marrying him?" He gestures with his head towards Archer. "You guys are already a thing." He can't meet my eyes as he speaks. "I like it here, Eliza. We have a family. I don't want to lose that."

"He left us in foster care, Kit," I remind him, shaking my head in exasperation. "He left us to face the world alone."

Kit finally looks over at me and the look in his eyes devastates me more than anything that has occurred tonight. "You can go, but I'm staying, and I think you should stay and think this through for once. Would it really be so bad to just marry him?"

I wipe at a stray tear that falls down my cheek. "You're choosing him? It's always been me and you, Kit. We've never needed anyone else before, and we don't now."

"Eliza, sit yourself down, young lady," Wilbur orders, his voice bellowing across the room, making everyone flinch. "You'll do your duty to this family, like your father should have done. You'll repair the damage he did, and you'll marry Archer Savage."

"Go to hell, Wilbur, and take all these poisonous snakes with you." I spin on my heels and storm from the room. I hear Wilbur shouting after me, demanding I sit back down. Edith rushes through from the kitchen to see what all the commotion is, and she stops still in her tracks when she takes in my tear-stained face.

"Eliza, what's wrong?"

I snicker and raise my hands to the ceiling. "What's wrong is that I should never have stepped foot in this god-damn house of lies. No wonder dad ran away. No wonder he went as far as he could from that man and did everything he could to start a new life."

I take the stairs, two at a time, to my room. Grabbing my old rucksack that I arrived with, I throw my clothes inside. I make sure to only take the clothes that I came with, none of the finery that was paid for with Wilbur's money. The last thing I throw in my bag is my teddy bear and my photos of my family. A family I no longer have now that he has taken Kit from me.

The door bursts open and Archer strides into the room. "Scarlet, just breathe a minute." He runs a hand through his hair and his dark eyes plead with me. "Look, I wanted to tell you. I even tired this morning."

I take a step back as he takes a step forward. "You stay the fuck away from me. I hate you," I hiss with tears spilling down my face. "There you go. I hate you. Isn't this what you wanted? To destroy me." I clap my hands together in applause. "Well congratulations. You fucking did it. I broke my rules for you. I let you in. One day you'll regret losing me, because I was the first real thing you had in your life, and I wasn't there because it was my duty or because I wanted the status. I was there because there was something in you that called to me." I clench my hand over my heart. "You saw me. Just like I saw you, Archer Savage. But I'm a fool, a stupid fucking fool for ever thinking that there was anything more to you than your cunning and your deceit."

I throw my bag over my shoulder and try to move past him, but, he grabs me and pins me against the wall, gripping my chin between the fingers of one hand whilst the other keeps me pinned in place. "Don't go," he says as his dark eyes hold mine prisoner. He opens his mouth as if he is going to say more, but he hesitates.

"I've nothing to stay for." I lift my knee and hit him right between his legs and he staggers back, swearing under his breath and clutching at his groin. Taking my chance, I flee down the stairs and wrench the front door open. I run down that drive like my life depends on it. I keep running and I only stop once to take out my phone and throw it into a bush at the side of the road. There is no way I am giving that fucker the chance to track me down. I don't know where I'm going, but so long as it's far away from here, that is all that matters.

Somehow, I find myself at the cemetery in the bay. I have no idea what led me here, but I walk the rows of graves until I find the one I'm looking for. I trace the letters of my grandmother's name where it is carved into the stone, and I sit myself down and rest my head against her headstone. I wonder what she would make of all this if she were here. She had an arranged marriage planned, and she defied her family and married Wilbur.

I miss my mum and dad so much that my heart physically aches. I just wish they were here to fold me into their arms and tell me everything is going to be okay. But nothing is okay. I've lost my brother to that poisonous bastard, and I fooled myself into believing I actually had friends here. What a complete idiot I have been. So desperate to have a family and belong somewhere that I failed to see what was staring me in the face all along. I am nothing more than a pawn in a rich man's game.

I shiver as the coolness of the night closes in. It's getting late and I need to find somewhere to stay, but where can I go? There is no one around here I can rely on or trust. I shake my head and swear at myself. Of course, there is one person who has always looked out for me, who didn't give a shit about the Aces and their power and influence. I can only hope that when I ask him for help, he'll be there to support me.

IT TAKES A BIT OF A WALK AND WHEN I FINALLY ARRIVE, I'M shivering from the cold. Deep down, I've always known that this is the side of the bay I belong on. Hitching my bag up my shoulder, I walk up the drive to the large house that looks so out of place on this side of the Bay until I find myself at the front door. Taking a deep breath, I rap on the door hard, and I keep knocking.

"Okay, fuck, quit hammering. I'm coming." The door opens and Silver's eyes flash with surprise when he sees me. He leans against the door and cocks his head. "Well, well. To what do I owe the pleasure?"

I drop my rucksack on the floor in front of me. "I need a place to stay."

He grins at me, straightening up from the door, and then holds it open for me. "Well, come on in. Welcome to the dark side, princess."

The End.

Book Two coming
January 2023

BOOKS BY CARA. E HOLT.

The Soul Mark series.

Soul Matched.

Soul Bound.

Soul Surrender.

The Endgame series.

Endgame.

Grayson's Endgame.

Playing Games.

The Hexborn series.

Inescapable.

Infusion (coming 2023).

The Boy I Once Loved.

(Standalone).

Hawk Bay Duet.

Ruthless Legacy.

Fallen Legacy (coming soon).

ABOUT THE AUTHOR

Cara lives in the northwest of England with her two sons, her husband, and the family dog, Bella. When not writing, she can be found immersed in a good book or binge-watching her favourite Netflix series.

Connect with Cara on social media to hear about upcoming book releases, teasers and cover reveals, etc.

Facebook:
https://www.facebook.com/caraeholtofficial
Instagram:
https://www.instagram.com/caraeholt_author
TikTok:
https://www.tiktok.com/@caraeholt_author

Sign up to my newsletter to hear news and updates on my next book, teasers, and cover reveals.
https://subscribepage.io/yCXNOV

Printed in Great Britain
by Amazon

86640568R00159